The Collected Supernatural & Weird Fiction of D. H. Lawrence

The Collected Supernatural
& Weird Fiction of
D. H. Lawrence

Three Novelettes—Glad Ghosts,
The Man Who Died & The Border Line
—and Five Short Stories of the Macabre
and Unusual

D. H. Lawrence

LEONAUR

The Collected Supernatural & Weird Fiction of D. H. Lawrence
Three Novelettes—Glad Ghosts, The Man Who Died & The Border Line
—and Five Short Stories of the Macabre and Unusual
by D. H. Lawrence

Leonaur is an imprint of Oakpast Ltd

Material original to this edition and
this editorial selection
copyright © 2009 Oakpast Ltd

ISBN: 978-1-84677-844-5 (hardcover)
ISBN: 978-1-84677-843-8 (softcover)

http://www.leonaur.com

Publisher's Notes

Contents

Glad Ghosts

I knew Carlotta Fell in the early days before the war. Then she was escaping into art, and was just "Fell". That was at our famous but uninspired school of art, the Thwaite, where I myself was diligently murdering my talent. At the Thwaite they always gave Carlotta the Still-life prizes. She accepted them calmly, as one of our conquerors, but the rest of the students felt vicious about it. They called it buttering the laurels, because Carlotta was Hon., and her father a well-known peer.

She was by way of being a beauty too. Her family was not rich, yet she had come into five hundred a year of her own, when she was eighteen; and that, to us, was an enormity. Then she appeared in the fashionable papers, affecting to be wistful, with pearls, slanting her eyes. Then she went and did another of her beastly still-lives, a cactus-in-a-pot.

At the Thwaite, being snobs, we were proud of her too. She showed off a bit, it is true, playing bird of paradise among the pigeons. At the same time, she *was* thrilled to be with us, and out of her own set. Her wistfulness and yearning "for something else" was absolutely genuine. Yet she was not going to hobnob with us either, at least not indiscriminately.

She was ambitious, in a vague way. She wanted to coruscate, somehow or other. She had a family of clever and "distinguished" uncles, who had flattered her. What then?

Her cactuses-in-a-pot were admirable. But even she didn't expect them to start a revolution. Perhaps she would rather glow in the wide if dirty skies of life than in the somewhat remote and unsatisfactory ether of Art.

7

She and I were "friends" in a bare, stark, but real sense. I was poor, but I didn't really care. She didn't really care either. Whereas I did care about some passionate vision which, I could feel, lay embedded in the half-dead body of this life. The quick body within the dead. I could *feel* it. And I wanted to get at it, if only for myself.

She didn't know what I was after. Yet she could feel that I was It, and, being an aristocrat of the Kingdom of It, as well as the realm of Great Britain, she was loyal—loyal to me because of It, the quick body which I imagined within the dead.

Still, we never had much to do with one another. I had no money. She never wanted to introduce me to her own people. I didn't want it either. Sometimes we had lunch together, sometimes we went to a theatre, or we drove in the country, in some car that belonged to neither of us. We never flirted or talked love. I don't think she wanted it, any more than I did. She wanted to marry into her own surroundings, and I knew she was of too frail a paste to face my future.

Now I come to think of it, she was always a bit sad when we were together. Perhaps she looked over seas she would never cross. She belonged finally, fatally, to her own class. Yet I think she hated them. When she was in a group of people who talked "smart", titles and *beau monde* and all that, her rather short nose would turn up, her wide mouth press into discontent, and a languor of bored irritation come even over her broad shoulders. Bored irritation, and a loathing of climbers, a loathing of the ladder altogether. She hated her own class: yet it was also sacrosanct to her. She disliked, even to me, mentioning the titles of her friends. Yet the very hurried resentment with which she said, when I asked her: Who is it—?

"Lady Nithsdale, Lord Staines—old friends of my mother," proved that the coronet was wedged into her brow, like a ring of iron grown into a tree.

She had another kind of reverence for a true artist: perhaps more genuine, perhaps not; anyhow, more free and easy.

She and I had a curious understanding in common: an inkling, perhaps, of the unborn body of life hidden within the body of this half-death which we call life: and hence a tacit hostility to the commonplace world, its inert laws. We were rather like two soldiers on a secret mission into enemy country. Life, and people, was an enemy country to us both. But she would never declare herself.

She always came to me to find out what I thought, particularly in a moral issue. Profoundly, fretfully discontented with the conventional moral standards, she didn't know how to take a stand of her own. So she came to me. She had to try to get her own feelings straightened out. In that she showed her old British fibre. I told her what, as a young man, I thought: and usually she was resentful. She did so want to be conventional. She would even act quite perversely, in her determination to be conventional. But she always had to come back to me, to ask me again. She depended on me morally. Even when she disagreed with me, it soothed her, and restored her to know my point of view. Yet she disagreed with me.

We had then a curious abstract intimacy, that went very deep, yet showed no obvious contact. Perhaps I was the only person in the world with whom she felt, in her uneasy self, at home, at peace. And to me, she was always of my own *intrinsic* sort, of my own species. Most people are just another species to me. They might as well be turkeys.

But she would always *act* according to the conventions of her class, even perversely. And I knew it.

So, just before the war she married Lord Lathkill. She was twenty-one. I did not see her till war was declared; then she asked me to lunch with her and her husband, in town. He was an officer in a Guards regiment, and happened to be in uniform, looking very handsome and well set-up, as if he expected to find the best of life served up to him for ever. He was very dark, with dark eyes and fine black hair, and a very beautiful, diffident voice, almost womanish in its slow, delicate inflections. He seemed pleased and flattered at having Carlotta for a wife.

To me he was beautifully attentive, almost deferential, because I was poor, and of the other world, those poor devils of outsiders. I laughed at him a little, and laughed at Carlotta, who was a bit irritated by the gentle delicacy with which he treated me.

She was elated too. I remember her saying:

"We need war, don't you think? Don't you think men need the fight, to keep life chivalrous and put martial glamour into it?"

And I remember saying: "I think we need some sort of fight; but my sort isn't the war sort." It was August, we could take it lightly.

"What's your sort?" she asked quickly.

"I don't know: single-handed, anyhow," I said, with a grin. Lord Lathkill made me feel like a lonely *sansculotte*, he was so completely unostentatious, so very willing to pay all the attention to me, and yet so subtly complacent, so unquestionably sure of his position. Whereas I was not a very sound earthenware pitcher which had already gone many times to the well.

He was not conceited, not half as *conceited* as I was. He was willing to leave me all the front of the stage, even with Carlotta. He felt so sure of some things, like a tortoise in a glittering, polished tortoise-shell that mirrors eternity. Yet he was not quite easy with me.

"You are Derbyshire?" I said to him, looking into his face. "So am I! I was born in Derbyshire."

He asked me with a gentle, uneasy sort of politeness, where? But he was a bit taken aback. And his dark eyes, brooding over me, had a sort of fear in them. At the centre they were hollow with a certain misgiving. He was so sure of *circumstances*, and not by any means sure of the man in the middle of the circumstances. Himself! Himself! That was already a ghost.

I felt that he saw in me something crude but real, and saw himself as something in its own way perfect, but quite unreal. Even his love for Carlotta, and his marriage, was a circumstance that was inwardly unreal to him. One could tell by the curious way in which he waited, before he spoke. And by the hollow look, almost a touch of madness, in his dark eyes, and in his soft, melancholy voice.

I could understand that she was fascinated by him. But God help him if ever circumstances went against him!

She had to see me again, a week later, to talk about him. So she asked me to the opera. She had a box, and we were alone, and the notorious Lady Perth was two boxes away. But this was one of Carlotta's conventional perverse little acts, with her husband in France. She only wanted to talk to me about him.

So she sat in the front of her box, leaning a little to the audience and talking sideways to me. Anyone would have known at once there was a liaison between us, how *dangereuse* they would never have guessed. For there, in the full view of the world—her world at least, not mine—she was talking sideways to me, saying in a hurried, yet stony voice:

"What do you think of Luke?"

She looked up at me heavily, with her sea-coloured eyes, waiting for my answer.

"He's tremendously charming," I said, above the theatreful of faces.

"Yes, he's that!" she replied, in the flat, plangent voice she had when she was serious, like metal ringing flat, with a strange far-reaching vibration. "Do you think he'll be happy?"

"*Be* happy!" I ejaculated. "When, *be* happy?"

"With me," she said, giving a sudden little snort of laughter, like a schoolgirl, and looking up me shyly, mischievously, anxiously.

"If you make him," I said, still casual.

"How can I make him?"

She said it with flat plangent earnestness. She was always like that, pushing me deeper in than I wanted to go.

"Be happy yourself, I suppose: and quite sure about it. And then *tell* him you're happy, and tell him he is, too, and he'll be it."

"Must I do all that?" she said rapidly. "Not otherwise?"

I knew I was frowning at her, and she was watching my frown.

"Probably not," I said roughly. "He'll never make up his mind about it himself."

"How did you know?" she asked, as if it had been a mystery.

"I didn't. It only seems to me like that."

"Seems to you like that," she re-echoed, in that sad, clean monotone of finality, always like metal. I appreciate it in her, that

11

she does not murmur or whisper. But I wished she left me alone, in that beastly theatre.

She was wearing emeralds, on her snow-white skin, and leaning forward gazing fixedly down into the auditorium, as a crystal-gazer into a crystal. Heaven knows if she saw all those little facets of faces and plastrons. As for me, I knew that, like a *sansculotte*, I should never be king till breeches were off.

"I had terrible work to make him marry me," she said, in her swift, clear, low tones.

"Why?"

"He was frightfully in love with me. *He is!* But he thinks he's unlucky. . . ."

"Unlucky, how? In cards or in love?" I mocked.

"In both," she said briefly, with sudden cold resentment at my flippancy. There was over her eyes a glaze of fear. "It's in their family."

"What did you say to him?" I asked, rather laboured feeling the dead weight.

"I promised to have luck for two," she said. "And war was declared a fortnight later."

"Ah, well!" I said. "That's the world's luck, not yours."

"Quite!" she said.

There was a pause.

"Is his family supposed to be unlucky?" I asked.

"The Worths? Terribly! They really are!"

It was interval, and the box door had opened. Carlotta always had her eye, a good half of it at least, on the external happenings. She rose, like a reigning beauty—which she wasn't, and never became—to speak to Lady Perth, and out of spite, did not introduce me.

Carlotta and Lord Lathkill came, perhaps a year later, to visit us when we were in a cottage in Derbyshire, and he was home on leave. She was going to have a child, and was slow, and seemed depressed. He was vague, charming, talking about the country and the history of the lead-mines. But the two of them seemed vague, as if they never got anywhere.

The last time I saw them was when the war was over, and

I was leaving England. They were alone at dinner, save for me. He was still haggard, with a wound in the throat. But he said he would soon be well. His slow, beautiful voice was a bit husky now. And his velvety eyes were hardened, haggard, but there was weariness, emptiness in the hardness.

I was poorer than ever, and felt a little weary myself. Carlotta was struggling with his silent emptiness. Since the war, the melancholy fixity of his eyes was more noticeable, the fear at the centre was almost monomania. She was wilting and losing her beauty.

There were twins in the house. After dinner, we went straight up to look at them, to the night nursery. They were two boys, with their father's fine dark hair, both of them.

He had put out his cigar, and leaned over the cots, gazing in silence. The nurse, dark-faced and faithful, drew back. Carlotta glanced at her children; but more helplessly, she gazed at him.

"Bonny children! Bonny boys, aren't they, nurse?" I said softly.

"Yes, sir!" she said quickly. "They are!"

"Ever think I'd have twins, roistering twins?" said Carlotta, looking at me.

"I never did," said I.

"Ask Luke whether it's bad luck or bad management," she said, with that schoolgirl's snort of laughter, looking up apprehensively at her husband.

"Oh, I!" he said, turning suddenly and speaking loud, in his wounded voice. "I call it amazing good luck, myself! Don't know what other people think about it." Yet he had the fine, wincing fear in his body, of an injured dog.

After that, for years I did not see her again. I heard she had a baby girl. Then a catastrophe happened: both the twins were killed in a motor-car accident in America, motoring with their aunt.

I learned the news late, and did not write to Carlotta. What could I say?

A few months later, crowning disaster, the baby girl died of some sudden illness. The Lathkill ill-luck seemed to be working surely.

Poor Carlotta! I had no further news of her, only I heard that she and Lord Lathkill were both living in seclusion, with his mother, at the place in Derbyshire.

When circumstances brought me to England, I debated within myself, whether I should write or not to Carlotta. At last I sent a note to the London address.

I had a reply from the country: "So glad you are within reach again! When will you come and see us?"

I was not very keen on going to Riddings. After all, it was Lord Lathkill's place, and Lady Lathkill, his mother, was old and of the old school. And I always something of a *sansculotte*, who will only be king when breeches are off.

"Come to town," I wrote, "and let us have lunch together."

She came. She looked older, and pain had drawn horizontal lines across her face.

"You're not a bit different," she said to me.

"And you're only a little bit," I said.

"Am I!" she replied, in a deadened, melancholic voice. "Perhaps! I suppose while we live we've got to live. What do you think?"

"Yes, I think it. To be the living dead, that's awful."

"Quite!" she said, with terrible finality.

"How is Lord Lathkill?" I asked.

"Oh," she said. "It's finished him, as far as living is concerned. But he's very willing for *me* to live."

"And you, are you willing?" I said.

She looked up into my eyes, strangely.

"I'm not sure," she said. "I need help. What do you think about it?"

"Oh, God, live if you can!"

"Even take help?" she said, with her strange involved simplicity.

"Ah, certainly."

"Would you recommend it?"

"Why, yes! You are a young thing—" I began.

"Won't you come down to Riddings?" she said quickly.

"And Lord Lathkill—and his mother?" I asked.

"They want you."

"Do you want me to come?"

"I want you to, yes! Will you?"

"Why, yes, if you want me."

"When, then?"

14

"When you wish."

"Do you mean it?"

"Why, of course."

"You're not afraid of the Lathkill ill-luck?"

"*I*!" I exclaimed in amazement; such amazement, that she gave her schoolgirl snort of laughter.

"Very well, then," she said. "Monday? Does that suit you?" We made arrangements, and I saw her off at the station.

I knew Riddings, Lord Lathkill's place, from the outside. It was an old Derbyshire stone house, at the end of the village of Middleton: a house with three sharp gables, set back not very far from the high road, but with a gloomy moor for a park behind.

Monday was a dark day over the Derbyshire hills. The green hills were dark, dark green, the stone fences seemed almost black. Even the little railway station, deep in the green, cleft hollow, was of stone, and dark and cold, and seemed in the underworld.

Lord Lathkill was at the station. He was wearing spectacles, and his brown eyes stared strangely. His black hair fell lank over his forehead.

"I'm so awfully glad you've come," he said. "It is cheering Carlotta up immensely."

Me, as a man myself, he hardly seemed to notice. I was something which had arrived, and was expected. Otherwise he had an odd, unnatural briskness of manner.

"I hope I shan't disturb your mother, Lady Lathkill," I said as he tucked me up in the car.

"On the contrary," he sang, in his slow voice, "she is looking forward to your coming as much as we both are. Oh no, don't look on mother as too old-fashioned, she's not so at all. She's tremendously up to date in art and literature and that kind of thing. She has her leaning towards the uncanny—spiritualism, and that kind of thing—nowadays, but Carlotta and I think that if it gives her an interest, all well and good."

He tucked me up most carefully in the rugs, and the servant put a foot-warmer at my feet.

"Derbyshire, you know, is a cold county," continued Lord Lathkill, "especially among the hills."

"It's a very dark county," I said.

"Yes, I suppose it is, to one coming from the tropics. We, of course, don't notice it; we rather like it."

He seemed curiously smaller, shrunken, and his rather long cheeks were sallow. His manner, however, was much more cheerful, almost communicative. But he talked, as it were, to the faceless air, not really to me. I wasn't really there at all. He was talking to himself. And when once he looked at me, his brown eyes had a hollow look, like gaps with nothing in them except a haggard, hollow fear. He was gazing through the windows of nothingness, to see if I were really there.

It was dark when we got to Riddings. The house had no door in the front, and only two windows upstairs were lit. It did not seem very hospitable. We entered at the side, and a very silent manservant took my things.

We went upstairs in silence, in the dead-seeming house. Carlotta had heard us, and was at the top of the stairs. She was already dressed; her long white arms were bare; she had something glittering on a dull green dress.

"I was so afraid you wouldn't come," she said, in a dulled voice, as she gave me her hand. She seemed as if she would begin to cry. But of course she wouldn't. The corridor, dark-panelled and with blue carpet on the floor, receded dimly, with a certain dreary gloom. A servant was diminishing in the distance, with my bags, silently. There was a curious, unpleasant sense of the fixity of the materials of the house, the obscene triumph of dead matter. Yet the place was warm, central-heated. Carlotta pulled herself together and said, dulled: "Would you care to speak to my mother-in-law before you go to your room? She would like it."

We entered a small drawing-room abruptly. I saw the water-colours on the walls and a white-haired lady in black bending round to look at the door as she rose cautiously.

"This is Mr. Morier, Mother-in-law," said Carlotta, in her dull, rather quick way, "on his way to his room."

The dowager Lady Lathkill came a few steps forward, leaning from heavy hips, and gave me her hand. Her crest of hair was snow white, and she had curious blue eyes, fixed, with a tiny dot of a pupil, peering from her pink, soft-skinned face of an old and well-preserved woman. She wore a lace *fichu*. The upper part of her body was moderately slim, leaning forward slightly from her heavy black-silk hips.

She murmured something to me, staring at me fixedly for a long time, but as a bird does, with shrewd, cold far-distant sight. As a hawk, perhaps, looks shrewdly far down, in his search. Then, muttering, she presented to me the other two people in the room: a tall, short-faced, swarthy young woman with the hint of a black moustache; and a plump man in a dinner-jacket, rather bald and ruddy, with a little grey moustache, but yellow under the eyes. He was Colonel Hale.

They all seemed awkward, as if I had interrupted them at a séance. I didn't know what to say: they were utter strangers to me.

"Better come and choose your room, then," said Carlotta, and I bowed dumbly, following her out of the room. The old Lady Lathkill still stood planted on her heavy hips, looking half round after us with her ferret's blue eyes. She had hardly any eyebrows, but they were arched high up on her pink, soft forehead, under the crest of icily white hair. She had never emerged for a second from the remote place where she unyieldingly kept herself.

Carlotta, Lord Lathkill and I tramped in silence down the corridor and round a bend. We could none of us get a word out. As he suddenly rather violently flung open a door at the end of the wing, he said, turning round to me with a resentful, hang-dog air:

"We did you the honour of offering you our ghost room. It doesn't look much, but it's our equivalent for a royal apartment."

It was a good-sized room with faded, red-painted panelling showing remains of gilt, and the usual big, old mahogany furniture, and a big pinky-faded carpet with big, whitish, faded roses. A bright fire was burning in the stone fire-place.

"Why?" said I, looking at the stretches of the faded, once handsome carpet.

"Why what?" said Lord Lathkill. "Why did we offer you this room?"

"Yes! No! Why is it your equivalent for a royal apartment?"

"Oh, because our ghost is as rare as sovereignty in her visits, and twice as welcome. Her gifts are infinitely more worth having."

"What sort of gifts?"

"The family fortune. She invariably restores the family fortune. That's why we put you here, to tempt her."

"What temptation should *I* be?—especially to restoring your family fortunes. I didn't think they needed it, anyhow."

"Well!" he hesitated. "Not exactly in money: we can manage modestly that way; but in everything else but money—"

There was a pause. I was thinking of Carlotta's "luck for two". Poor Carlotta! She looked worn now. Especially her chin looked worn, showing the edge of the jaw. She had sat herself down in a chair by the fire, and put her feet on the stone fender, and was leaning forward, screening her face with her hand, still careful of her complexion. I could see her broad, white shoulders, showing the shoulder-blades, as she leaned forward, beneath her dress. But it was as if some bitterness had soaked all the life out of her, and she was only weary, or inert, drained of her feelings. It grieved me, and the thought passed through my mind that a man should take her in his arms and cherish her body, and start her flame again. If she would let him, which was doubtful.

Her courage was fallen, in her body; only her spirit fought on. She would have to restore the body of her life, and only a living body could do it.

"What *about* your ghost?" I said to him. "Is she really ghastly?"

"Not at all!" he said. "She's supposed to be lovely. But I have no experience, and I don't know anybody who has. We hoped you'd come, though, and tempt her. Mother had a message about you, you know."

"No, I didn't know."

"Oh yes! When you were still in Africa. The medium said: 'There is a man in Africa. I can only see M, a double M. He is thinking of your family. It would be good if he entered your family.' Mother was awfully puzzled, but Carlotta said 'Mark Morier' at once."

"That's not why I asked you down," said Carlotta quickly, looking round, shading her eyes with her hand as she looked at me.

I laughed, saying nothing.

"But, of course," continued Lord Lathkill, "you *needn't* have this room. We have another one ready as well. Would you like to see it?"

"How does your ghost manifest herself?" I said, parrying.

"Well, I hardly know. She seems to be a very grateful *presence*, and that's about all I do know. She was apparently quite persona grata to everyone she visited. *Gratissima*, apparently!"

"*Benissimo!*" said I.

A servant appeared in the doorway, murmuring something I could not hear. Everybody in the house, except Carlotta and Lord Lathkill, seemed to murmur under their breath.

"What's she say?" I asked.

"If you will stay in this room? I told her you might like a room on the front. And if you'll take a bath?" said Carlotta.

"Yes!" said I. And Carlotta repeated to the maidservant.

"And for heaven's sake speak to me loudly," said I to that elderly correct female in her starched collar, in the doorway.

"Very good, sir!" she piped up. "And shall I make the bath hot or medium?"

"Hot!" said I, like a cannon-shot.

"Very good, sir!" she piped up again, and her elderly eyes twinkled as she turned and disappeared.

Carlotta laughed, and I sighed. We were six at table. The pink Colonel with the yellow creases under his blue eyes sat opposite me, like an old boy with a liver. Next him sat Lady Lathkill, watching from her distance. Her pink, soft old face, naked-seeming, with its pin-point blue eyes, was a real modern witch-face.

Next me, on my left, was the dark young woman, whose slim, swarthy arms had an indiscernible down on them. She had a blackish neck, and her expressionless yellow-brown eyes said nothing, under level black brows. She was inaccessible. I made some remarks, without result. Then I said:

"I didn't hear your name when Lady Lathkill introduced me to you."

Her yellow-brown eyes stared into mine for some moments before she said:

"Mrs Hale!" Then she glanced across the table. "Colonel Hale is my husband."

My face must have signalled my surprise. She stared into my eyes very curiously, with a significance I could not grasp, a long, hard stare. I looked at the bald, pink head of the Colonel bent over his soup, and I returned to my own soup.

"Did you have a good time in London?" said Carlotta.

"No," said I. "It was dismal."

"Not a good word to say for it?"

"Not one."

"No nice people?"

"Not my sort of nice."

"What's your sort of nice?" she asked, with a little laugh.

The other people were stone. It was like talking into a chasm.

"Ah! If I knew myself, I'd look for them! But not sentimental, with a lot of soppy emotions on top, and nasty ones underneath."

"Who are you thinking of?" Carlotta looked up at me as the man brought the fish. She had a crushed sort of roguishness. The other diners were images.

"I? Nobody. Just everybody. No, I think I was thinking of the Obelisk Memorial Service."

"Did you go to it?"

"No, but I fell into it."

"Wasn't it moving?"

"Rhubarb, senna, that kind of moving!"

She gave a little laugh, looking up into my face, from the fish.

"What was wrong with it?"

I noticed that the Colonel and Lady Lathkill each had a little dish of rice, no fish, and that they were served second—oh, humility!—and that neither took the white wine. No, they had no wine-glasses. The remoteness gathered about them, like the snows on Everest. The dowager peered across at me occasionally, like a white ermine of the snow, and she had that cold air about her, of being good, and containing a secret of goodness:

20

remotely, ponderously, fixedly knowing better. And I, with my chatter, was one of those fabulous fleas that are said to hop upon glaciers.

"Wrong with it? *It* was wrong, all wrong. In the rain, a soppy crowd, with soppy bare heads, soppy emotions, soppy chrysanthemums and prickly laurustinus! A steam of wet mob-emotions! Ah, no, it shouldn't be allowed."

Carlotta's face had fallen. She again could feel death in her bowels, the kind of death the war signifies.

"Wouldn't you have us honour the dead?" came Lady Lathkill's secretive voice across at me, as if a white ermine had barked.

"Honour the dead!" My mind opened in amazement. "Do you think they'd be honoured?"

I put the question in all sincerity.

"They would understand the *intention* was to honour them," came her reply.

I felt ashamed.

"If I were dead, would I be honoured if a great, steamy wet crowd came after me with soppy chrysanthemums and prickly laurustinus? Ugh! I'd run to the nethermost ends of Hades. Lord, how I'd run from them!"

The manservant gave us roast mutton, and Lady Lathkill and the Colonel chestnuts in sauce. Then he poured the burgundy. It was good wine. The pseudo-conversation was interrupted.

Lady Lathkill ate in silence, like an ermine in the snow, feeding on his prey. Sometimes she looked round the table, her blue eyes peering fixedly, completely uncommunicative. She was very watchful to see that we were all properly attended to; "The currant jelly for Mr. Morier," she would murmur, as if it were her table. Lord Lathkill, next her, ate in complete absence. Sometimes she murmured to him, and he murmured back, but I never could hear what they said. The Colonel swallowed the chestnuts in dejection, as if all were weary duty to him now. I put it down to his liver.

It was an awful dinner-party. I never could hear a word anybody said, except Carlotta. They all let their words die in their throats, as if the larynx were the coffin of sound.

Carlotta tried to keep her end up, the cheerful hostess sort of thing. But Lady Lathkill somehow, in silence and apparent humility, had stolen the authority that goes with hostess, and she clung on to it grimly, like a white ermine sucking a rabbit. Carlotta kept glancing miserably at me, to see what I thought. I didn't think anything. I just felt frozen within the tomb. And I drank the good, good warm burgundy.

"Mr. Morier's glass!" murmured Lady Lathkill, and her blue eyes with their black pin-points rested on mine a moment.

"Awfully nice to drink good burgundy!" said I pleasantly.

She bowed her head slightly, and murmured something inaudible.

"I beg your pardon?"

"Very glad you like it!" she repeated, with distaste at having to say it again, out loud.

"Yes, I do. It's good."

Mrs. Hale, who had sat tall and erect and alert, like a black she-fox, never making a sound, looked round at me to see what sort of specimen I was. She was just a bit intrigued.

"Yes, thanks," came a musical murmur from Lord Lathkill. "I think I *will* take some more."

The man, who had hesitated, filled his glass.

"I'm awfully sorry I can't drink wine," said Carlotta absently. "It has the wrong effect on me."

"I should say it has the wrong effect on everybody," said the Colonel, with an uneasy attempt to be there. "But some people like the effect, and some don't."

I looked at him in wonder. Why was he chipping in? He looked as if he'd liked the effect well enough, in his day.

"Oh no!" retorted Carlotta coldly. "The effect on different people is quite different."

She closed with finality, and a further frost fell on the table.

"Quite so," began the Colonel, trying, since he'd gone off the deep end, to keep afloat.

But Carlotta turned abruptly to me.

"Why is it, do you think, that the effect is so different on different people?"

"And on different occasions," said I, grinning through my burgundy. "Do you know what they say? They say that alcohol, if it has an effect on your psyche, takes you back to old states of consciousness, and old reactions. But some people it doesn't stimulate at all, there is only a nervous reaction of repulsion."

"There's certainly a nervous reaction of repulsion in me," said Carlotta.

"As there is in all higher natures," murmured Lady Lathkill.

"Dogs hate whisky," said I.

"That's quite right," said the Colonel. "Scared of it!"

"I've often thought," said I, "about those old states of consciousness. It's supposed to be an awful retrogression, reverting back to them. Myself, my desire to go onwards takes me back a little."

"Where to?" said Carlotta.

"Oh, I don't know! To where you feel it a bit warm, and like smashing the glasses, don't you know?"

J'avons bien bu et nous boirons!
Cassons les verres nous les payerons!
Compagnons! Voyez vous bien!
Voyez vous bien!
Voyez! voyez! voyez vous bien
Que les d'moiselles sont belles
Où nous allons!

I had the effrontery to sing this verse of an old soldier's song while Lady Lathkill was finishing her celery and nut salad. I sang it quite nicely, in a natty, well-balanced little voice, smiling all over my face meanwhile. The servant, as he went round for Lady Lathkill's plate, furtively fetched a look at me. Look! thought I. You chicken that's come untrussed!

The partridges had gone, we had swallowed the flan, and were at dessert. They had accepted my song in complete silence. Even Carlotta! My flan had gone down in one gulp, like an oyster.

"You're quite right!" said Lord Lathkill, amid the squashing of walnuts. "I mean the state of mind of a Viking, shall we say, or of a Catiline conspirator, might be frightfully good for us, if we could recapture it."

"A Viking!" said I, stupefied. And Carlotta gave a wild snort of laughter.

"Why not a Viking?" he asked in all innocence.

"A Viking!" I repeated, and swallowed my port. Then I looked round at my black-browed neighbour.

"Why do you never say anything?" I asked.

"What should I say?" she replied, frightened at the thought.

I was finished. I gazed into my port as if expecting the ultimate revelation.

Lady Lathkill rustled her finger-tips in the finger-bowl, and laid down her napkin decisively. The Colonel, old buck, rose at once to draw back her chair. *Place aux hommes!* I bowed to my neighbour, Mrs. Hale, a most disconcerting bow, and she made a circuit to get by me.

"You won't be awfully long?" said Carlotta, looking at me with her slow, hazel-green eyes, between mischief and wistfulness and utter depression.

Lady Lathkill steered heavily past me as if I didn't exist, perching rather forward, with her crest of white hair, from her big hips. She seemed abstracted, concentrated on something, as she went.

I closed the door, and turned to the men.

"Dans la première auberge

"J'eus b'en bu!" Sang I in a little voice.

"Quite right," said Lord Lathkill. "You're quite right."

And we sent the port round.

"This house," I said, "needs a sort of spring-cleaning."

"You're quite right," said Lord Lathkill.

"There's a bit of a dead smell!" said I. "We need Bacchus, and Eros, to sweeten it up, to freshen it."

"You think Bacchus and Eros?" said Lord Lathkill, with complete seriousness; as if one might have telephoned for them.

"In the best sense," said I. As if we were going to get them from Fortnum and Mason's, at least.

"What exactly is the best sense?" asked Lord Lathkill.

24

"Ah! The flame of life! There's a dead smell here."

The Colonel fingered his glass with thick, inert fingers uneasily.

"Do you think so?" he said, looking up at me heavily.

"Don't you?"

He gazed at me with blank, glazed blue eyes, that had deathly yellow stains underneath. Something was wrong with him, some sort of breakdown. He should have been a fat, healthy, jolly old boy. Not very old either: probably not quite sixty. But with this collapse on him, he seemed, somehow, to smell.

"You know," he said, staring at me with a sort of gruesome challenge, then looking down at his wine, "there's more things than we're aware of happening to us!" He looked up at me again, shutting his full lips under his little grey moustache, and gazing with a glazed defiance.

"Quite!" said I.

He continued to gaze at me with glazed, gruesome defiance.

"Ha!" He made a sudden movement, and seemed to break up, collapse and become brokenly natural. "There, you've said it. I married my wife when I was a kid of twenty."

"Mrs. Hale?" I exclaimed.

"Not this one"—he jerked his head towards the door—"my first wife." There was a pause; he looked at me with shamed eyes, then turned his wine-glass round and his head dropped. Staring at his twisting glass, he continued: "I married her when I was twenty, and she was twenty-eight. You might say, she married me. Well, there it was! We had three children—I've got three married daughters—and we got on all right. I suppose she mothered me, in a way. And I never thought a thing. I was content enough, wasn't tied to her apron-strings, and she never asked questions. She was always fond of me, and I took it for granted. I took it for granted. Even when she died—I was away in Salonika—I took it for granted, if you understand me. It was part of the rest of things—war—life—death. I knew I should feel lonely when I got back. Well, then I got buried—shell dropped, and the dugout caved in—and that queered me. They sent me home. And the minute I saw the Lizard light—it was evening when we got

25

up out of the Bay—I realised that Lucy had been waiting for me. I could feel her there, at my side, more plainly than I feel you now. And do you know, at that moment I woke up to her, and she made an awful impression on me. She seemed, if you get me, tremendously powerful, important; everything else dwindled away. There was the Lizard light blinking a long way off, and that meant home. And all the rest was my wife, Lucy: as if her skirts filled all the darkness. In a way, I was frightened; but that was because I couldn't quite get myself into line. I felt: Good God! I never knew her! And she was this tremendous thing! I felt like a child, and as weak as a kitten. And, believe me or not, from that day to this she's never left me. I know quite well she can hear what I'm saying. But she'll let me tell you. I knew that at dinner-time."

"But what made you marry again?" I said.

"She made me!" He went a trifle yellow on his cheek-bones. "I could feel her telling me: 'Marry! Marry!' Lady Lathkill had messages from her too; she was her great friend in life. I didn't think of marrying. But Lady Lathkill had the same message, that I must marry. Then a medium described the girl in detail: my present wife. I knew her at once, friend of my daughters. After that the messages became more insistent, waking me three and four times in the night. Lady Lathkill urged me to propose, and I did it, and was accepted. My present wife was just twenty-eight, the age Lucy had been—"

"How long ago did you marry the present Mrs. Hale?"

"A little over a year ago. Well, I thought I had done what was required of me. But directly after the wedding, such a state of terror came over me—perfectly unreasonable—I became almost unconscious. My present wife asked me if I was ill, and I said I was. We got to Paris. I felt I was dying. But I said I was going out to see a doctor, and I found myself kneeling in a church. Then I found peace—and Lucy. She had her arms round me, and I was like a child at peace. I must have knelt there for a couple of hours in Lucy's arms. I *never* felt like that when she was alive: why, I couldn't stand that sort of thing! It's all come on after—after—And now, I daren't offend Lucy's spirit. If I do, I suffer tortures till I've made peace again, till she folds me in her arms. Then I can live. But she won't let me go near the present Mrs. Hale. I—I—I daren't go near her."

He looked up at me with fear, and shame, and shameful secrecy, and a sort of gloating showing in his unmanned blue eyes. He had been talking as if in his sleep.

"Why did your dead wife urge you to marry again?" I said.

"I don't know," he replied. "I don't know. She was older than I was, and all the cleverness was on her side. She was a very clever woman, and I was never much in the intellectual line myself. I just took it for granted she liked me. She never showed jealousy, but I think now, perhaps she was jealous all the time, and kept it under. I don't know. I think she never felt quite straight about having married me. It seems like that. As if she had something on her mind. Do you know, while she was alive, I never gave it a thought. And now I'm aware of nothing else but her. It's as if her spirit wanted to live in my body, or at any rate—I don't know—"

His blue eyes were glazed, almost fishy, with fear and gloating shame. He had a short nose, and full, self-indulgent lips, and a once-comedy chin. Eternally a careless boy of thirteen. But now, care had got him in decay.

"And what does your present wife say?" I asked.

He poured himself some more wine.

"Why," he replied, "except for her, I shouldn't mind so much. She says nothing. Lady Lathkill has explained everything to her, and she agrees that—that—a spirit from the other side is more important than mere pleasure—you know what I mean. Lady Lathkill says that this is a preparation for my next incarnation, when I am going to serve Woman, and help Her to take Her place."

He looked up again, trying to be proud in his shame.

"Well, what a damned curious story!" exclaimed Lord Lathkill. "Mother's idea for herself—she had it in a message too—is that she is coming on earth the next time to save the animals from the cruelty of man. That's why she hates meat at table, or anything that has to be killed."

"And does Lady Lathkill encourage you in this business with your dead wife?" said I.

"Yes. She helps me. When I get as you might say at cross-purposes with Lucy—with Lucy's spirit, that is—Lady Lathkill helps to put it right between us. Then I'm all right, when I know I'm loved."

He looked at me stealthily, cunningly.

"Then you're all wrong," said I, "surely."

"And do you mean to say," put in Lord Lathkill, "that you don't live with the present Mrs. Hale at all? Do you mean to say you never *have* lived with her?"

"I've got a higher claim on me," said the unhappy Colonel.

"My God!" said Lord Lathkill.

I looked in amazement: the sort of chap who picks up a woman and has a good time with her for a week, then goes home as nice as pie, and now look at him! It was obvious that he had a terror of his black-browed new wife, as well as of Lucy's spirit. A devil and a deep blue sea with a *vengenace*!

"A damned curious story!" mused Lord Lathkill. "I'm not so sure I like it. Something's wrong somewhere. We shall have to go upstairs."

"Wrong!" said I. "Why, Colonel, don't you turn round and quarrel with the spirit of your first wife, fatally and finally, and get rid of her?"

The Colonel looked at me, still diminished and afraid, but perking up a bit, as we rose from table.

"How would you go about it?" he said.

"I'd just face her, wherever she seemed to be, and say: 'Lucy, go to blazes!'"

Lord Lathkill burst into a loud laugh, then was suddenly silent as the door noiselessly opened, and the dowager's white hair and pointed, uncanny eyes peered in, then entered.

"I think I left my papers in here, Luke," she murmured.

"Yes, mother. There they are. We're just coming up."

"Take your time." He held the door, and ducking forward, she went out again, clutching some papers. The Colonel had blenched yellow on his cheek-bones.

28

We went upstairs to the small drawing-room.

"You were a long time," said Carlotta, looking in all our faces. "Hope the coffee's not cold. We'll have fresh if it is."

She poured out, and Mrs. Hale carried the cups. The dark young woman thrust out her straight, dusky arm, offering me sugar, and gazing at me with her unchanging, yellow-brown eyes. I looked back at her, and being clairvoyant in this house, was conscious of the curves of her erect body, the sparse black hairs there would be on her strong-skinned dusky thighs. She was a woman of thirty, and she had had a great dread lest she should never marry. Now she was as if mesmerised.

"What do you do usually in the evenings?" I said.

She turned to me as if startled, as she nearly always did when addressed.

"We do nothing," she replied. "Talk; and sometimes Lady Lathkill reads."

"What does she read?"

"About spiritualism."

"Sounds pretty dull."

She looked at me again, but she did not answer. It was difficult to get anything out of her. She put up no fight, only remained in the same swarthy, passive, negative resistance. For a moment I wondered that no men made love to her: it was obvious they didn't. But then, modern young men are accustomed to being attracted, flattered, impressed: they expect an effort to please. And Mrs. Hale made none: didn't know how. Which for me was her mystery. She was passive, static, locked up in a resistant passivity that had fire beneath it.

Lord Lathkill came and sat by us. The Colonel's confession had had an effect on him.

"I'm afraid," he said to Mrs. Hale, "you have a thin time here."

"Why?" she asked.

"Oh, there is so little to amuse you. Do you like to dance?"

"Yes," she said.

"Well, then," he said, "let us go downstairs and dance to the Victrola. There are four of us. You'll come, of course?" he said to me.

Then he turned to his mother.

"Mother, we shall go down to the morning-room and dance. Will you come? Will you, Colonel?"

The dowager gazed at her son.

"I will come and look on," she said.

"And I will play the pianola, if you like," volunteered the Colonel. We went down and pushed aside the chintz chairs and the rugs. Lady Lathkill sat in a chair, the Colonel worked away at the pianola. I danced with Carlotta, Lord Lathkill with Mrs. Hale.

A quiet soothing came over me, dancing with Carlotta. She was very still and remote, and she hardly looked at me. Yet the touch of her was wonderful, like a flower that yields itself to the morning. Her warm, silken shoulder was soft and grateful under my hand, as if it knew me with that second knowledge which is part of one's childhood, and which so rarely blossoms again in manhood and womanhood. It was as if we had known each other perfectly, as children, and now, as man and woman met in the full, further sympathy. Perhaps, in modern people, only after long suffering and defeat, can the naked intuition break free between woman and man.

She, I knew, let the strain and the tension of all her life depart from her then, leaving her nakedly still, within my arm. And I only wanted to be with her, to have her in my touch.

Yet after the second dance she looked at me, and suggested that she should dance with her husband. So I found myself with the strong, passive shoulder of Mrs. Hale under my hand, and her inert hand in mine, as I looked down at her dusky, dirty-looking neck—she wisely avoided powder. The duskiness of her mesmerised body made me see the faint dark sheen of her thighs, with intermittent black hairs. It was as if they shone through the silk of her mauve dress, like the limbs of a half-wild animal that is locked up in its own helpless dumb winter, a prisoner.

She knew, with the heavy intuition of her sort, that I glimpsed her crude among the bushes, and felt her attraction. But she kept looking away over my shoulder, with her yellow eyes, towards Lord Lathkill.

Myself or him, it was a question of which got there first. But she preferred him. Only for some things she would rather it were me.

Luke had changed curiously. His body seemed to have come alive, in the dark cloth of his evening suit; his eyes had a devil-may-care light in them, his long cheeks a touch of scarlet, and his black hair fell loose over his forehead. He had again some of that Guardsman's sense of well-being and claim to the best in life, which I had noticed the first time I saw him. But now it was a little more florid, defiant, with a touch of madness.

He looked down at Carlotta with uncanny kindness and affection. Yet he was glad to hand her over to me. He, too, was afraid of her: as if with her his bad luck had worked. Whereas, in a throb of crude brutality, he felt it would not work with the dark young woman. So, he handed Carlotta over to me with relief, as if, with me, she would be safe from the doom of his bad luck. And he, with the other woman, would be safe from it too. For the other woman was outside the circle.

I was glad to have Carlotta again: to have that inexpressible delicate and complete quiet of the two of us, resting my heart in a balance now at last physical as well as spiritual. Till now, it had always been a fragmentary thing. Now, for this hour at least, it was whole, a soft, complete, physical flow, and a unison deeper even than childhood.

As she danced she shivered slightly, and I seemed to smell frost in the air. The Colonel, too, was not keeping the rhythm.

"Has it turned colder?" I said.

"I wonder," she answered, looking up at me with a slow beseeching. Why, and for what was she beseeching me? I pressed my hand a little closer, and her small breasts seemed to speak to me. The Colonel recovered the rhythm again. But at the end of the dance she shivered again, and it seemed to me I too was chilled.

"Has it suddenly turned colder?" I said, going to the radiator. It was quite hot.

"It seems to me it has," said Lord Lathkill in a queer voice.

The Colonel was sitting abjectly on the music-stool, as if broken.

31

"Shall we have another? Shall we try a tango?" said Lord Lathkill. "As much of it as we can manage?"

"I—I—" the Colonel began, turning round on the seat, his face yellow. "I'm not sure—"

Carlotta shivered. The frost seemed to touch my vitals. Mrs. Hale stood stiff, like a pillar of brown rock-salt, staring at her husband.

"We had better leave off," murmured Lady Lathkill, rising.

Then she did an extraordinary thing. She lifted her face, staring to the other side, and said suddenly, in a clear, cruel sort of voice:

"Are you here, Lucy?"

She was speaking across to the spirits. Deep inside me leaped a jump of laughter. I wanted to howl with laughter. Then instantly I went inert again. The chill gloom seemed to deepen suddenly in the room, everybody was overcome. On the piano-seat the Colonel sat yellow and huddled, with a terrible hang-dog look of guilt on his face. There was a silence, in which the cold seemed to creak. Then came again the peculiar bell-like ringing of Lady Lathkill's voice:

"Are you here? What do you wish us to do?"

A dead and ghastly silence, in which we all remained transfixed. Then from somewhere came two slow thuds, and a sound of drapery moving. The Colonel, with mad fear in his eyes, looked round at the uncurtained windows, and crouched on his seat.

"We must leave this room," said Lady Lathkill.

"I'll tell you what, mother," said Lord Lathkill curiously; "you and the Colonel go up, and we'll just turn on the Victrola."

That was almost uncanny of him. For myself, the cold effluence of these people had paralysed me. Now I began to rally. I felt that Lord Lathkill was sane, it was these other people who were mad.

Again from somewhere indefinite came two slow thuds.

"We must leave this room," repeated Lady Lathkill in monotony.

"All right, mother. You go. I'll just turn on the Victrola."

And Lord Lathkill strode across the room. In another moment the monstrous barking howl of the opening of a jazz tune, an event far more extraordinary than thuds, poured from the unmoving bit of furniture called a Victrola.

Lady Lathkill silently departed. The Colonel got to his feet.

"I wouldn't go if I were you, Colonel," said I. "Why not dance? I'll look on this time."

I felt as if I were resisting a rushing, cold, dark current.

Lord Lathkill was already dancing with Mrs. Hale, skating delicately along, with a certain smile of obstinacy, secrecy, and excitement kindled on his face. Carlotta went up quietly to the Colonel, and put her hand on his broad shoulder. He let himself be moved into the dance, but he had no heart in it.

There came a heavy crash, out of the distance. The Colonel stopped as if shot: in another moment he would go down on his knees. And his face was terrible. It was obvious he really felt another presence, other than ours, blotting us out. The room seemed dree and cold. It was heavy work, bearing up.

The Colonel's lips were moving, but no sound came forth. Then, absolutely oblivious of us, he went out of the room.

The Victrola had run down. Lord Lathkill went to wind it up again, saying:

"I suppose mother knocked over a piece of furniture."

But we were all of us depressed, in abject depression.

"Isn't it awful!" Carlotta said to me, looking up beseechingly.

"Abominable!" said I.

"What do you think there is in it?"

"God knows. The only thing is to stop it, as one does hysteria. It's on a par with hysteria."

"Quite," she said.

Lord Lathkill was dancing, and smiling very curiously down into his partner's face. The Victrola was at its loudest.

Carlotta and I looked at one another, with hardly the heart to start again. The house felt hollow and gruesome. One wanted to get out, to get away from the cold, uncanny blight which filled the air.

"Oh, I say, keep the ball rolling," called Lord Lathkill.

"Come," I said to Carlotta.

Even then she hung back a little. If she had not suffered, and lost so much, she would have gone upstairs at once to struggle in the silent wrestling of wills with her mother-in-law. Even now, *that* particular fight drew her, almost the strongest. But I took her hand.

"Come," I said. "Let us dance it down. We'll roll the ball the opposite way."

She danced with me, but she was absent, unwilling. The empty gloom of the house, the sense of cold, and of deadening opposition, pressed us down. I was looking back over my life, and thinking how the cold weight of an unliving spirit was slowly crushing all warmth and vitality out of everything. Even Carlotta herself had gone numb again, cold and resistant even to me. The thing seemed to happen wholesale in her.

"One has to choose to live," I said, dancing on. But I was powerless. With a woman, when her spirit goes inert in opposition, a man can do nothing. I felt my life-flow sinking in my body.

"This house is awfully depressing," I said to her, as we mechanically danced. "Why don't you *do* something? Why don't you get out of this tangle? Why don't you break it?"

"How?" she said.

I looked down at her, wondering why she was suddenly hostile.

"You needn't fight," I said. "You needn't fight it. Don't get tangled up in it. Just side-step, on to another ground."

She made a pause of impatience before she replied:

"I don't see where I am to side-step to, precisely."

"You do," said I. "A little while ago, you were warm and unfolded and good. Now you are shut up and prickly, in the cold. You needn't be. Why not stay warm?"

"It's nothing I do," she said coldly.

"It is. Stay warm to me. I am here. Why clutch in a tug-of-war with Lady Lathkill?"

"Do I clutch in a tug-of-war with my mother-in-law?"

"You know you do."

She looked up at me, with a faint little shadow of guilt and beseeching, but with a moue of cold obstinacy dominant.

"Let's have done," said I.

And in cold silence we sat side by side on the lounge.

The other two danced on. They at any rate were in unison. One could see from the swing of their limbs. Mrs. Hale's yellow-brown eyes looked at me every time she came round.

"Why does she look at me?" I said.

"I can't imagine," said Carlotta, with a cold grimace.

"I'd better go upstairs and see what's happening," she said, suddenly rising and disappearing in a breath.

Why should she go? Why should she rush off to the battle of wills with her mother-in-law? In such a battle, while one has any life to lose, one can only lose it. There is nothing positively to be done, but to withdraw out of the hateful tension.

The music ran down. Lord Lathkill stopped the Victrola.

"Carlotta gone?" he said.

"Apparently."

"Why didn't you stop her?"

"Wild horses wouldn't stop her."

He lifted his hand with a mocking gesture of helplessness.

"The lady loves her will," he said. "Would you like to dance?"

I looked at Mrs. Hale.

"No," I said. "I won't butt in. I'll play the pianola. The Victrola's a brute."

I hardly noticed the passage of time. Whether the others danced or not, I played, and was unconscious of almost everything. In the midst of one rattling piece, Lord Lathkill touched my arm.

"Listen to Carlotta. She says closing time," he said, in his old musical voice, but with the sardonic ring of war in it now.

Carlotta stood with her arms dangling, looking like a penitent schoolgirl.

"The Colonel has gone to bed. He hasn't been able to manage a reconciliation with Lucy," she said. "My mother-in-law thinks we ought to let him try to sleep."

Carlotta's slow eyes rested on mine, questioning, penitent— or so I imagined—and somewhat sphinx-like.

"Why, of course," said Lord Lathkill. "I wish him all the sleep in the world."

Mrs. Hale said never a word.

"Is mother retiring too?" asked Luke.

"I think so."

"Ah! then supposing we up and look at the supper-tray."

We found Lady Lathkill mixing herself some nightcap brew over a spirit-lamp: something milky and excessively harmless. She stood at the sideboard stirring her potations, and hardly noticed us. When she had finished she sat down with her steaming cup.

"Colonel Hale all right, mother?" said Luke, looking across at her.

The dowager, under her uplift of white hair, stared back at her son. There was an eye-battle for some moments, during which he maintained his arch, debonair ease, just a bit crazy.

"No," said Lady Lathkill, "he is in great trouble."

"Ah!" replied her son. "Awful pity we can't do anything for him. But if flesh and blood can't help him, I'm afraid I'm a dud. Suppose he didn't mind our dancing? Frightfully good for US! We've been forgetting that we're flesh and blood, mother."

He took another whisky and soda, and gave me one. And in a paralysing silence Lady Lathkill sipped her hot brew, Luke and I sipped our whiskies, the young woman ate a little sandwich. We all preserved an extraordinary aplomb, and an obstinate silence.

It was Lady Lathkill who broke it. She seemed to be sinking downwards, crouching into herself like a skulking animal.

"I suppose," she said, "we shall all go to bed?"

"You go mother. We'll come along in a moment."

She went, and for some time we four sat silent. The room seemed to become pleasanter, the air was more grateful.

"Look here," said Lord Lathkill at last. "What do you think of this ghost business?"

"I?" said I. "I don't like the atmosphere it produces. There may be ghosts, and spirits, and all that. The dead must be somewhere; there's no such place as nowhere. But they don't affect me particularly. Do they you?"

"Well," he said, "no, not directly. Indirectly I suppose it does."

"I think it makes a horribly depressing atmosphere, spiritualism," said I. "I want to kick."

"Exactly! And ought one?" he asked in his terribly sane-seeming way.

This made me laugh. I knew what he was up to.

"I don't know what you mean by *ought*," said I. "If I really want to kick, if I know I can't stand a thing, I kick. Who's going to authorise me, if my own genuine feeling doesn't?"

"Quite," he said, staring at me like an owl, with a fixed, meditative stare.

"Do you know," he said, "I suddenly thought at dinner-time, what corpses we all were, sitting eating our dinners. I thought it when I saw you look at those little Jerusalem artichoke things in a white sauce. Suddenly it struck me, you were alive and twinkling, and we were all bodily dead. Bodily dead, if you understand. Quite alive in other directions, but bodily dead. And whether we ate vegetarian or meat made no difference. We were bodily dead."

"Ah, with a slap in the face," said I, "we come to life! You or I or anybody."

"I *do* understand poor Lucy," said Luke. "Don't you? She forgot to be flesh and blood while she was alive, and now she can't forgive herself, nor the Colonel. That must be pretty rough, you know, not to realise it till you're dead, and you haven't, so to speak, anything left to go on. I mean, it's awfully important to be flesh and blood."

He looked so solemnly at us, we three broke simultaneously into an uneasy laugh.

"Oh, but I *do* mean it," he said. "I've only realised how very extraordinary it is to be a man of flesh and blood, alive. It seems so ordinary, in comparison, to be dead, and merely spirit. That seems so commonplace. But fancy having a living face, and arms, and thighs. Oh, my God, I'm glad I've realised in time!"

He caught Mrs. Hale's hand, and pressed her dusky arm against his body.

"Oh, but if one had died without realising it!" he cried.

"Think how ghastly for Jesus, when He was risen and wasn't touchable! How very awful, to have to say *Noli me tangere!* Ah, touch me, touch me *alive!*"

He pressed Mrs. Hale's hand convulsively against his breast. The tears had already slowly gathered in Carlotta's eyes and were dropping on to her hands in her lap.

"Don't cry, Carlotta," he said. "Really, don't. We haven't killed one another. We're too decent, after all. We've almost become two spirits side by side. We've almost become two ghosts to one another, wrestling. Oh, but I want you to get back your body, even if I can't give it to you. I want my flesh and blood, Carlotta, and I want you to have yours. We've suffered so much the other way. And the children, it is as well they are dead. They were born of our will and our disembodiment. Oh, I feel like the Bible. Clothe me with flesh again, and wrap my bones with sinew, and let the fountain of blood cover me. My spirit is like a naked nerve on the air."

Carlotta had ceased to weep. She sat with her head dropped, as if asleep. The rise and fall of her small, slack breasts was still heavy, but they were lifting on a heaving sea of rest. It was as if a slow, restful dawn were rising in her body, while she slept. So slack, so broken she sat, it occurred to me that in this crucifixion business the crucified does not put himself alone on the cross. The woman is nailed even more inexorably up, and crucified in the body even more cruelly.

It is a monstrous thought. But the deed is even more monstrous. Oh, Jesus, didn't you know that you couldn't be crucified alone?—that the two thieves crucified along with you were the two women, your wife and mother! You called them two thieves. But what would they call you, who had their women's bodies on the cross? The abominable trinity on Calvary!

I felt an infinite tenderness for my dear Carlotta. She could not yet be touched. But my soul streamed to her like warm blood. So she sat slack and drooped, as if broken. But she was not broken. It was only the great release.

Luke sat with the hand of the dark young woman pressed against his breast. His face was warm and fresh, but he too breathed heavily, and stared unseeing. Mrs. Hale sat at his side erect and mute. But she loved him, with erect, black-faced, remote power.

"Morier!" said Luke to me. "If you can help Carlotta, you will, won't you? I can't do any more for her now. We are in mortal fear of each other."

"As much as she'll let me," said I, looking at her drooping figure, that was built on such a strong frame.

The fire rustled on the hearth as we sat in complete silence. How long it lasted I cannot say. Yet we were none of us startled when the door opened.

It was the Colonel, in a handsome brocade dressing-gown, looking worried.

Luke still held the dark young woman's hand clasped against his thigh. Mrs. Hale did not move.

"I thought you fellows might help me," said the Colonel, in a worried voice, as he closed the door.

"What is wrong, Colonel?" said Luke.

The Colonel looked at him, looked at the clasped hands of Luke and the dark young woman, looked at me, looked at Carlotta, without changing his expression of anxiety, fear, and misery. He didn't care about us.

"I can't sleep," he said. "It's gone wrong again. My head feels as if there was a cold vacuum in it, and my heart beats, and something screws up inside me. I know it's Lucy. She hates me again. I can't stand it."

He looked at us with eyes half-glazed, obsessed. His face seemed as if the flesh were breaking under the skin, decomposing.

"Perhaps, poor thing," said Luke, whose madness seemed really sane this night, "perhaps you hate *her*."

Luke's strange concentration instantly made us feel a tension, as of hate, in the Colonel's body.

"I?" The Colonel looked up sharply, like a culprit. "I! I wouldn't say that, if I were you."

"Perhaps that's what's the matter," said Luke, with mad, beautiful calm. "Why can't you feel kindly towards her, poor thing! She must have been done out of a lot while she lived."

It was as if he had one foot in life and one in death, and knew both sides. To us it was like madness.

"I—I!" stammered the Colonel; and his face was a study. Expression after expression moved across it: of fear, repudiation, dismay, anger, repulsion, bewilderment, guilt. "I was good to her."

"Ah, yes," said Luke. "Perhaps *you* were good to her. But was your body good to poor Lucy's body, poor dead thing!"

He seemed to be better acquainted with the ghost than with us.

The Colonel gazed blankly at Luke, and his eyes went up and down, up and down, up and down, up and down.

"My body!" he said blankly.

And he looked down amazedly at his little round stomach, under the silk gown, and his stout knee, in its blue-and-white pyjama.

"My body!" he repeated blankly.

"Yes," said Luke. "Don't you see, you may have been awfully good to her. But her poor woman's body, were you ever good to that?"

"She had everything she wanted. She had three of my children," said the Colonel dazedly.

"Ah yes, that may easily be. But your body of a man, was it ever good to her body of a woman? That's the point. If you understand the marriage service: with my body I thee worship. That's the point. No getting away from it."

The queerest of all accusing angels did Lord Lathkill make, as he sat there with the hand of the other man's wife clasped against his thigh. His face was fresh and naïve, and the dark eyes were bright with a clairvoyant candour, that was like madness, and perhaps was supreme sanity.

The Colonel was thinking back, and over his face a slow understanding was coming.

"It may be," he said. "It may be. Perhaps, that way, I despised her. It may be, it may be."

"I know," said Luke. "As if she weren't worth noticing, what you did to her. Haven't I done it myself? And don't I know now, it's a horrible thing to do, to oneself as much as to her? Her poor ghost, that ached, and never had a real body! It's not so easy to worship with the body. Ah, if the Church taught us *that* sacrament: with my body I thee worship! that would easily make up for any honouring and obeying the woman might do. But that's why she haunts you. You ignored and disliked her body, and she was only a living ghost. Now she wails in the afterworld, like a still-wincing nerve."

The Colonel hung his head, slowly pondering. Pondering with all his body. His young wife watched the sunken, bald head in a kind of stupor. His day seemed so far from her day. Carlotta had lifted her face; she was beautiful again, with the tender before-dawn freshness of a new understanding.

She was watching Luke, and it was obvious he was another man to her. The man she knew, the Luke who was her husband was gone, and this other strange, uncanny creature had taken his place. She was filled with wonder. Could one so change, as to become another creature entirely? Ah, if it were so! If she herself could cease to be! If that woman who was married to Luke, married to him in an intimacy of misfortune that was like a horror, could only cease to be, and let a new, delicately-wild Carlotta take her place!

"It may be," said the Colonel, lifting his head. "It may be." There seemed to come a relief over his soul, as he realised. "I didn't worship her with my body. I think maybe I worshipped other women that way; but maybe I never did. But I thought I was good to her. And I thought she didn't want it."

"It's no good thinking. We all want it," asserted Luke. "And before we die, we know it. I say, before we die. It may be after. But everybody wants it, let them say and do what they will. Don't you agree, Morier?"

I was startled when he spoke to me. I had been thinking of Carlotta: how she was looking like a girl again, as she used to look at the Thwaite, when she painted cactuses-in-a-pot. Only now, a certain rigidity of the will had left her, so that she looked even younger than when I first knew her, having now a virginal, flower-like *stillness* which she had not had then. I had always believed that people could be born again: if they would only let themselves.

"I'm sure they do," I said to Luke.

But I was thinking, if people were born again, the old circumstances would not fit the new body.

"What about yourself, Luke?" said Carlotta abruptly.

"I!" he exclaimed, and the scarlet showed in his cheek. "I! I'm not fit to be spoken about. I've been moaning like the ghost of disembodiment myself, ever since I became a man."

The Colonel said never a word. He hardly listened. He was pondering, pondering. In this way, he, too, was a brave man.

"I have an idea what you mean," he said. "There's no denying it, I didn't like her body. And now, I suppose it's too late."

He looked up bleakly: in a way, willing to be condemned, since he knew vaguely that something was wrong. Anything better than the blind torture.

"Oh, I don't know," said Luke. "Why don't you, even now, love her a little with your real heart? Poor disembodied thing! Why don't you take her to your warm heart, even now, and comfort her inside there? Why don't you be kind to her poor ghost, bodily?"

The Colonel did not answer. He was gazing fixedly at Luke. Then he turned, and dropped his head, alone in a deep silence. Then, deliberately, but not lifting his head, he pulled open his dressing-gown at the breast, unbuttoned the top of his pyjama jacket, and sat perfectly still, his breast showing white and very pure, so much younger and purer than his averted face. He breathed with difficulty, his white breast rising irregularly. But in the deep isolation where he was, slowly a gentleness of compassion came over him, moulding his elderly features with strange freshness, and softening his blue eye with a look it had never had before. Something of the tremulous gentleness of a young bridegroom had come upon him, in spite of his baldness, his silvery little moustache, the weary marks of his face.

The passionate, compassionate soul stirred in him and was pure, his youth flowered over his face and eyes.

We sat very still, moved also in the spirit of compassion. There seemed a presence in the air, almost a smell of blossom, as if time had opened and gave off the perfume of spring. The Colonel gazed in silence into space, his smooth white chest, with the few dark hairs, open and rising and sinking with life.

Meanwhile his dark-faced young wife watched as if from afar. The youngness that was on him was not for her.

I knew that Lady Lathkill would come. I could feel her far off in her room, stirring and sending forth her rays. Swiftly I steeled myself to be in readiness. When the door opened I rose and walked across the room.

She entered with characteristic noiselessness, peering in round the door, with her crest of white hair, before she ventured bodily in. The Colonel looked at her swiftly, and swiftly covered his breast, holding his hand at his bosom, clutching the silk of his robe.

"I was afraid," she murmured, "that Colonel Hale might be in trouble."

"No," said I. "We are all sitting very peacefully. There is no trouble."

Lord Lathkill also rose.

"No trouble at all, I assure you, mother!" he said.

Lady Lathkill glanced at us both, then turned heavily to the Colonel.

"She is unhappy to-night?" she asked.

The Colonel winced.

"No," he said hurriedly. "No, I don't think so." He looked up at her with shy, wincing eyes.

"Tell me what I can do," she said in a very low tone, bending towards him.

"Our ghost is walking to-night, mother," said Lord Lathkill. "Haven't you felt the air of spring, and smelt the plum-blossom? Don't you feel us all young? Our ghost is walking, to bring Lucy home. The Colonel's breast is quite extraordinary, white as plum-blossom, mother, younger-looking than mine, and he's already taken Lucy into his bosom, in his breast, where he breathes like the wind among trees. The Colonel's breast is white and extraordinarily beautiful, mother. I don't wonder poor Lucy yearned for it, to go home into it at last. It's like going into an orchard of plum-blossom for a ghost."

His mother looked round at him, then back at the Colonel, who was still clutching his hand over his chest, as if protecting something.

"You see, I didn't understand where I'd been wrong," he said, looking up at her imploringly. "I never realised that it was my body which had not been good to her."

Lady Lathkill curved sideways to watch him. But her power was gone. His face had come smooth with the tender glow of compassionate life, that flowers again. She could not get at him.

"It's no good, mother. You know our ghost is walking. She's supposed to be absolutely like a crocus, if you know what I mean: harbinger of spring in the earth. So it says in my great-grandfather's diary: for she rises with silence like a crocus at the feet, and violets in the hollows of the heart come out. For she is of the feet and the hands, the thighs and breast, the face and the all-concealing belly, and her name is silent, but her odour is of spring, and her contact is the all-in-all." He was quoting from his great-grandfather's diary, which only the sons of the family read. And as he quoted he rose curiously on his toes, and spread his fingers, bringing his hands together till the finger-tips touched. His father had done that before him, when he was deeply moved.

Lady Lathkill sat down heavily in the chair next the Colonel.

"How do you feel?" she asked him, in a secretive mutter.

He looked round at her, with the large blue eyes of candour.

"I never knew what was wrong," he said, a little nervously. "She only wanted to be looked after a bit, not to be a homeless, houseless ghost. It's all right! She's all right here." He pressed his clutched hand on his breast. "It's all right; it's all right. She'll be all right now."

He rose, a little fantastic in his brocade gown, but once more manly, candid, and sober.

"With your permission," he said, "I will retire."—He made a little bow.—"I am glad you helped me. I didn't know—didn't know."

But the change in him, and his secret wondering were so strong in him, he went out of the room scarcely being aware of us.

Lord Lathkill threw up his arms, and stretched quivering.

"Oh, pardon, pardon," he said, seeming, as he stretched, quivering, to grow bigger and almost splendid, sending out rays of fire to the dark young woman. "Oh, mother, thank you for my limbs, and my body! Oh, mother, thank you for my knees and my shoulders at this moment! Oh, mother, thank you that my body is straight and alive! Oh, mother, torrents of spring, torrents of spring, whoever said that?"

"Don't you forget yourself, my boy?" said his mother.

"Oh no, dear no! Oh, mother dear, a man has to be in love in his thighs, the way you ride a horse. Why don't we stay in love that way all our lives? Why do we turn into corpses with consciousness? Oh, mother of my body, thank you for my body, you strange woman with white hair! I don't know much about you, but my body came from you, so thank you, my dear. I shall think of you to-night!"

"Hadn't we better go?" she said, beginning to tremble.

"Why, yes," he said, turning and looking strangely at the dark woman. "Yes, let us go; let us go!"

Carlotta gazed at him, then, with strange, heavy, searching look, at me. I smiled to her, and she looked away. The dark young woman looked over her shoulder as she went out. Lady Lathkill hurried past her son, with head ducked. But still he laid his hand on her shoulder, and she stopped dead.

"Good night, mother; mother of my face and my thighs. Thank you for the night to come, dear mother of my body."

She glanced up at him rapidly, nervously, then hurried away. He stared after her, then switched off the light.

"Funny old mother!" he said. "I never realised before that she was the mother of my shoulders and my hips, as well as my brain. Mother of my thighs!"

He switched off some of the lights as we went, accompanying me to my room.

"You know," he said, "I can understand that the Colonel is happy, now the forlorn ghost of Lucy is comforted in his heart. After all, he married her! And she must be content at last: he has a beautiful chest, don't you think? Together they will sleep well.

And then he will begin to live the life of the living again. How friendly the house feels tonight! But, after all, it is my old home. And the smell of plum-blossom—don't you notice it? It is our ghost, in silence like a crocus. There, your fire has died down! But it's a nice room! I hope our ghost will come to you. I think she will. Don't speak to her. It makes her go away. She, too, is a ghost of silence. We talk far too much. But now I am going to be silent too, and a ghost of silence. Good night!"

He closed the door softly and was gone. And softly, in silence, I took off my things. I was thinking of Carlotta, and a little sadly, perhaps, because of the power of circumstance over us. This night I could have worshipped her with my body, and she, perhaps, was stripped in the body to be worshipped. But it was not for me, at this hour, to fight against circumstances.

I had fought too much, even against the most imposing circumstances, to use any more violence for love. Desire is a sacred thing, and should not be violated.

"Hush!" I said to myself. "I will sleep, and the ghost of my silence can go forth, in the subtle body of desire, to meet that which is coming to meet it. Let my ghost go forth, and let me not interfere. There are many intangible meetings, and unknown fulfilments of desire."

So I went softly to sleep, as I wished to, without interfering with the warm, crocus-like ghost of my body.

And I must have gone far, far down the intricate galleries of sleep, to the very heart of the world. For I know I passed on beyond the strata of images and words, beyond the iron veins of memory, and even the jewels of rest, to sink in the final dark like a fish, dumb, soundless, and imageless, yet alive and swimming.

And at the very core of the deep night the ghost came to me, at the heart of the ocean of oblivion, which is also the heart of life. Beyond hearing, or even knowledge of contact, I met her and knew her. How I know it I don't know. Yet I know it with eyeless, wingless knowledge.

For man in the body is formed through countless ages, and at the centre is the speck, or spark upon which all his formation has taken place. It is even not himself, deep beyond his many

46

depths. Deep from him calls to deep. And according as deep answers deep, man glistens and surpasses himself.

Beyond all the pearly mufflings of consciousness, of age upon age of consciousness, deep calls yet to deep, and sometimes is answered. It is calling and answering, new-awakened God calling within the deep of man, and new God calling answer from the other deep. And sometimes the other deep is a woman, as it was with me, when my ghost came.

Women were not unknown to me. But never before had woman come, in the depths of night, to answer my deep with her deep. As the ghost came, came as a ghost of silence, still in the depth of sleep.

I know she came. I know she came even as a woman, to my man. But the knowledge is darkly naked as the event. I only know, it was so. In the deep of sleep a call was called from the deeps of me, and answered in the deeps, by a woman among women. Breasts or thighs or face. I remember not a touch, no, nor a movement of my own. It is all complete in the profundity of darkness. Yet I know it was so.

I awoke towards dawn, from far, far away. I was vaguely conscious of drawing nearer and nearer, as the sun must have been drawing towards the horizon, from the complete beyond. Till at last the faint pallor of mental consciousness coloured my waking.

And then I was aware of a pervading scent, as of plum-blossom, and a sense of extraordinary silkiness—though where, and in what contact, I could not say. It was as the first blemish of dawn.

And even with so slight a conscious registering, *it* seemed to disappear. Like a whale that has sounded to the bottomless seas. That knowledge of *it*, which was the mating of the ghost and me, disappeared from me, in its rich weight of certainty, as the scent of the plum-blossom moved down the lanes of my consciousness, and my limbs stirred in a silkiness for which I have no comparison.

As I became aware, I also became uncertain. I wanted to be certain of *it*, to have definite evidence. And as I sought for evidence, *it* disappeared, my perfect knowledge was gone. I no longer knew in full.

Now as the daylight slowly amassed, in the windows from which I had put back the shutters, I sought in myself for evidence, and in the room.

But I shall never know. I shall never know if it was a ghost, some sweet spirit from the innermost of the ever-deepening cosmos; or a woman, a very woman, as the silkiness of my limbs seems to attest; or a dream, a hallucination! I shall never know. Because I went away from Riddings in the morning on account of the sudden illness of Lady Lathkill.

"You will come again," Luke said to me. "And in any case, you will never really go away from us."

"Good-bye," she said to me. "At last it was perfect!"

She seemed so beautiful, when I left her, as if it were the ghost again, and I was far down the deeps of consciousness.

The following autumn, when I was overseas once more, I had a letter from Lord Lathkill. He wrote very rarely.

"Carlotta has a son," he said, "and I an heir. He has yellow hair, like a little crocus, and one of the young plum trees in the orchard has come out of all season into blossom. To me he is flesh and blood of our ghost itself. Even mother doesn't look over the wall, to the other side, any more. It's all this side for her now.

"So our family refuses to die out, by the grace of our ghost. We are calling him Gabriel.

"Dorothy Hale also is a mother, three days before Carlotta. She has a black lamb of a daughter, called Gabrielle. By the bleat of the little thing, I know its father. Our own is a blue-eyed one, with the dangerous repose of a pugilist. I have no fears of our family misfortune for him, ghost-begotten and ready-fisted.

"The Colonel is very well, quiet, and self-possessed. He is farming in Wiltshire, raising pigs. It is a passion with him, the crème de la crème of swine. I admit, he has golden sows as elegant as a young Diane de Poictiers, and young hogs like Perseus in the first red-gold flush of youth. He looks me in the eye, and I look him back, and we understand. He is quiet, and proud now, and very hale and hearty, raising swine *ad maiorem gloriam Dei*. A good sport!

"I am in love with this house and its inmates, including the plum-blossom-scented one, she who visited you, in all the peace. I cannot understand why you wander in uneasy and distant parts of the earth. For me, when I am at home, I am there. I have peace upon my bones, and if the world is going to come to a violent and untimely end, as prophets aver, I feel the house of Lathkill will survive, built upon our ghost. So come back, and you'll find we shall not have gone away. . . ."

Smile

He had decided to sit up all night, as a kind of penance. The telegram had simply said: "Ophelia's condition critical." He felt, under the circumstances, that to go to bed in the *wagon-lit* would be frivolous. So he sat wearily in the first-class compartment as night fell over France.

He ought, of course, to be sitting by Ophelia's bedside. But Ophelia didn't want him. So he sat up in the train.

Deep inside him was a black and ponderous weight: like some tumour filled with sheer gloom, weighing down his vitals. He had always taken life seriously. Seriousness now overwhelmed him. His dark, handsome, clean-shaven face would have done for Christ on the Cross, with the thick black eyebrows tilted in the dazed agony.

The night in the train was like an inferno: nothing was real. Two elderly Englishwomen opposite him had died long ago, perhaps even before he had. Because, of course, he was dead himself.

Slow, grey dawn came in the mountains of the frontier, and he watched it with unseeing eyes. But his mind repeated:

And when the dawn came, dim and sad
And chill with early showers,
Her quiet eyelids closed: she had
Another morn than ours.

And his monk's changeless, tormented face showed no trace of the contempt he felt, even self-contempt, for this bathos, as his critical mind judged it.

He was in Italy: he looked at the country with faint aversion.

Not capable of much feeling any more, he had only a tinge of aversion as he saw the olives and the sea. A sort of poetic swindle.

It was night again when he reached the home of the Blue Sisters, where Ophelia had chosen to retreat. He was ushered into the Mother Superior's room, in the palace. She rose and bowed to him in silence, looking at him along her nose. Then she said in French:

"It pains me to tell you. She died this afternoon."

He stood stupefied, not feeling much, anyhow, but gazing at nothingness from his handsome, strong-featured monk's face.

The Mother Superior softly put her white, handsome hand on his arm and gazed up into his face, leaning to him.

"Courage!" she said softly. "Courage, no?"

He stepped back. He was always scared when a woman leaned at him like that. In her voluminous skirts, the Mother Superior was very womanly.

"Quite!" he replied in English. "Can I see her?"

The Mother Superior rang a bell, and a young sister appeared. She was rather pale, but there was something naïve and mischievous in her hazel eyes. The elder woman murmured an introduction, the young woman demurely made a slight reverence. But Matthew held out his hand, like a man reaching for the last straw. The young nun unfolded her white hands and shyly slid one into his, passive as a sleeping bird.

And out of the fathomless Hades of his gloom he thought: "What a nice hand!"

They went along a handsome but cold corridor, and tapped at a door. Matthew, walking in far-off Hades, still was aware of the soft, fine voluminousness of the women's black skirts, moving with soft, fluttered haste in front of him.

He was terrified when the door opened, and he saw the candles burning round the white bed, in the lofty, noble room. A sister sat beside the candles, her face dark and primitive, in the white coif, as she looked up from her breviary. Then she rose, a sturdy woman, and made a little bow, and Matthew was aware of creamy-dusky hands twisting a black rosary, against the rich, blue silk of her bosom.

The three sisters flocked silent, yet fluttered and very feminine, in their volumes of silky black skirts, to the bedhead. The Mother Superior leaned, and with utmost delicacy lifted the veil of white lawn from the dead face.

Matthew saw the dead, beautiful composure of his wife's face, and instantly, something leaped like laughter in the depths of him, he gave a little grunt, and an extraordinary smile came over his face.

The three nuns, in the candle glow that quivered warm and quick like a Christmas tree, were looking at him with heavily compassionate eyes, from under their coif-bands. They were like a mirror. Six eyes suddenly started with a little fear, then changed, puzzled, into wonder. And over the three nuns' faces, helplessly facing him in the candle-glow, a strange, involuntary smile began to come. In the three faces, the same smile growing so differently, like three subtle flowers opening. In the pale young nun, it was almost pain, with a touch of mischievous ecstasy. But the dark Ligurian face of the watching sister, a mature, level-browed woman, curled with a pagan smile, slow, infinitely subtle in its archaic humour. It was the Etruscan smile, subtle and unabashed, and unanswerable.

The Mother Superior, who had a large-featured face something like Matthew's own, tried hard not to smile. But he kept his humorous, malevolent chin uplifted at her, and she lowered her face as the smile grew, grew and grew over her face.

The young, pale sister suddenly covered her face with her sleeve, her body shaking. The Mother Superior put her arm over the girl's shoulder, murmuring with Italian emotion: "Poor little thing! Weep, then, poor little thing!" But the chuckle was still there, under the emotion. The sturdy dark sister stood unchanging, clutching the black beads, but the noiseless smile immovable.

Matthew suddenly turned to the bed, to see if his dead wife had observed him. It was a movement of fear.

Ophelia lay so pretty and so touching, with her peaked, dead little nose sticking up, and her face of an obstinate child fixed in the final obstinacy. The smile went away from Matthew, and the look of super-martyrdom took its place. He did not weep:

he just gazed without meaning. Only, on his face deepened the look: I knew this martyrdom was in store for me!

She was so pretty, so childlike, so clever, so obstinate, so worn—and so dead! He felt so blank about it all.

They had been married ten years. He himself had not been perfect—no, no, not by any means! But Ophelia had always wanted her own will. She had loved him, and grown obstinate, and left him, and grown wistful, or contemptuous, or angry, a dozen times, and a dozen times come back to him.

They had no children. And he, sentimentally, had always wanted children. He felt very largely sad.

Now she would never come back to him. This was the thirteenth time, and she was gone for ever.

But was she? Even as he thought it, he felt her nudging him somewhere in the ribs, to make him smile. He writhed a little, and an angry frown came on his brow. He was not *going* to smile! He set his square, naked jaw, and bared his big teeth, as he looked down at the infinitely provoking dead woman. "At it again!"— he wanted to say to her, like the man in Dickens.

He himself had not been perfect. He was going to dwell on his own imperfections.

He turned suddenly to the three women, who had faded backwards beyond the candles, and now hovered, in the white frames of their coifs, between him and nowhere. His eyes glared, and he bared his teeth.

"*Mea culpa! Mea culpa!*" he snarled.

"*Macchè!*" exclaimed the daunted Mother Superior, and her two hands flew apart, then together again, in the density of the sleeves, like birds nesting in couples.

Matthew ducked his head and peered round, prepared to bolt. The Mother Superior, in the background, softly intoned a *Pater Noster*, and her beads dangled. The pale young sister faded farther back. But the black eyes of the sturdy, black-*avised* sister twinkled like eternally humorous stars upon him, and he felt the smile digging him in the ribs again.

"Look here!" he said to the women, in expostulation, "I'm awfully upset. I'd better go."

They hovered in fascinating bewilderment. He ducked for the door. But even as he went, the smile began to come on his face, caught by the tail of the sturdy sister's black eye, with its everlasting twink. And, he was secretly thinking, he wished he could hold both her creamy-dusky hands, that were folded like mating birds, voluptuously.

But he insisted on dwelling upon his own imperfections. *Mea culpa!* he howled at himself. And even as he howled it, he felt something nudge him in the ribs, saying to him: *Smile!*

The three women left behind in the lofty room looked at one another, and their hands flew up for a moment, like six birds flying suddenly out of the foliage, then settling again.

"Poor thing!" said the Mother Superior, compassionately.

"Yes! Yes! Poor thing!" cried the young sister, with naïve, shrill impulsiveness.

"Già!" said the dark-*avised* sister.

The Mother Superior noiselessly moved to the bed, and leaned over the dead face.

"She seems to know, poor soul!" she murmured. "Don't you think so?"

The three coifed heads leaned together. And for the first time they saw the faint ironical curl at the corners of Ophelia's mouth. They looked in fluttering wonder.

"She has seen him!" whispered the thrilling young sister.

The Mother Superior delicately laid the fine-worked veil over the cold face. Then they murmured a prayer for the anima, fingering their beads. Then the Mother Superior set two of the candles straight upon their spikes, clenching the thick candle with firm, soft grip, and pressing it down.

The dark-faced, sturdy sister sat down again with her little holy book. The other two rustled softly to the door, and out into the great white corridor. There softly, noiselessly sailing in all their dark drapery, like dark swans down a river, they suddenly hesitated. Together they had seen a forlorn man's figure, in a melancholy overcoat, loitering in the cold distance at the corridor's end. The Mother Superior suddenly pressed her pace into an appearance of speed.

Matthew saw them bearing down on him, these voluminous figures with framed faces and lost hands. The young sister trailed a little behind.

"*Pardon, ma Mère!*" he said, as if in the street. "I left my hat somewhere. . . ."

He made a desperate, moving sweep with his arm, and never was man more utterly smileless.

The Last Laugh

There was a little snow on the ground, and the church clock had just struck midnight. Hampstead in the night of winter for once was looking pretty, with clean white earth and lamps for moon, and dark sky above the lamps.

A confused little sound of voices, a gleam of hidden yellow light. And then the garden door of a tall, dark Georgian house suddenly opened, and three people confusedly emerged. A girl in a dark blue coat and fur turban, very erect: a fellow with a little dispatch-case, slouching: a thin man with a red beard, bare-headed, peering out of the gateway down the hill that swung in a curve downwards towards London.

"Look at it! A new world!" cried the man in the beard, ironically, as he stood on the step and peered out.

"No, Lorenzo! It's only white-wash!" cried the young man in the overcoat. His voice was handsome, resonant, plangent, with a weary sardonic touch. As he turned back his face was dark in shadow.

The girl with the erect, alert head, like a bird, turned back to the two men.

"What was that?" she asked, in her quick, quiet voice.

"Lorenzo says it's a new world. I say it's only white-wash," cried the man in the street.

She stood still and lifted her woolly, gloved finger. She was deaf and was taking it in.

Yes, she had got it. She gave a quick, chuckling laugh, glanced very quickly at the man in the bowler hat, then back at the man in the stucco gateway, who was grinning like a satyr and waving good-bye.

"Good-bye, Lorenzo!" came the resonant, weary cry of the man in the bowler hat.

"Good-bye!" came the sharp, night-bird call of the girl.

The green gate slammed, then the inner door. The two were alone in the street, save for the policeman at the corner. The road curved steeply downhill.

"You'd better mind how you *step!*" shouted the man in the bowler hat, leaning near the erect, sharp girl, and slouching in his walk. She paused a moment, to make sure what he had said.

"Don't mind me, I'm quite all right. Mind yourself!" she said quickly. At that very moment he gave a wild lurch on the slippery snow, but managed to save himself from falling. She watched him on tiptoes of alertness. His bowler hat bounced away in the thin snow. They were under a lamp near the curve. As he ducked for his hat he showed a bald spot, just like a tonsure, among his dark, thin, rather curly hair. And when he looked up at her, with his thick black brows sardonically arched, and his rather hooked nose self-derisive, jamming his hat on again, he seemed like a satanic young priest. His face had beautiful lines, like a faun, and a doubtful martyred expression. A sort of faun on the Cross, with all the malice of the complication.

"Did you hurt yourself?" she asked in her quick, cool, unemotional way.

"No!" he shouted derisively.

"Give me the machine, won't you?" she said, holding out her woolly hand. "I believe I'm safer."

"Do you *want* it?" he shouted.

"Yes, I'm sure I'm safer."

He handed her the little brown dispatch-case, which was really a Marconi listening machine for her deafness. She marched erect as ever. He shoved his hands deep in his overcoat pockets and slouched along beside her, as if he wouldn't make his legs firm. The road curved down in front of them, clean and pale with snow under the lamps. A motorcar came churning up. A few dark figures slipped away into the dark recesses of the houses, like fishes among rocks above a sea-bed of white sand. On the left was a tuft of trees sloping upwards into the dark.

He kept looking around, pushing out his finely shaped chin and his hooked nose as if he were listening for something. He could still hear the motor-car climbing on to the Heath. Below was the yellow, foul-smelling glare of the Hampstead Tube Station. On the right the trees.

The girl, with her alert pink-and-white face, looked at him sharply, inquisitively. She had an odd nymph-like inquisitiveness, sometimes like a bird, sometimes a squirrel, sometimes a rabbit: never quite like a woman. At last he stood still, as if he would go no farther. There was a curious, baffled grin on his smooth, cream-coloured face.

"James," he said loudly to her, leaning towards her ear. "Do you hear somebody *laughing*?"

"Laughing?" she retorted quickly. "Who's laughing?"

"I don't know. *somebody*!" he shouted, showing his teeth at her in a very odd way.

"No, I hear nobody," she announced.

"But it's most *extraordinary*!" he cried, his voice slurring up and down. "Put on your machine."

"Put it on?" she retorted. "What for?"

"To see if you can *hear* it," he cried.

"Hear what?"

"The *laughing*. Somebody laughing. It's most *extraordinary*."

She gave her odd little chuckle and handed him her machine. He held it while she opened the lid and attached the wires, putting the band over her head and the receivers at her ears, like a wireless operator. Crumbs of snow fell down the cold darkness. She switched on: little yellow lights in glass tubes shone in the machine. She was connected, she was listening. He stood with his head ducked, his hands shoved down in his overcoat pockets.

Suddenly he lifted his face and gave the weirdest, slightly neighing laugh, uncovering his strong, spaced teeth, and arching his black brows, and watching her with queer, gleaming, goat-like eyes.

She seemed a little dismayed.

"There!" he said. "Didn't you hear it?"

"I heard *you*!" she said, in a tone which conveyed that *that* was enough.

"But didn't you hear *it*!" he cried, unfurling his lips oddly again.

"No!" she said.

He looked at her vindictively, and stood again with ducked head. She remained erect, her fur hat in her hand, her fine bobbed hair banded with the machine-band and catching crumbs of snow, her odd, bright-eyed, deaf nymph's face lifted with blank listening.

"There!" he cried, suddenly jerking up his gleaming face. "You mean to tell me you can't—" He was looking at her almost diabolically. But something else was too strong for him. His face wreathed with a startling, peculiar smile, seeming to gleam, and suddenly the most extraordinary laugh came bursting out of him, like an animal laughing. It was a strange, neighing sound, amazing in her ears. She was startled, and switched her machine quieter.

A large form loomed up: a tall, clean-shaven young policeman.

"A radio?" he asked laconically.

"No, it's my machine. I'm deaf!" said Miss James quickly and distinctly. She was not the daughter of a peer for nothing.

The man in the bowler hat lifted his face and glared at the fresh-faced young policeman with a peculiar white glare in his eyes.

"Look here!" he said distinctly. "Did you hear someone laughing?"

"Laughing? I heard you, sir."

"No, *not* me." He gave an impatient jerk of his arm, and lifted his face again. His smooth, creamy face seemed to gleam, there were subtle curves of derisive triumph in all its lines. He was careful not to look directly at the young policeman. "The most extraordinary laughter I ever heard," he added, and the same touch of derisive exultation sounded in his tones.

The policeman looked down on him cogitatingly.

"It's perfectly all right," said Miss James coolly. "He's not drunk. He just hears something that we don't hear."

"Drunk!" echoed the man in the bowler hat, in profoundly amused derision. "If I were merely drunk—" And off he went again in the wild, neighing, animal laughter, while his averted face seemed to flash.

At the sound of the laughter something roused in the blood of the girl and of the policeman. They stood nearer to one another, so that their sleeves touched and they looked wonderingly across at the man in the bowler hat. He lifted his black brows at them.

"Do you mean to say you heard nothing?" he asked.

"Only you," said Miss James.

"Only you, sir!" echoed the policeman.

"What was it like?" asked Miss James.

"Ask me to *describe* it!" retorted the young man, in extreme contempt. "It's the most marvellous sound in the world."

And truly he seemed wrapped up in a new mystery.

"Where does it come from?" asked Miss James, very practical.

"Apparently," it answered in contempt, "from over there." And he pointed to the trees and bushes inside the railings over the road.

"Well, let's go and see!" she said. "I can carry my machine and go on listening."

The man seemed relieved to get rid of the burden. He shoved his hands in his pockets again and sloped off across the road. The policeman, a queer look flickering on his fresh young face, put his hand round the girl's arm carefully and subtly, to help her. She did not lean at all on the support of the big hand, but she was interested, so she did not resent it. Having held herself all her life intensely aloof from physical contact, and never having let any man touch her, she now, with a certain nymph-like voluptuousness, allowed the large hand of the young policeman to support her as they followed the quick wolf-like figure of the other man across the road uphill. And she could feel the presence of the young policeman, through all the thickness of his dark-blue uniform, as something young and alert and bright.

When they came up to the man in the bowler hat, he was standing with his head ducked, his ears pricked, listening beside the iron rail inside which grew big black holly trees tufted with snow, and old, ribbed, silent English elms.

The policeman and the girl stood waiting. She was peering into the bushes with the sharp eyes of a deaf nymph, deaf to the world's noises. The man in the bowler hat listened intensely. A lorry rolled downhill, making the earth tremble.

"There!" cried the girl, as the lorry rumbled darkly past. And she glanced round with flashing eyes at her policeman, her fresh soft face gleaming with startled life. She glanced straight into the puzzled, amused eyes of the young policeman. He was just enjoying himself.

"Don't you see?" she said, rather imperiously.

"What is it, Miss?" answered the policeman.

"I mustn't point," she said. "Look where I look."

And she looked away with brilliant eyes, into the dark holly bushes. She must see something, for she smiled faintly, with subtle satisfaction, and she tossed her erect head in all the pride of vindication. The policeman looked at her instead of into the bushes. There was a certain brilliance of triumph and vindication in all the poise of her slim body.

"I always knew I should see him," she said triumphantly to herself.

"Whom do you see?" shouted the man in the bowler hat.

"Don't you see him too?" she asked, turning round her soft, arch, nymph-like face anxiously. She was anxious for the little man to see.

"No, I see nothing. What do you see, James?" cried the man in the bowler hat, insisting.

"A man."

"Where?"

"There. Among the holly bushes."

"Is he there now?"

"No! He's gone."

"What sort of a man?"

"I don't know."

"What did he look like?"

"I can't tell you."

But at that instant the man in the bowler hat turned suddenly, and the arch, triumphant look flew to his face.

"Why, he must be *there!*" he cried, pointing up the grove. "Don't you hear him laughing? He must be behind those trees."

And his voice, with curious delight, broke into a laugh again, as he stood and stamped his feet on the snow, and danced to his own laughter, ducking his head. Then he turned away and ran swiftly up the avenue lined with old trees.

He slowed down as a door at the end of a garden path, white with untouched snow, suddenly opened, and a woman in a long-fringed black shawl stood in the light. She peered out into the night. Then she came down to the low garden gate. Crumbs of snow still fell. She had dark hair and a tall dark comb.

"Did you knock at my door?" she asked of the man in the bowler hat.

"I? No!"

"Somebody knocked at my door."

"Did they? Are you sure? They can't have done. There are no footmarks in the snow."

"Nor are there!" she said. "But somebody knocked and called something."

"That's very curious," said the man. "Were you expecting someone?"

"No. Not exactly expecting anyone. Except that one is always expecting Somebody, you know." In the dimness of the snow-lit night he could see her making big, dark eyes at him.

"Was it someone laughing?" he said.

"No. It was no one laughing, exactly. Someone knocked, and I ran to open, hoping as one always hopes, you know—"

"What?"

"Oh—that something wonderful is going to happen."

He was standing close to the low gate. She stood on the opposite side. Her hair was dark, her face seemed dusky, as she looked up at him with her dark, meaningful eyes.

"Did you wish someone would come?" he asked.

"Very much," she replied, in her plangent Jewish voice. She must be a Jewess.

"No matter who?" he said, laughing.

"So long as it was a man I could like," she said, in a low, meaningful, falsely shy voice.

"Really!" he said. "Perhaps after all it was I who knocked—without knowing."

"I think it was," she said. "It must have been."

"Shall I come in?" he asked, putting his hand on the little gate.

"Don't you think you'd better?" she replied.

He bent down, unlatching the gate. As he did so the woman in the black shawl turned, and, glancing over her shoulder, hurried back to the house, walking unevenly in the snow, on her high-heeled shoes. The man hurried after her, hastening like a hound to catch up.

Meanwhile the girl and the policeman had come up. The girl stood still when she saw the man in the bowler hat going up the garden walk after the woman in the black shawl with the fringe.

"Is he going in?" she asked quickly.

"Looks like it, doesn't it?" said the policeman.

"Does he know that woman?"

"I can't say. I should say he soon will," replied the policeman.

"But who is she?"

"I couldn't say who she is."

The two dark, confused figures entered the lighted doorway, then the door closed on them.

"He's gone," said the girl outside on the snow. She hastily began to pull off the band of her telephone receiver, and switched off her machine. The tubes of secret light disappeared, she packed up the little leather case. Then, pulling on her soft fur cap, she stood once more ready.

The slightly martial look which her long dark-blue military-seeming coat gave her was intensified, while the slightly anxious, bewildered look on her face had gone. She seemed to stretch herself, to stretch her limbs free. And the inert look had left her full soft cheeks. Her cheeks were alive with the glimmer of pride and a new dangerous surety.

She looked quickly at the tall young policeman. He was clean-shaven, fresh-faced, smiling oddly under his helmet, waiting in subtle patience, a few yards away. She saw that he was a decent young man, one of the waiting sort.

The second of ancient fear was followed at once in her by a blithe, unaccustomed sense of power.

"Well!" she said. "I should say it's no use waiting." She spoke decisively.

"You don't have to wait for him, do you?" asked the policeman.

"Not at all. He's much better where he is." She laughed an odd, brief laugh. Then glancing over her shoulder, she set off down the hill, carrying her little case. Her feet felt lighter, her legs felt long and strong. She glanced over her shoulder again. The young policeman was following her, and she laughed to herself. Her limbs felt so lithe and so strong, if she wished she could easily run faster than he. If she wished she could easily kill him, even with her hands.

So it seemed to her. But why kill him? He was a decent young fellow. She had in front of her eyes the dark face among the holly bushes, with the brilliant, mocking eyes. Her breast felt full of power, and her legs felt long and strong and wild. She was surprised herself at the strong, bright, throbbing sensation beneath her breasts, a sensation of triumph and rosy anger. Her hands felt keen on her wrists. She who had always declared she had not a muscle in her body! Even now, it was not muscle, it was a sort of flame.

Suddenly it began to snow heavily, with fierce frozen puffs of wind. The snow was small, in frozen grains, and hit sharp on her face. It seemed to whirl round her as if she herself were whirling in a cloud. But she did not mind. There was a flame in her, her limbs felt flamey and strong, amid the whirl.

And the whirling snowy air seemed full of presences, full of strange unheard voices. She was used to the sensation of noises taking place which she could not hear. This sensation became very strong. She felt something was happening in the wild air.

The London air was no longer heavy and clammy, saturated with ghosts of the unwilling dead. A new, clean tempest swept down from the Pole, and there were noises.

Voices were calling. In spite of her deafness she could hear someone, several voices, calling and whistling, as if many people were hallooing through the air:

"He's come back! Aha! He's come back!"

There was a wild, whistling, jubilant sound of voices in the storm of snow. Then obscured lightning winked through the snow in the air.

"Is that thunder and lightning?" she asked of the young policeman, as she stood still, waiting for his form to emerge through the veil of whirling snow.

"Seems like it to me," he said.

And at that very moment the lightning blinked again, and the dark, laughing face was near her face, it almost touched her cheek.

She started back, but a flame of delight went over her.

"There!" she said. "Did you see that?"

"It lightened," said the policeman.

She was looking at him almost angrily. But then the clean, fresh animal look of his skin, and the tame-animal look in his frightened eyes amused her, she laughed her low, triumphant laugh. He was obviously afraid, like a frightened dog that sees something uncanny.

The storm suddenly whistled louder, more violently, and, with a strange noise like castanets, she seemed to hear voices clapping and crying:

"He is here! He's come back!"

She nodded her head gravely.

The policeman and she moved on side by side. She lived alone in a little stucco house in a side street down the hill. There was a church and a grove of trees and then the little old row of houses. The wind blew fiercely, thick with snow. Now and again a taxi went by, with its lights showing weirdly. But the world seemed empty, uninhabited save by snow and voices.

As the girl and the policeman turned past the grove of trees near the church, a great whirl of wind and snow made them stand still, and in the wild confusion they heard a whirling of sharp, delighted voices, something like seagulls, crying:

"He's here! He's here!"

"Well, I'm jolly glad he's back," said the girl calmly.

"What's that?" said the nervous policeman, hovering near the girl.

The wind let them move forward. As they passed along the railings it seemed to them the doors of the church were open, and the windows were out, and the snow and the voices were blowing in a wild career all through the church.

"How extraordinary that they left the church open!" said the girl.

The policeman stood still. He could not reply.

And as they stood they listened to the wind and the church full of whirling voices all calling confusedly.

"*Now* I hear the laughing," she said suddenly.

It came from the church: a sound of low, subtle, endless laughter, a strange, naked sound.

"Now I hear it!" she said.

But the policeman did not speak. He stood cowed, with his tail between his legs, listening to the strange noises in the church.

The wind must have blown out one of the windows, for they could see the snow whirling in volleys through the black gap, and whirling inside the church like a dim light. There came a sudden crash, followed by a burst of chuckling, naked laughter. The snow seemed to make a queer light inside the building, like ghosts moving, big and tall.

There was more laughter, and a tearing sound. On the wind, pieces of paper, leaves of books, came whirling among the snow through the dark window. Then a white thing, soaring like a crazy bird, rose up on the wind as if it had wings, and lodged on a black tree outside, struggling. It was the altar-cloth.

There came a bit of gay, trilling music. The wind was running over the organ-pipes like pan-pipes, quickly up and down. Snatches of wild, gay, trilling music, and bursts of the naked low laughter.

"Really!" said the girl. "This is most extraordinary. Do you hear the music and the people laughing?"

"Yes, I hear somebody on the organ!" said the policeman.

"And do you get the puff of warm wind? Smelling of spring. Almond blossom, that's what it is! A most marvellous scent of almond blossom. *isn't* it an extraordinary thing!"

She went on triumphantly past the church, and came to the row of little old houses. She entered her own gate in the little railed entrance.

"Here I am!" she said finally. "I'm home now. Thank you very much for coming with me."

She looked at the young policeman. His whole body was white as a wall with snow, and in the vague light of the arc-lamp from the street his face was humble and frightened.

"Can I come in and warm myself a bit?" he asked humbly. She knew it was fear rather than cold that froze him. He was in mortal fear.

"Well!" she said. "Stay down in the sitting-room if you like. But don't come upstairs, because I am alone in the house. You can make up the fire in the sitting-room, and you can go when you are warm."

She left him on the big, low couch before the fire, his face bluish and blank with fear. He rolled his blue eyes after her as she left the room. But she went up to her bedroom and fastened her door.

In the morning she was in her studio upstairs in her little house, looking at her own paintings and laughing to herself. Her canaries were talking and shrilly whistling in the sunshine that followed the storm. The cold snow outside was still clean, and the white glare in the air gave the effect of much stronger sunshine than actually existed.

She was looking at her own paintings, and chuckling to herself over their comicalness. Suddenly they struck her as absolutely absurd. She quite enjoyed looking at them, they seemed to her so grotesque. Especially her self-portrait, with its nice brown hair and its slightly opened rabbit-mouth and its baffled uncertain rabbit-eyes. She looked at the painted face and laughed in a long, rippling laugh, till the yellow canaries like faded daffodils almost went mad in an effort to sing louder. The girl's long, rippling laugh sounded through the house uncannily.

The house-keeper, a rather sad-faced young woman of a superior sort—nearly all people in England are of the superior sort, superiority being an English ailment—came in with an inquiring and rather disapproving look.

"Did you call, Miss James?" she asked loudly.

"No. No, I didn't call. Don't shout, I can hear quite well," replied the girl.

The housekeeper looked at her again.

"You knew there was a young man in the sitting-room?" she said.

"No. Really!" cried the girl. "What, the young policeman? I'd forgotten all about him. He came in in the storm to warm himself. Hasn't he gone?"

"No, Miss James."

"How extraordinary of him! What time is it? Quarter to nine! Why didn't he go when he was warm? I must go and see him, I suppose."

"He says he's lame," said the housekeeper censoriously and loudly.

"Lame! That's extraordinary. He certainly wasn't last night. But don't shout. I can hear quite well."

"Is Mr. Marchbanks coming in to breakfast, Miss James?" said the housekeeper, more and more censorious.

"I couldn't say. But I'll come down as soon as mine is ready. I'll be down in a minute, anyhow, to see the policeman. Extraordinary that he is still here."

She sat down before her window, in the sun, to think a while. She could see the snow outside, the bare, purplish trees. The air all seemed rare and different. Suddenly the world had become quite different: as if some skin or integument had broken, as if the old, mouldering London sky had crackled and rolled back, like an old skin, shrivelled, leaving an absolutely new blue heaven.

"It really is extraordinary!" she said to herself. "I certainly saw that man's face. What a wonderful face it was! I shall never forget it. Such laughter! He laughs longest who laughs last. He certainly will have the last laugh. I like him for that: he will laugh last. Must be someone really extraordinary! How very nice to be the one to laugh last. He certainly will. What a wonderful being! I suppose I must call him a being. He's not a person exactly.

"But how wonderful of him to come back and alter all the world immediately! *Isn't* that extraordinary. I wonder if he'll have altered Marchbanks. Of course Marchbanks never SAW him. But he heard him. Wouldn't that do as well, I wonder!—*I wonder!*"

She went off into a muse about Marchbanks. She and he were *such* friends. They had been friends like that for almost two years. Never lovers. Never that at all. But *friends*.

And after all, she had been in love with him: in her head. This seemed now so funny to her: that she had been, in her head, so much in love with him. After all, life was too absurd.

Because now she saw herself and him as such a funny pair. He so funnily taking life terribly seriously, especially his own life. And she so ridiculously *determined* to save him from himself. Oh, how absurd! *Determined* to save him from himself, and wildly in love with him in the effort. The determination to save him from himself.

Absurd! Absurd! Absurd! Since she had seen the man laughing among the holly bushes—*such* extraordinary, wonderful laughter—she had seen her own ridiculousness. Really, what fantastic silliness, saving a man from himself! Saving anybody. What fantastic silliness! How much more amusing and lively to let a man go to perdition in his own way. Perdition was more amusing than salvation anyhow, and a much better place for most men to go to.

She had never been in love with any man, and only spuriously in love with Marchbanks. She saw it quite plainly now. After all, what nonsense it all was, this being-in-love business. Thank goodness she had never made the humiliating mistake.

No, the man among the holly bushes had made her see it all so plainly: the ridiculousness of being in love, the infra dig. business of chasing a man or being chased by a man.

"Is love *really* so absurd and infra dig?" she said aloud to herself.

"Why, of course!" came a deep, laughing voice.

She started round, but nobody was to be seen.

"I expect it's that man again!" she said to herself. "It really *is* remarkable, you know. I consider it's a remarkable thing that I never really wanted a man, *any* man. And there I am over thirty. It *is* curious. Whether it's something wrong with me, or right with me, I can't say. I don't know till I've proved it. But I believe, if that man kept on laughing something would happen to me."

She smelt the curious smell of almond blossom in the room, and heard the distant laugh again.

"I do wonder why Marchbanks went with that woman last night—that Jewish-looking woman. Whatever could he want of her?—or she of him? So strange, as if they both had made up their minds to something! How extraordinarily puzzling life is! So messy, it all seems.

"Why does nobody laugh in life like that man? He *did* seem so wonderful. So scornful! And so proud! And so real! With those laughing, scornful, amazing eyes, just laughing and disappearing again. I can't imagine him chasing a Jewish-looking woman. Or chasing any woman, thank goodness. It's all so messy. My policeman would be messy if one would let him: like a dog. I do dislike dogs, really I do. And men do seem so doggy!—"

But even while she mused, she began to laugh again to herself with a long, low chuckle. How wonderful of that man to come and laugh like that and make the sky crack and shrivel like an old skin! Wasn't he wonderful! Wouldn't it be wonderful if he just touched her. Even touched her. She felt, if he touched her, she herself would emerge new and tender out of the old, hard skin. She was gazing abstractedly out of the window.

"There he comes, just now," she said abruptly. But she meant Marchbanks, not the laughing man.

There he came, his hands still shoved down in his overcoat pockets, his head still rather furtively ducked in the bowler hat, and his legs still rather shambling. He came hurrying across the road, not looking up, deep in thought, no doubt. Thinking profoundly, with agonies of agitation, no doubt about his last night's experience. It made her laugh.

She, watching from the window above, burst into a long laugh, and the canaries went off their heads again.

70

He was in the hall below. His resonant voice was calling, rather imperiously: "James! Are you coming down?"

"No," she called. "You come up."

He came up two at a time, as if his feet were a bit savage with the stairs for obstructing him.

In the doorway he stood staring at her with a vacant, sardonic look, his grey eyes moving with a queer light. And she looked back at him with a curious, rather haughty carelessness.

"Don't you want your breakfast?" she asked. It was his custom to come and take breakfast with her each morning.

"No," he answered loudly. "I went to a tea-shop."

"Don't shout," she said. "I can hear you quite well."

He looked at her with mockery and a touch of malice.

"I believe you always could," he said, still loudly.

"Well, anyway, I can now, so you needn't shout," she replied.

And again his grey eyes, with the queer, greyish phosphorescent gleam in them, lingered malignantly on her face.

"Don't look at me," she said calmly. "I know all about everything."

He burst into a pouf of malicious laughter.

"Who taught you—the policeman?" he cried.

"Oh, by the way, he must be downstairs! No, he was only incidental. So, I suppose, was the woman in the shawl. Did you stay all night?"

"Not entirely. I came away before dawn. What did you do?"

"Don't shout. I came home long before dawn." And she seemed to hear the long, low laughter.

"Why, what's the matter?" he said curiously. "What have you been doing?"

"I don't quite know. Why?—are you going to call me to account?"

"Did you hear that laughing?"

"Oh yes. And many more things. And saw things too."

"Have you seen the paper?"

"No. Don't shout, I can hear."

"There's been a great storm, blew out the windows and doors of the church outside here, and pretty well wrecked the place."

"I saw it. A leaf of the church Bible blew right in my face: from the Book of Job—" She gave a low laugh.

"But what else did you see?" he cried loudly.

"I saw *him*."

"Who?"

"Ah, that I can't say."

"But what was he like?"

"That I can't tell you. I don't really know."

"But you must know. Did your policeman see him too?"

"No, I don't suppose he did. My policeman!" And she went off into a long ripple of laughter. "He is by no means mine. But I *must* go downstairs and see him."

"It's certainly made you very strange," Marchbanks said. "You've got no *soul*, you know."

"Oh, thank goodness for that!" she cried. "My policeman has one, I'm sure. *My policeman!*" And she went off again into a long peal of laughter, the canaries pealing shrill accompaniment.

"What's the matter with you?" he said.

"Having no soul. I never had one really. It was always fobbed off on me. Soul was the only thing there was between you and me. Thank goodness it's gone. Haven't you lost yours? The one that seemed to worry you, like a decayed tooth?"

"But what are you *talking* about?" he cried.

"I don't know," she said. "It's all so extraordinary. But look here, I *must* go down and see my policeman. He's downstairs in the sitting-room. You'd better come with me."

They went down together. The policeman in his waistcoat and shirtsleeves was lying on the sofa, with a very long face.

"Look here!" said Miss James to him. "Is it true you're lame?"

"It is true. That's why I'm here. I can't walk," said the fair-haired young man as tears came to his eyes.

"But how did it happen? You weren't lame last night," she said.

"I don't know how it happened—but when I woke up and tried to stand up, I couldn't do it." The tears ran down his distressed face.

"How very extraordinary!" she said. "What can we do about it?"

"Which foot is it?" asked Marchbanks. "Let us have a look at it."

"I don't like to," said the poor devil.

"You'd better," said Miss James.

He slowly pulled off his stocking, and showed his white left foot curiously clubbed, like the weird paw of some animal. When he looked at it himself, he sobbed.

And as he sobbed, the girl heard again the low, exulting laughter. But she paid no heed to it, gazing curiously at the weeping young policeman.

"Does it hurt?" she asked.

"It does if I try to walk on it," wept the young man.

"I'll tell you what," she said. "We'll telephone for a doctor, and he can take you home in a taxi."

The young fellow shamefacedly wiped his eyes.

"But have you no idea how it happened?" asked Marchbanks anxiously.

"I haven't myself," said the young fellow.

At that moment the girl heard the low, eternal laugh right in her ear. She started, but could see nothing.

She started round again as Marchbanks gave a strange, yelping cry, like a shot animal. His white face was drawn, distorted in a curious grin, that was chiefly agony but partly wild recognition. He was staring with fixed eyes at something. And in the rolling agony of his eyes was the horrible grin of a man who realises he had made a final, and this time fatal, fool of himself.

"Why," he yelped in a high voice, "I knew it was he!" And with a queer shuddering laugh he pitched forward on the carpet and lay writhing for a moment on the floor. Then he lay still, in a weird, distorted position, like a man struck by lightening.

Miss James stared with round, staring brown eyes.

"Is he dead?" she asked quickly.

The young policeman was trembling so that he could hardly speak. She could hear his teeth chattering.

"Seems like it," he stammered.

There was a faint smell of almond blossom in the air.

The Lovely Lady

At seventy-two, Pauline Attenborough could still sometimes be mistaken, in the half-light, for thirty. She really was a wonderfully-preserved woman, of perfect chic. Of course it helps a great deal to have the right frame. She would be an exquisite skeleton, and her skull would be an exquisite skull, like that of some Etruscan woman with feminine charm still in the swerve of the bone and the pretty, naïve teeth.

Mrs Attenborough's face was of the perfect oval and slightly flat type that wears best. There is no flesh to sag. Her nose rode serenely, in its finely-bridged curve. Only the big grey eyes were a tiny bit prominent, on the surface of her face, and they gave her away most. The bluish lids were heavy, as if they ached sometimes with the strain of keeping the eyes beneath them arch and bright; and at the corners of the eyes were fine little wrinkles which would slacken into haggardness, then be pulled up tense again to that bright, gay look like a Leonardo woman who really could laugh outright.

Her niece Cecilia was perhaps the only person in the world who was aware of the invisible little wire which connected Pauline's eye-wrinkles with Pauline's willpower. Only Cecilia consciously watched the eyes go haggard and old and tired, and remain so, for hours; until Robert came home. Then *ping!*—the mysterious little wire that worked between Pauline's will and her face went taut, the weary, haggard, prominent eyes suddenly began to gleam, the eyelids arched, the queer, curved eyebrows which floated in such frail arches on Pauline's forehead began to gather a mocking significance, and you had the *real* lovely lady, in all her charm.

She really had the secret of everlasting youth; that is to say, she could don her youth again like an eagle. But she was sparing of it. She was wise enough not to try being young for too many people. Her son Robert, in the evenings, and Sir Wilfrid Knipe sometimes in the afternoon to tea; then occasional visitors on Sunday, when Robert was home—for these she was her lovely and changeless self, that age could not wither, nor custom stale; so bright and kindly and yet subtly mocking, like Mona Lisa, who knew a thing or two. But Pauline knew more, so she needn't be smug at all. She could laugh that lovely, mocking Bacchante laugh of hers, which was at the same time never malicious, always good-naturedly tolerant, both of virtues and vices—the former, of course, taking much more tolerating. So she suggested, roguishly.

Only with her niece Cecilia she did not trouble to keep up the glamour. Ciss was not very observant, anyhow; and, more than that, she was plain; more still, she was in love with Robert; and most of all, she was thirty, and dependent on her aunt Pauline. Oh, Cecilia—why make music for her?

Cecilia, called by her aunt and by her cousin Robert just Ciss, like a cat spitting, was a big, dark-complexioned, pug-faced young woman who very rarely spoke, and when she did couldn't get it out. She was the daughter of a poor Congregational clergyman who had been, while he lived, brother to Ronald, Aunt Pauline's husband. Ronald and the Congregational minister were both well dead, and Aunt Pauline had had charge of Ciss for the last five years.

They lived all together in a quite exquisite though rather small Queen Anne house some twenty-five miles out of town, secluded in a little dale, and surrounded by small but very quaint and pleasant grounds. It was an ideal place and an ideal life for Aunt Pauline, at the age of seventy-two. When the kingfishers flashed up the little stream in her garden, going under the alders, something still flashed in her heart. She was that kind of woman.

Robert, who was two years older than Ciss, went every day to town, to his chambers in one of the Inns. He was a barrister, and, to his secret but very deep mortification, he earned about a hundred pounds a year. He simply *couldn't* get above that figure, though it was rather easy to get below it. Of course, it didn't matter. Pauline had money. But then, what was Pauline's was Pauline's, and though she could give almost lavishly, still, one was always aware of having a *lovely* and *undeserved* present made to one. Presents are so much nicer when they're undeserved, Aunt Pauline would say.

Robert, too, was plain, and almost speechless. He was medium sized, rather broad and stout, though not fat. Only his creamy, clean-shaven face was rather fat, and sometimes suggestive of an Italian priest, in its silence and its secrecy. But he had grey eyes like his mother, but very shy and uneasy, not bold like hers. Perhaps Ciss was the only person who fathomed his awful shyness and malaise, his habitual feeling that he was in the wrong place: almost like a soul that has got into a wrong body. But he never did anything about it. He went up to Chambers, and read law. It was, however, all the weird old processes that interested him. He had, unknown to everybody but his mother, a quite extraordinary collection of old Mexican legal documents—reports of processes and trials, pleas, accusations: the weird and awful mixture of ecclesiastical law and common law in seventeenth-century Mexico. He had started a study in this direction through coming across the report of a trial of two English sailors, for murder, in Mexico, in 1620, and he had gone on, when the next document was an accusation against a Don Miguel Estrada for seducing one of the nuns of the Sacred Heart Convent in Oaxaca in 1680.

Pauline and her son Robert had wonderful evenings with these old papers. The lovely lady knew a little Spanish. She even looked a trifle Spanish herself, with a high comb and a marvellous dark-brown shawl embroidered in thick silvery silk embroidery. So she would sit at the perfect old table, soft as velvet in its deep brown surface, a high comb in her hair, earrings with dropping pendants in her ears, her arms bare and still beautiful, a few strings of pearls round her throat, a puce velvet dress on and this or another beautiful shawl, and by candlelight she looked, yes, a Spanish high-bred beauty of thirty-two or three. She set the candles to give her face just the chiaroscuro she knew suited her; her high chair that rose behind her face was done in old green brocade, against which her face emerged like a Christmas rose.

They were always three at table, and they always drank a bottle of champagne: Pauline two glasses, Ciss two glasses, Robert the rest. The lovely lady sparkled and was radiant. Ciss, her black hair bobbed, her broad shoulders in a very nice and becoming dress that Aunt Pauline had helped her to make, stared from her aunt to her cousin and back again, with rather confused, mute hazel eyes, and played the part of an audience suitably impressed. She WAS impressed, somewhere, all the time. And even rendered speechless by Pauline's brilliancy, even after five years. But at the bottom of her consciousness was the data of as weird a document as Robert ever studied: all the things she knew about her aunt and her cousin.

Robert was always a gentleman, with an old-fashioned, punctilious courtesy that covered his shyness quite completely. He was, and Ciss knew it, more confused than shy. He was worse than she was. Cecilia's own confusion dated from only five years back. Robert's must have started before he was born. In the lovely lady's womb he must have felt *very* confused.

He paid all his attention to his mother, drawn to her as a humble flower to the sun. And yet, priest-like, he was all the time aware, with the tail of his consciousness, that Ciss was there, and that she was a bit shut out of it, and that something wasn't right. He was aware of the third consciousness in the room. Whereas to Pauline, her niece Cecilia was an appropriate part of her own setting, rather than a distinct consciousness.

Robert took coffee with his mother and Ciss in the warm drawing-room, where all the furniture was so lovely, all collectors' pieces—Mrs Attenborough had made her own money, dealing privately in pictures and furniture and rare things from barbaric countries—and the three talked desultorily till about eight or half-past. It was very pleasant, very cosy, very homely even; Pauline made a real home cosiness out of so much elegant material. The chat was simple, and nearly always bright. Pauline was her *real* self, emanating a friendly mockery and an odd, ironic gaiety—till there came a little pause.

At which Ciss always rose and said good-night, and carried out the coffee-tray, to prevent Burnett from intruding any more.

And then! ah, then, the lovely, glowing intimacy of the evening, between mother and son, when they deciphered manuscripts and discussed points, Pauline with that eagerness of a girl for which she was famous. And it was quite genuine. In some mysterious way she had *saved up* her power for being thrilled, in connection with a man. Robert, solid, rather quiet and subdued, seemed like the elder of the two—almost like a priest with a young girl pupil. And that was rather how he felt.

Ciss had a flat for herself just across the courtyard, over the old coach-house and stables. There were no horses. Robert kept his car in the coach-house. Ciss had three very nice rooms up there, stretching along in a row one after the other, and she had got used to the ticking of the stable clock.

But sometimes she did not go to her rooms. In the summer she would sit on the lawn, and from the open window of the drawing-room upstairs she would hear Pauline's wonderful, heart-searching laugh. And in winter the young woman would put on a thick coat and walk slowly to the little balustraded bridge over the stream, and then look back at the three lighted windows of that drawing-room where mother and son were so happy together.

Ciss loved Robert, and she believed that Pauline intended the two of them to marry—when she was dead. But poor Robert, he was so convulsed with shyness already, with man or woman. What would he be when his mother was dead?—in a dozen more years. He would be just a shell, the shell of a man who had never lived.

The strange, unspoken sympathy of the young with one another, when they are overshadowed by the old, was one of the bonds between Robert and Ciss. But another bond, which Ciss did not know how to draw tight, was the bond of passion. Poor Robert was by nature a passionate man. His silence and his agonised, though hidden, shyness were both the result of a secret physical passionateness. And how Pauline could play on this! Ah, Ciss was not blind to the eyes which he fixed on his mother—eyes fascinated yet humiliated, full of shame. He was ashamed that he was not a man. And he did not love his mother. He was fascinated by her. Completely fascinated. And for the rest, paralysed in a life-long confusion.

Ciss stayed in the garden till the lights leapt up in Pauline's bedroom—about ten o'clock. The lovely lady had retired. Robert would now stay another hour or so, alone. Then he, too, would retire. Ciss, in the dark outside, sometimes wished she could creep up to him and say: "Oh, Robert! It's all wrong!" But Aunt Pauline would hear. And, anyhow, Ciss couldn't do it. She went off to her own rooms, once more, once more, and so for ever.

In the morning coffee was brought up on a tray to each of the rooms of the three relatives. Ciss had to be at Sir Wilfrid Knipe's at nine o'clock, to give two hours' lessons to his little grand-daughter. It was her sole serious occupation, except that she played the piano for the love of it. Robert set off to town about nine. And as a rule, Aunt Pauline appeared to lunch, though sometimes not till tea-time. When she appeared, she looked fresh and young. But she was inclined to fade rather rapidly, like a flower without water, in the daytime. Her hour was the candle hour.

So she always rested in the afternoon. When the sun shone, if possible she took a sun-bath. This was one of her secrets. Her lunch was very light; she could take her sun-and-air-bath before noon or after, as it pleased her. Often it was in the afternoon, when the sun shone very warmly into a queer little yew-walled square just behind the stables. Here Ciss stretched out the lying-chair and rugs, and put the light parasol handy in the silent little enclosure of thick dark yew-hedges beyond the old red walls of the unused stables. And hither came the lovely lady with her book. Ciss then had to be on guard in one of her own rooms, should her aunt, who was very keen-eared, hear a footstep.

One afternoon it occurred to Cecilia that she herself might

while away this rather long afternoon hour by taking a sun-bath. She was growing restive. The thought of the flat roof of the stable buildings, to which she could climb from a loft at the end, started her on a new adventure. She often went on to the roof; she had to, to wind up the stable clock, which was a job she had assumed to herself. Now she took a rug, climbed out under the heavens, looked at the sky and the great elm-tops, looked at the sun, then took off her things and lay down perfectly securely, in a corner of the roof under the parapet, full in the sun.

It was rather lovely, to bask all one's length like this in warm sun and air. Yes, it was very lovely! It even seemed to melt some of the hard bitterness of her heart, some of that core of unspoken resentment which never dissolved. Luxuriously, she spread herself, so that the sun should touch her limbs fully, fully. If she had no other lover, she should have the sun! She rolled over voluptuously.

And suddenly her heart stood still in her body, and her hair almost rose on end as a voice said very softly, musingly, in her ear:

"No, Henry dear! It was not my fault you died instead of marrying that Claudia. No, darling. I was quite, quite willing for you to marry her, unsuitable though she was."

Cecilia sank down on her rug, powerless and perspiring with dread. That awful voice, so soft, so musing, yet so unnatural. Not a human voice at all. Yet there must, there MUST be someone on the roof! Oh, how unspeakably awful!

She lifted her weak head and peeped across the sloping leads. Nobody! The chimneys were too narrow to shelter anybody. There was nobody on the roof. Then it must be someone in the trees, in the elms. Either that, or—terror unspeakable—a bodiless voice! She reared her head a little higher.

And as she did so, came the voice again:

"No, darling! I told you you would tire of her in six months. And you see it was true, dear. It was true, true, true! I wanted to spare you that. So it wasn't I who made you feel weak and disabled, wanting that very silly Claudia—poor thing, she looked so woebegone afterwards!—wanting her and not wanting her. You got yourself into that perplexity, my dear. I only warned you.

What else could I do? And you lost your spirit and died without ever knowing me again. It was bitter, bitter—"

The voice faded away. Cecilia subsided weakly on to her rug, after the anguished tension of listening. Oh, it was awful. The sun shone, the sky was blue, all seemed so lovely and afternoony and summery. And yet, oh, horror!—she was going to be forced to believe in the supernatural! And she loathed the supernatural, ghosts and voices and rappings and all the rest.

But that awful, creepy, bodiless voice, with its rusty sort of whispers of an overtone! It had something so fearfully familiar in it, too! And yet was so utterly uncanny. Poor Cecilia could only lie there unclothed, and so all the more agonisingly help-less, inert, collapsed in sheer dread.

And then she heard the thing sigh!—a deep sigh that seemed weirdly familiar, yet was not human. "Ah well, ah well! the heart must bleed. Better it should bleed than break. It is grief, grief! But it wasn't my fault, dear. And Robert could marry our poor, dull Ciss tomorrow, if he wanted her. But he doesn't care about it, so why force him into anything?" The sounds were very un-even, sometimes only a husky sort of whisper. Listen! Listen!

Cecilia was about to give vent to loud and piercing screams of hysteria, when the last two sentences arrested her. All her caution and her cunning sprang alert. It was Aunt Pauline! It *must* be Aunt Pauline, practising ventriloquism, or something like that. What a devil she was!

Where was she? She must be lying down there, right below where Cecilia herself was lying. And it was either some fiend's trick of ventriloquism, or else thought-transference. The sounds were very uneven; sometimes quite inaudible, sometimes only a brushing sort of noise. Ciss listened intently. No, it could not be ventriloquism. It was worse: some form of thought-transference that conveyed itself like sound. Some horror of that sort! Cecilia still lay weak and inert, too terrified to move; but she was grow-ing calmer with suspicion. It was some diabolic trick of that unnatural woman.

But *what* a devil of a woman! She even knew that she, Ce-cilia, had mentally accused her of killing her son Henry. Poor

Henry was Robert's elder brother, twelve years older than Robert. He had died suddenly when he was twenty-two, after an awful struggle with himself, because he was passionately in love with a young and very good-looking actress, and his mother had humorously despised him for the attachment. So he had caught some sudden ordinary disease, but the poison had gone to his brain and killed him before he ever regained consciousness. Ciss knew the few facts from her own father. And lately she had been thinking that Pauline was going to kill Robert as she had killed Henry. It was clear murder: a mother murdering her sensitive sons, who were fascinated by her: the Circe!

"I suppose I may as well get up," murmured the dim, unbreathing voice. "Too much sun is as bad as too little. Enough sun, enough love-thrill, enough proper food, and not too much of any of them, and a woman might live for ever. I verily believe, for ever. If she absorbs as much vitality as she expends. Or perhaps a trifle more!"

It was certainly Aunt Pauline! How—how terrible! She, Ciss, was hearing Aunt Pauline's thoughts. Oh, how ghastly! Aunt Pauline was sending out her thoughts in a sort of radio, and she, Ciss, had to *hear* what her aunt was thinking. How ghastly! How insufferable! One of them would surely have to die.

She twisted and lay inert and crumpled, staring vacantly in front of her. Vacantly! Vacantly! And her eyes were staring almost into a hole. She was staring in it unseeing, a hole going down in the corner, from the lead gutter. It meant nothing to her. Only it frightened her a little more.

When suddenly, out of the hole came a sigh and a last whisper: "Ah well! Pauline! Get up, it's enough for to-day." Good God! Out of the hole of the rain-pipe! The rain-pipe was acting as a speaking-tube! Impossible! No, quite possible. She had read of it even in some book. And Aunt Pauline, like the old and guilty woman she was talked aloud to herself. That was it!

A sullen exultance sprang in Ciss's breast. *That* was why she would never have anybody, not even Robert, in her bedroom. That was why she never dozed in a chair, never sat absent-minded anywhere, but went to her room, and kept to her room, except when she roused herself to be alert. When she slackened off she talked to herself! She talked in a soft little crazy voice to herself. But she was not crazy. It was only her thoughts murmuring themselves aloud.

So she had qualms about poor Henry! Well she might have! Ciss believed that Aunt Pauline had loved her big, handsome, brilliant first-born much more than she loved Robert, and that his death had been a terrible blow and a chagrin to her. Poor Robert had been only ten years old when Henry died. Since then he had been the substitute.

Ah, how awful!

But Aunt Pauline was a strange woman. She had left her husband when Henry was a small child, some years even before Robert was born. There was no quarrel. Sometimes she saw her husband again, quite amiably, but a little mockingly. And she even gave him money.

For Pauline earned all her own. Her father had been a Consul in the East and in Naples, and a devoted collector of beautiful exotic things. When he died, soon after his grandson Henry was born, he left his collection of treasures to his daughter. And Pauline, who had really a passion and a genius for loveliness, whether in texture or form or colour, had laid the basis of her fortune on her father's collection. She had gone on collecting, buying where she could, and selling to collectors or to museums. She was one of the first to sell old, weird African figures to the museums, and ivory carvings from New Guinea. She bought Renoir as soon as she saw his pictures. But not Rousseau. And all by herself she made a fortune.

After her husband died she had not married again. She was not even *known* to have had lovers. If she did have lovers, it was not among the men who admired her most and paid her devout and open attendance. To these she was a "friend".

Cecilia slipped on her clothes and caught up her rug, hastening carefully down the ladder to the loft. As she descended she heard the ringing, musical call: "All right, Ciss"—which meant that the lovely lady was finished, and returning to the house. Even her voice was wonderfully young and sonorous, beautifully balanced and self-possessed. So different from the little voice in which she talked to herself. *That* was much more the voice of an old woman.

Ciss hastened round to the yew enclosure, where lay the comfortable chaise longue with the various delicate rugs. Everything Pauline had was choice, to the fine straw mat on the floor. The great yew walls were beginning to cast long shadows. Only in the corner where the rugs tumbled their delicate colours was there hot, still sunshine.

The rugs folded up, the chair lifted away, Cecilia stooped to look at the mouth of the rain-pipe. There it was, in the corner, under a little hood of masonry and just projecting from the thick leaves of the creeper on the wall. If Pauline, lying there, turned her face towards the wall, she would speak into the very mouth of the tube. Cecilia was reassured. She had heard her aunt's thoughts indeed, but by no uncanny agency.

That evening, as if aware of something, Pauline was a little quieter than usual, though she looked her own serene, rather mysterious self. And after coffee she said to Robert and Ciss:

"I'm so sleepy. The sun has made me so sleepy. I feel full of sunshine like a bee. I shall go to bed, if you don't mind. You two sit and have a talk."

Cecilia looked quickly at her cousin.

"Perhaps you'd rather be alone?" she said to him.

"No—no," he replied. "Do keep me company for a while, if it doesn't bore you."

The windows were open, the scent of honeysuckle wafted in, with the sound of an owl. Robert smoked in silence. There was a sort of despair in his motionless, rather squat body. He looked like a caryatid bearing a weight.

"Do you remember Cousin Henry?" Cecilia asked him suddenly.

He looked up in surprise.

"Yes. Very well," he said.

"What did he look like?" she said, glancing into her cousin's big, secret-troubled eyes, in which there was so much frustration.

"Oh, he was handsome: tall, and fresh-coloured, with mother's soft brown hair." As a matter of fact, Pauline's hair was grey. "The ladies admired him very much; and he was at all the dances."

"And what kind of character had he?"

"Oh, very good-natured and jolly. He liked to be amused. He was rather quick and clever, like mother, and very good company."

"And did he love your mother?"

"Very much. She loved him too—better than she does me, as a matter of fact. He was so much more nearly her idea of a man."

"Why was he more her idea of a man?"

"Tall—handsome—attractive, and very good company—and would, I believe, have been very successful at law. I'm afraid I am merely negative in all those respects."

Ciss looked at him attentively, with her slow-thinking hazel eyes. Under his impassive mask she knew he suffered.

"Do you think you are so much more negative than he?" she said.

He did not lift his face. But after a few moments he replied:

"My life, certainly, is a negative affair."

She hesitated before she dared ask him:

"And do you mind?"

He did not answer her at all. Her heart sank.

"You see, I'm afraid my life is as negative as yours is," she said. "And I'm beginning to mind bitterly. I'm thirty."

She saw his creamy, well-bred hand tremble.

"I suppose," he said, without looking at her, "one will rebel when it is too late."

That was queer, from him.

"Robert!" she said. "Do you like me at all?"

She saw his dusky-creamy face, so changeless in its folds, go pale.

"I am very fond of you," he murmured.

"Won't you kiss me? Nobody ever kisses me," she said pathetically.

He looked at her, his eyes strange with fear and a certain haughtiness. Then he rose, and came softly over to her, and kissed her gently on the cheek.

"It's an awful shame, Ciss!" he said softly.

She caught his hand and pressed it to her breast.

"And sit with me sometimes in the garden," she said, murmuring with difficulty. "Won't you?"

He looked at her anxiously and searchingly.

"What about mother?"

Ciss smiled a funny little smile, and looked into his eyes. He suddenly flushed crimson, turning aside his face. It was a painful sight.

"I know," he said. "I am no lover of women."

He spoke with sarcastic stoicism, against himself, but even she did not know the shame it was to him.

"You never try to be," she said.

Again his eyes changed uncannily.

"Does one have to try?" he said.

"Why, yes. One never does anything if one doesn't try."

He went pale again.

"Perhaps you are right," he said.

In a few minutes she left him, and went to her rooms. At least she had tried to take off the everlasting lid from things.

The weather continued sunny, Pauline continued her sunbaths, and Ciss lay on the roof eavesdropping, in the literal sense of the word. But Pauline was not to be heard. No sound came up the pipe. She must be lying with her face away into the open. Ciss listened with all her might. She could just detect the faintest, faintest murmur away below, but no audible syllable.

And at night, under the stars, Cecilia sat and waited in silence, on the seat which kept in view the drawing-room windows and the side door into the garden. She saw the light go up in her aunt's room. She saw the lights at last go out in the drawing-room. And she waited. But he did not come. She stayed on in the darkness half the night, while the owl hooted. But she stayed alone.

Two days she heard nothing; her aunt's thoughts were not revealed; and at evening nothing happened. Then, the second night, as she sat with heavy, helpless persistence in the garden, suddenly she started. He had come out. She rose and went softly over the grass to him.

"Don't speak!" he murmured.

And in silence, in the dark, they walked down the garden and over the little bridge to the paddock, where the hay, cut very late, was in cock. There they stood disconsolate under the stars.

"You see," he said, "how can I ask for love, if I don't feel any love in myself? You know I have a real regard for you—"

"How *can* you feel any love, when you never feel anything?" she said.

"That is true," he replied.

And she waited for what next.

"And how can I marry?" he said. "I am a failure even at making money. I can't ask my mother for money."

She sighed deeply.

"Then don't bother yet about marrying," she said. "Only love me a little. Won't you?"

He gave a short laugh.

"It sounds so atrocious, to say it is hard to begin," he said.

She sighed again. He was so stiff to move.

"Shall we sit down a minute?" she said. And then, as they sat on the hay, she added: "May I touch you? Do you mind?"

"Yes, I mind. But do as you wish," he replied, with that mixture of shyness and queer candour which made him a little ridiculous, as he knew quite well. But in his heart there was almost murder.

She touched his black, always tidy, hair, with her fingers.

"I suppose I shall rebel one day," he said again suddenly.

They sat some time, till it grew chilly. And he held her hand fast, but he never put his arms round her. At last she rose, and went indoors, saying good-night.

The next day, as Cecilia lay stunned and angry on the roof, taking her sun-bath, and becoming hot and fierce with sunshine, suddenly she started. A terror seized her in spite of herself. It was the voice.

"*Caro, caro, tu non l'hai visto!*" it was murmuring away, in a language Cecilia did not understand. She lay and writhed her limbs in the sun, listening intently to words she could not follow. Softly, whisperingly, with infinite caressiveness and yet with

87

that subtle, insidious arrogance under its velvet, came the voice, murmuring in Italian: *"Bravo, si, molto bravo, poverino, ma uomo come te non sarà mai, mai, mai!"* Oh, especially in Italian Cecilia heard the poisonous charm of the voice, so caressive, so soft and flexible, yet so utterly egoistic. She hated it with intensity as it sighed and whispered out of nowhere. Why, why should it be so delicate, so subtle and flexible and beautifully controlled, when she herself was so clumsy? Oh, poor Cecilia, she writhed in the afternoon sun, knowing her own clownish clumsiness and lack of suavity, in comparison.

"No, Robert dear, you will never be the man your father was, though you have some of his looks. He was a marvellous lover, soft as a flower yet piercing as a humming-bird. *Cara, cara mia bellissima, ti ho aspettato come l'agonissante aspetta la morte, morte deliziosa, quasi quasi troppo deliziosa per una mera anima humana.* He gave himself to a woman as he gave himself to God. Mauro! Mauro! How you loved me! How you loved me!"

The voice ceased in reverie, and Cecilia knew what she had guessed before—that Robert was not the son of her Uncle Ronald, but of some Italian.

"I am disappointed in you, Robert. There is no poignancy in you. Your father was a Jesuit, but he was the most perfect and poignant lover in the world. You are a Jesuit like a fish in a tank. And that Ciss of yours is the cat fishing for you. It is less edifying even than poor Henry."

Cecilia suddenly bent her mouth down to the tube, and said in a deep voice:

"Leave Robert alone! Don't kill him as well."

There was dead silence in the hot July afternoon that was lowering for thunder. Cecilia lay prostrate, her heart beating in great thumps. She was listening as if her whole soul were an ear. At last she caught the whisper:

"Did someone speak?"

She leaned again to the mouth of the tube:

"Don't kill Robert as you killed me," she said, with slow enunciation, and a deep but small voice.

"Ah!" came the sharp little cry. "Who is that speaking?"

"Henry," said the deep voice.

There was dead silence. Poor Cecilia lay with all the use gone out of her. And there was dead silence. Till at last came the whisper:

"I didn't kill Henry. No, no! No, no! Henry, surely you can't blame me! I loved you, dearest; I only wanted to help you."

"You killed me!" came the deep, artificial, accusing voice. "Now let Robert live. Let him go! Let him marry!"

There was a pause.

"How very, very awful!" mused the whispering voice. "Is it possible, Henry, you are a spirit, and you condemn me?"

"Yes, I condemn you!"

Cecilia felt all the pent-up rage going down that rain-pipe. At the same time, she almost laughed. It was awful.

She lay and listened and listened. No sound! As if time had ceased, she lay inert in the weakening sun, till she heard a far-off rumble of thunder. She sat up. The sky was yellowing. Quickly she dressed herself, went down, and out to the corner of the stables.

"Aunt Pauline!" she called discreetly. "Did you hear thunder?"

"Yes. I am going in. Don't wait," came a feeble voice.

Cecilia retired, and from the loft watched, spying, as the figure of the lovely lady, wrapped in a lovely wrap of old blue silk, went rather totteringly to the house.

The sky gradually darkened. Cecilia hastened in with the rugs. Then the storm broke. Aunt Pauline did not appear to tea. She found the thunder trying. Robert also did not arrive till after tea, in the pouring rain. Cecilia went down the covered passage to her own house, and dressed carefully for dinner, putting some white columbines at her breast.

The drawing-room was lit with a softly-shaded lamp. Robert, dressed, was waiting, listening to the rain. He too seemed strangely crackling and on edge. Cecilia came in, with the white flowers nodding at her dusky breast. Robert was watching her curiously, a new look on his face. Cecilia went to the bookshelves near the door, and was peering for something, listening acutely. She heard a rustle, then the door softly opening. And as it opened, Ciss suddenly switched on the strong electric light by the door.

Her aunt, in a dress of black lace over ivory colour, stood in the doorway. Her face was made up, but haggard with a look of unspeakable irritability, as if years of suppressed exasperation and dislike of her fellow-men had suddenly crumpled her into an old witch.

"Oh, aunt!" cried Cecilia.

"Why, mother, you're a little old lady!" came the astounded voice of Robert—like an astonished boy, as if it were a joke.

"Have you only just found it out?" snapped the old woman venomously.

"Yes! Why, I thought—" his voice tailed out in misgiving.

The haggard, old Pauline, in a frenzy of exasperation, said:
"Aren't we going down?"

She had not even noticed the excess of light, a thing she shunned. And she went downstairs almost tottering.

At table she sat with her face like a crumpled mask of unspeakable irritability. She looked old, very old, and like a witch. Robert and Cecilia fetched furtive glances at her. And Ciss, watching Robert, saw that he was so astonished and repelled by his mother's looks that he was another man.

"What kind of a drive home did you have?" snapped Pauline, with an almost gibbering irritability.

"It rained, of course," he said.

"How clever of you to have found that out!" said his mother, with the grisly grin of malice that had succeeded her arch smile.

"I don't understand," he said, with quiet suavity.

"It's apparent," said his mother, rapidly and sloppily eating her food.

She rushed through the meal like a crazy dog, to the utter consternation of the servant. And the moment it was over she darted in a queer, crab-like way upstairs. Robert and Cecilia followed her, thunderstruck, like two conspirators.

"You pour the coffee. I loathe it! I'm going. Good-night!" said the old woman, in a succession of sharp shots. And she scrambled out of the room.

There was a dead silence. At last he said:

"I'm afraid mother isn't well. I must persuade her to see a doctor."

"Yes," said Cecilia.

The evening passed in silence. Robert and Ciss stayed on in the drawing-room, having lit a fire. Outside was cold rain. Each pretended to read. They did not want to separate. The evening passed with ominous mysteriousness, yet quickly.

At about ten o'clock the door suddenly opened, and Pauline appeared, in a blue wrap. She shut the door behind her, and came to the fire. Then she looked at the two young people in hate, real hate.

"You two had better get married quickly," she said, in an ugly voice. "It would look more decent; such a passionate pair of lovers!"

Robert looked up at her quietly.

"I thought you believed that cousins should not marry, mother," he said.

"I do. But you're not cousins. Your father was an Italian priest." Pauline held her daintily-slippered foot to the fire, in an old coquettish gesture. Her body tried to repeat all the old graceful gestures. But the nerve had snapped, so it was a rather dreadful caricature.

"Is that really true, mother?" he asked.

"True! What do you think? He was a distinguished man, or he wouldn't have been my lover. He was far too distinguished a man to have had you for a son. But that joy fell to me."

"How unfortunate all round," he said slowly.

"Unfortunate for you? *You* were lucky. It was *my* misfortune," she said acidly to him.

She was really a dreadful sight, like a piece of lovely Venetian glass that has been dropped and gathered up again in horrible, sharp-edged fragments.

Suddenly she left the room again.

For a week it went on. She did not recover. It was as if every nerve in her body had suddenly started screaming in an insanity of discordance. The doctor came, and gave her sedatives, for she never slept. Without drugs she never slept at all, only paced back and forth in her room, looking hideous and evil, reeking with malevolence. She could not bear to see either her son or her niece. Only when either of them came she asked, in pure malice:

"Well! When's the wedding? Have you celebrated the nuptials yet?"

At first Cecilia was stunned by what she had done. She realised vaguely that her aunt, once a definite thrust of condemnation had penetrated her beautiful armour, had just collapsed, squirming, inside her shell. It was too terrible. Ciss was almost terrified into repentance. Then she thought: "This is what she always was. Now let her live the rest of her days in her true colours."

But Pauline would not live long. She was literally shrivelling away. She kept her room, and saw no one. She had her mirrors taken away.

Robert and Cecilia sat a good deal together. The jeering of the mad Pauline had not driven them apart, as she had hoped. But Cecilia dared not confess to him what she had done.

"Do you think your mother ever loved anybody?" Ciss asked him tentatively, rather wistfully, one evening.

He looked at her fixedly.

"Herself!" he said at last.

"She didn't even *love* herself," said Ciss. "It was something else. What was it?" She lifted a troubled, utterly puzzled face to him.

"Power," he said curtly.

"But what power?" she asked. "I don't understand."

"Power to feed on other lives," he said bitterly. "She was beautiful, and she fed on life. She has fed on me as she fed on Henry. She put a sucker into one's soul, and sucked up one's essential life."

"And don't you forgive her?"

"No."

"Poor Aunt Pauline!"

But even Ciss did not mean it. She was only aghast.

"I *know* I've got a heart," he said, passionately striking his breast. "But it's almost sucked dry. I *know* I've got a soul, some-where. But it's gnawed bare. I *hate* people who want power over others."

Ciss was silent. What was there to say?

And two days later Pauline was found dead in her bed, having taken too much *veronal*, for her heart was weakened.

From the grave even she hit back at her son and her niece. She left Robert the noble sum of one thousand pounds, and Ciss one hundred. All the rest, with the nucleus of her valuable antiques, went to form the "Pauline Attenborough Museum".

The Man Who Died

1

There was a peasant near Jerusalem who acquired a young gamecock which looked a shabby little thing, but which put on brave feathers as spring advanced, and was resplendent with arched and orange neck by the time the fig trees were letting out leaves from their end-tips.

This peasant was poor, he lived in a cottage of mud-brick, and had only a dirty little inner courtyard with a tough fig tree for all his territory. He worked hard among the vines and olives and wheat of his master, then came home to sleep in the mud-brick cottage by the path. But he was proud of his young rooster. In the shut-in yard were three shabby hens which laid small eggs, shed the few feathers they had, and made a disproportionate amount of dirt. There was also, in a corner under a straw roof, a dull donkey that often went out with the peasant to work, but sometimes stayed at home. And there was the peasant's wife, a black-browed youngish woman who did not work too hard. She threw a little grain, or the remains of the porridge mess, to the fowls, and she cut green fodder with a sickle for the ass.

The young cock grew to a certain splendour. By some freak of destiny, he was a dandy rooster, in that dirty little yard with three patchy hens. He learned to crane his neck and give shrill answers to the crowing of other cocks, beyond the walls, in a world he knew nothing of. But there was a special fiery colour to his crow, and the distant calling of the other cocks roused him to unexpected outbursts.

"How he sings," said the peasant, as he got up and pulled his day-shirt over his head.

"He is good for twenty hens," said the wife.

The peasant went out and looked with pride at his young rooster. A saucy, flamboyant bird, that has already made the final acquaintance of the three tattered hens. But the cockerel was tipping his head, listening to the challenge of far-off unseen cocks, in the unknown world. Ghost voices, crowing at him mysteriously out of limbo. He answered with a ringing defiance, never to be daunted.

"He will surely fly away one of these days," said the peasant's wife.

So they lured him with grain, caught him, though he fought with all his wings and feet, and they tied a cord round his shank, fastening it against the spur; and they tied the other end of the cord to the post that held up the donkey's straw pent-roof.

The young cock, freed, marched with a prancing stride of indignation away from the humans, came to the end of his string, gave a tug and a hitch of his tied leg, fell over for a moment, scuffled frantically on the unclean earthen floor, to the horror of the shabby hens, then with a sickening lurch, regained his feet, and stood to think. The peasant and the peasant's wife laughed heartily, and the young cock heard them. And he knew, with a gloomy, foreboding kind of knowledge that he was tied by the leg.

He no longer pranced and ruffled and forged his feathers. He walked within the limits of his tether sombrely. Still he gobbled up the best bits of food. Still, sometimes, he saved an extra-best bit for his favourite hen of the moment. Still he pranced with quivering, rocking fierceness upon such of his harem as came nonchalantly within range, and gave off the invisible lure. And still he crowed defiance to the cock-crows that showered up out of limbo, in the dawn.

But there was now a grim voracity in the way he gobbled his food, and a pinched triumph in the way he seized upon the shabby hens. His voice, above all, had lost the full gold of its clangour. He was tied by the leg, and he knew it. Body, soul and spirit were tied by that string.

Underneath, however, the life in him was grimly unbroken. It was the cord that should break. So one morning, just before the light of dawn, rousing from his slumbers with a sudden wave of strength, he leaped forward on his wings, and the string snapped. He gave a wild, strange squawk, rose in one lift to the top of the wall, and there he crowed a loud and splitting crow. So loud, it woke the peasant.

At the same time, at the same hour before dawn, on the same morning, a man awoke from a long sleep in which he was tied up. He woke numb and cold, inside a carved hole in the rock. Through all the long sleep his body had been full of hurt, and it was still full of hurt. He did not open his eyes. Yet he knew that he was awake, and numb, and cold, and rigid, and full of hurt, and tied up. His face was banded with cold bands, his legs were bandaged together. Only his hands were loose.

He could move if he wanted: he knew that. But he had no want. Who would want to come back from the dead? A deep, deep nausea stirred in him, at the premonition of movement. He resented already the fact of the strange, incalculable moving that had already taken place in him: the moving back into consciousness. He had not wished it. He had wanted to stay outside, in the place where even memory is stone dead.

But now, something had returned to him, like a returned letter, and in that return he lay overcome with a sense of nausea. Yet suddenly his hands moved. They lifted up, cold, heavy and sore. Yet they lifted up, to drag away the cloth from his face, and push at the shoulder-bands. Then they fell again, cold, heavy, numb, and sick with having moved even so much, unspeakably unwilling to move further.

With his face cleared and his shoulders free, he lapsed again, and lay dead, resting on the cold nullity of being dead. It was the most desirable. And almost, he had it complete: the utter cold nullity of being outside.

Yet when he was most nearly gone, suddenly, driven by an ache at the wrists, his hands rose and began pushing at the bandages of his knees, his feet began to stir, even while his breast lay cold and dead still.

And at last, the eyes opened. On to the dark. The same dark! Yet perhaps there was a pale chink, of the all-disturbing light, prising open the pure dark. He could not lift his head. The eyes closed. And again it was finished.

Then suddenly he leaned up, and the great world reeled. Bandages fell away. And narrow walls of rock closed upon him, and gave the new anguish of imprisonment. There were chinks of light. With a wave of strength that came from revulsion, he leaned forward, in that narrow well of rock, and leaned frail hands on the rock near the chinks of light.

Strength came from somewhere, from revulsion; there was a crash and a wave of light, and the dead man was crouching in his lair, facing the animal onrush of light. Yet it was hardly dawn. And the strange, piercing keenness of daybreak's sharp breath was on him. It meant full awakening.

Slowly, slowly he crept down from the cell of rock with the caution of the bitterly wounded. Bandages and linen and perfume fell away, and he crouched on the ground against the wall of rock, to recover oblivion. But he saw his hurt feet touching the earth again, with unspeakable pain, the earth they had meant to touch no more, and he saw his thin legs that had died, and pain unknowable, pain like utter bodily disillusion, filled him so full that he stood up, with one torn hand on the ledge of the tomb.

To be back! To be back again, after all that! He saw the linen swathing-bands fallen round his dead feet, and stooping, he picked them up, folded them, and laid them back in the rocky cavity from which he had emerged. Then he took the perfumed linen sheet, wrapped it round him as a mantle, and turned away, to the wanness of the chill dawn.

He was alone; and having died, was even beyond loneliness.

Filled still with the sickness of unspeakable disillusion, the man stepped with wincing feet down the rocky slope, past the sleeping soldiers, who lay wrapped in their woollen mantles under the wild laurels. Silent, on naked scarred feet, wrapped in a white linen shroud, he glanced down for a moment on the inert, heap-like bodies of the soldiers. They were repulsive, a slow squalor of limbs, yet he felt a certain compassion. He passed on towards the road, lest they should wake.

Having nowhere to go, he turned from the city that stood on her hills. He slowly followed the road away from the town, past the olives, under which purple anemones were drooping in the chill of dawn, and rich-green herbage was pressing thick. The world, the same as ever, the natural world, thronging with greenness, a nightingale winsomely, wistfully, coaxingly calling from the bushes beside a runnel of water, in the world, the natural world of morning and evening, forever undying, from which he had died.

He went on, on scarred feet, neither of this world nor of the next. Neither here nor there, neither seeing nor yet sightless, he passed dimly on, away from the city and its precincts, wondering why he should be travelling, yet driven by a dim, deep nausea of disillusion, and a resolution of which he was not even aware.

Advancing in a kind of half-consciousness under the dry stone wall of the olive orchard, he was roused by the shrill, wild crowing of a cock just near him, a sound which made him shiver as if electricity had touched him. He saw a black and orange cock on a bough above the road, then running through the olives of the upper level, a peasant in a grey woollen shirt-tunic. Leaping out of greenness, came the black and orange cock with the red comb, his tail-feathers streaming lustrous.

"O, stop him, master!" called the peasant. "My escaped cock!"

The man addressed, with a sudden flicker of smile, opened his great white wings of a shroud in front of the leaping bird. The cock fell back with a squawk and a flutter, the peasant jumped forward, there was a terrific beating of wings and whirring of feathers, then the peasant had the escaped cock safely under his arm, its wings shut down, its face crazily craning forward, its round eyes goggling from its white chops.

"It's my escaped cock!" said the peasant, soothing the bird with his left hand, as he looked perspiringly up into the face of the man wrapped in white linen.

The peasant changed countenance, and stood transfixed, as he looked into the dead-white face of the man who had died.

That dead-white face, so still, with the black beard growing on it as if in death; and those wide-open, black, sombre eyes, that had died! and those washed scars on the waxy forehead! The slow-blooded man of the field let his jaw drop, in childish inability to meet the situation.

"Don't be afraid," said the man in the shroud. "I am not dead. They took me down too soon. So I have risen up. Yet if they discover me, they will do it all over again..."

He spoke in a voice of old disgust. Humanity! Especially humanity in authority! There was only one thing it could do. He looked with black, indifferent eyes into the quick, shifty eyes of the peasant. The peasant quailed, and was powerless under the look of deathly indifference and strange, cold resoluteness. He could only say the one thing he was afraid to say:

"Will you hide in my house, master?"

"I will rest there. But if you tell anyone, you know what will happen. You will have to go before a judge."

"Me! I shan't speak. Let us be quick!"

The peasant looked round in fear, wondering sulkily why he had let himself in for this doom. The man with scarred feet climbed painfully up to the level of the olive garden, and followed the sullen, hurrying peasant across the green wheat among the olive trees. He felt the cool silkiness of the young wheat under his feet that had been dead, and the roughishness of its separate life was apparent to him. At the edges of rocks, he saw the silky, silvery-haired buds of the scarlet anemone bending downwards. And they, too, were in another world. In his own world he was alone, utterly alone. These things around him were in a world that had never died. But he himself had died, or had been killed from out of it, and all that remained now was the great void nausea of utter disillusion.

They came to a clay cottage, and the peasant waited dejectedly for the other man to pass.

"Pass!" he said. "Pass! We have not been seen."

The man in white linen entered the earthen room, taking with him the aroma of strange perfumes. The peasant closed the door, and passed through the inner doorway into the yard, where the ass stood within the high walls, safe from being stolen. There the peasant, in great disquietude, tied up the cock. The man with the waxen face sat down on a mat near the hearth, for he was spent and barely conscious. Yet he heard outside the whispering of the peasant to his wife, for the woman had been watching from the roof.

Presently they came in, and the woman hid her face. She poured water, and put bread and dried figs on a wooden platter.

"Eat, master!" said the peasant. "Eat! No one has seen."

But the stranger had no desire for food. Yet he moistened a little bread in the water, and ate it, since life must be. But desire was dead in him, even for food and drink. He had risen without desire, without even the desire to live, empty save for the all-overwhelming disillusion that lay like nausea where his life had been. Yet perhaps, deeper even than disillusion, was a desireless resoluteness, deeper even than consciousness.

The peasant and his wife stood near the door, watching. They saw with terror the livid wounds on the thin, waxy hands and the thin feet of the stranger, and the small lacerations in the still dead forehead. They smelled with terror the scent of rich perfumes that came from him, from his body. And they looked at the fine, snowy, costly linen. Perhaps really he was a dead king, from the region of terrors. And he was still cold and remote in the region of death, with perfumes coming from his transparent body as if from some strange flower.

Having with difficulty swallowed some, the moistened bread, he lifted his eyes to them. He saw them as they were: limited, meagre in their life, without any splendour of gesture and of courage. But they were what they were, slow, inevitable parts of the natural world. They had no nobility, but fear made them compassionate.

And the stranger had compassion on them again, for he knew that they would respond best to gentleness, giving back a clumsy gentleness again.

"Do not be afraid," he said to them gently. "Let me stay a little while with you. I shall not stay long. And then I shall go away for ever. But do not be afraid. No harm will come to you through me."

They believed him at once, yet the fear did not leave them. And they said:

"Stay, master, while ever you will. Rest! Rest quietly!" But they were afraid.

So he let them be, and the peasant went away with the ass. The sun had risen bright, and in the dark house with the door shut, the man was again as if in the tomb. So he said to the woman: "I would lie in the yard."

And she swept the yard for him, and laid him a mat, and he lay down under the wall in the morning sun. There he saw the first green leaves spurting like flames from the ends of the enclosed fig tree, out of the bareness to the sky of spring above. But the man who had died could not look, he only lay quite still in the sun, which was not yet too hot, and had no desire in him, not even to move. But he lay with his thin legs in the sun, his black, perfumed hair falling into the hollows of his neck, and his thin, colourless arms utterly inert. As he lay there, the hens clucked, and scratched, and the escaped cock, caught and tied by the leg again, cowered in a corner.

The peasant woman was frightened. She came peeping, and, seeing him never move, feared to have a dead man in the yard. But the sun had grown stronger, he opened his eyes and looked at her. And now she was frightened of the man who was alive, but spoke nothing.

He opened his eyes, and saw the world again bright as glass. It was life, in which he had no share any more. But it shone outside him, blue sky, and a bare fig tree with little jets of green leaf. Bright as glass, and he was not of it, for desire had failed.

Yet he was there, and not extinguished. The day passed in a kind of coma, and at evening he went into the house. The peasant man came home, but he was frightened, and had nothing to say. The stranger, too, ate of the mess of beans, a little. Then he washed his hands and turned to the wall, and was silent. The peasants were silent too. They watched their guest sleep. Sleep was so near death he could still sleep.

Yet when the sun came up, he went again to lie in the yard. The sun was the one thing that drew him and swayed him, and he still wanted to feel the cool air of the morning in his nostrils, see the pale sky overhead. He still hated to be shut up.

As he came out, the young cock crowed. It was a diminished, pinched cry, but there was that in the voice of the bird stronger than chagrin. It was the necessity to live, and even to cry out the triumph of life. The man who had died stood and watched the cock who had escaped and been caught, ruffling himself up, rising forward on his toes, throwing up his head, and parting his beak in another challenge from life to death. The brave sounds rang out, and though they were diminished by the cord round the bird's leg, they were not cut off. The man who had died looked nakedly on life, and saw a vast resoluteness everywhere flinging itself up in stormy or subtle wave-crests, foam-tips emerging out of the blue invisible, a black and orange cock or the green flame-tongues out of the extremes of the fig tree. They came forth, these things and creatures of spring, glowing with desire and with assertion. They came like crests of foam, out of the blue flood of the invisible desire, out of the vast invisible sea of strength, and they came coloured and tangible, evanescent, yet deathless in their coming. The man who had died looked on the great swing into existence of things that had not died, but he saw no longer their tremulous desire to exist and to be. He heard instead their ringing, ringing, defiant challenge to all other things existing.

The man lay still, with eyes that had died now wide open and darkly still, seeing the everlasting resoluteness of life. And the cock, with the flat, brilliant glance, glanced back at him, with a bird's half-seeing look. And always the man who had died saw not the bird alone, but the short, sharp wave of life of which the bird was the crest. He watched the queer, beaky motion of the creature as it gobbled into itself the scraps of food; its glancing of the eye of life, ever alert and watchful, over-weening and cautious, and the voice of its life, crowing triumph and assertion, yet strangled by a cord of circumstance. He seemed to hear the queer speech of very life, as the cock triumphantly imitated the clucking of the favourite hen, when she had laid an egg, a clucking which still had, in the male bird, the hollow chagrin of the cord round his leg. And when the man threw a bit of bread to the cock, it called with an extraordinary cooing tenderness, tousling and saving the morsel for the hens. The hens ran up greedily, and carried the morsel away beyond the reach of the string.

Then, walking complacently after them, suddenly the male bird's leg would hitch at the end of his tether, and he would yield with a kind of collapse. His flag fell, he seemed to diminish, he would huddle in the shade. And he was young, his tail-feathers, glossy as they were, were not fully grown. It was not till evening again that the tide of life in him made him forget. Then when his favourite hen came strolling unconcernedly near him, emitting the lure, he pounced on her with all his feathers vibrating. And the man who had died watched the unsteady, rocking vibration of the bent bird, and it was not the bird he saw, but one wave-tip of life overlapping for a minute another, in the tide of the swaying ocean of life. And the destiny of life seemed more fierce and compulsive to him even than the destiny of death. The doom of death was a shadow compared to the raging destiny of life, the determined surge of life.

At twilight the peasant came home with the ass, and he said: "Master! It is said that the body was stolen from the garden, and the tomb is empty, and the soldiers are taken away, accursed Romans! And the women are there to weep."

The man who had died looked at the man who had not died.

"It is well," he said. "Say nothing, and we are safe."

And the peasant was relieved. He looked rather dirty and stupid, and even as much flaminess as that of the young cock, which he had tied by. the leg, would never glow in him. He was without fire. But the man who had died thought to himself:

"Why, then, should he be lifted up? Clods of earth are turned over for refreshment, they are not to be lifted up. Let the earth remain earthy, and hold its own against the sky. I was to seek to lift it up. I was wrong to try to interfere. The ploughshare of devastation will be set in the soil of Judea, and the life of this peasant will be overturned like the sods of the field. No man can save the earth from tillage. It is tillage, not salvation..."

So he saw the man, the peasant, with compassion; but the

man who had died no longer wished to interfere in the soul of the man who had not died, and who could never die, save to return to earth. Let him return to earth in his own good hour, and let no one try to interfere when the earth claims her own.

So the man with scars let the peasant go from him, for the peasant had no rebirth in him. Yet the man who had died said to himself: "He is my host."

And at dawn, when he was better, the man who had died rose up, and on slow, sore feet retraced his way to the garden. For he had been betrayed in a garden, and buried in a garden. And as he turned round the screen of laurels, near the rock-face, he saw a woman hovering by the tomb, a woman in blue and yellow. She peeped again into the mouth of the hole, that was like a deep cupboard. But still there was nothing. And she wrung her hands and wept. And as she turned away, she saw the man in white, standing by the laurels, and she gave a cry, thinking it might be a spy, and she said:

"They have taken him away!"

So he said to her:

"Madeleine!"

Then she reeled as if she would fall, for she knew him. And he said to her:

"Madeleine! Do not be afraid. I am alive. They took me down too soon, so I came back to life. Then I was sheltered in a house."

She did not know what to say, but fell at his feet to kiss them.

"Don't touch me, Madeleine," he said. "Not yet! I am not yet healed and in touch with men."

So she wept because she did not know what to do. And he said: "Let us go aside, among the bushes, where we can speak unseen."

So in her blue mantle and her yellow robe, she followed him among the trees, and he sat down under a myrtle bush. And he said: "I am not yet quite come to. Madeleine, what is to be done next?"

"Master!" she said. "Oh, we have wept for you! And will you come back to us?"

"What is finished is finished, and for me the end is past," he said. "The stream will run till no more rains fill it, then it will dry up. For me, that life is over."

"And will you give up your triumph?" she said sadly.

"My triumph," he said, "is that I am not dead. I have outlived my mission and know no more of it. It is my triumph. I have survived the day and the death of my interference, and am still a man. I am young still, Madeleine, not even come to middle age. I am glad all that is over. It had to be. But now I am glad it is over, and the day of my interference is done. The teacher and the saviour are dead in me; now I can go about my business, into my own single life."

She heard him, and did not fully understand. But what he said made her feel disappointed.

"But you will come back to us?" she said, insisting.

"I don't know what I shall do," he said. "When I am healed, I shall know better. But my mission is over, and my teaching is finished, and death has saved me from my own salvation. Oh, Madeleine, I want to take my single way in life, which is my portion. My public life is over, the life of my self-importance. Now I can wait on life, and say nothing, and have no one betray me. I wanted to be greater than the limits of my hands and feet, so I brought betrayal on myself. And I know I wronged Judas, my poor Judas. For I have died, and now I know my own limits. Now I can live without striving to sway others any more. For my reach ends in my fingertips, and my stride is no longer than the ends of my toes. Yet I would embrace multitudes, I who have never truly embraced even one. But Judas and the high priests saved me from my own salvation, and soon I can turn to my destiny like a bather in the sea at dawn, who has just come down to the shore alone."

"Do you want to be alone henceforward?" she asked. "And was your mission nothing? Was it all untrue?"

"Nay!" he said. "Neither were your lovers in the past nothing. They were much to you, but you took more than you gave. Then you came to me for salvation from your own excess. And I, in my mission, I too ran to excess. I gave more than I took, and that also is woe and vanity. So Pilate and the high priests saved me from my own excessive salvation. Don't run to excess now in living, Madeleine. It only means another death."

She pondered bitterly, for the need for excessive giving was in her, and she could not bear to be denied.

"And will you not come back to us?" she said. "Have you risen for yourself alone?"

He heard the sarcasm in her voice, and looked at her beautiful face which still was dense with excessive need for salvation from the woman she had been, the female who had caught men at her will. The cloud of necessity was on her, to be saved from the old, wilful Eve, who had embraced many men and taken more than she gave. Now the other doom was on her. She wanted to give without taking. And that, too, is hard, and cruel to the warm body.

"I have not risen from the dead in order to seek death again," he said.

She glanced up at him, and saw the weariness settling again on his waxy face, and the vast disillusion in his dark eyes, and the underlying indifference. He felt her glance, and said to himself:

"Now my own followers will want to do me to death again, for having risen up different from their expectation."

"But you will come to us, to see us, us who love you?" she said.

He laughed a little and said:

"Ah, yes." Then he added: "Have you a little money? Will you give me a little money? I owe it."

She had not much, but it pleased her to give it to him.

"Do you think," he said to her, "that I might come and live with you in your house?"

She looked up at him with large blue eyes, that gleamed strangely.

"Now?" she said with peculiar triumph.

And he, who shrank now from triumph of any sort, his own or another's, said:

"Not now! Later, when I am healed, and...and I am in touch with the flesh."

The words faltered in him. And in his heart he knew he

would never go to live in her house. For the flicker of triumph had gleamed in her eyes; the greed of giving. But she murmured in a humming rapture:

"Ah, you know I would give up everything to you."

"Nay!" he said. "I didn't ask that."

A revulsion from all the life he had known came over him again, the great nausea of disillusion, and the spear-thrust through his bowels. He crouched under the myrtle bushes, without strength. Yet his eyes were open. And she looked at him again, and she saw that it was not the Messiah. The Messiah had not risen. The enthusiasm and the burning purity were gone, and the rapt youth. His youth was dead. This man was middle-aged and disillusioned, with a certain terrible indifference, and a resoluteness which love would never conquer. This was not the Master she had so adored, the young, flamy, unphysical exalter of her soul. This was nearer to the lovers she had known of old, but with a greater indifference to the personal issue, and a lesser susceptibility.

She was thrown out of the balance of her rapturous, anguished adoration. This risen man was the death of her dream.

"You should go now," he said to her. "Do not touch me, I am in death. I shall come again here, on the third day. Come if you will, at dawn. And we will speak again."

She went away, perturbed and shattered. Yet as she went, her mind discarded the bitterness of the reality, and she conjured up rapture and wonder, that the Master was risen and was not dead. He was risen, the Saviour, the exalter, the wonder-worker! He was risen, but not as man; as pure God, who should not be touched by flesh, and who should be rapt away into Heaven. It was the most glorious and most ghostly of the miracles.

Meanwhile the man who had died gathered himself together at last, and slowly made his way to the peasant's house. He was glad to go back to them, and away from Madeleine and his own associates. For the peasants had the inertia of earth and would let him rest, and as yet, would put no compulsion on him.

The woman was on the roof, looking for him. She was afraid that he had gone away. His presence in the house had become like gentle wine to her. She hastened to the door, to him.

"Where have you been?" she said. "Why did you go away?"

"I have been to walk in a garden, and I have seen a friend, who gave me a little money. It is for you."

He held out his thin hand, with the small amount of money, all that Madeleine could give him. The peasant's wife's eyes glistened, for money was scarce, and she said:

"Oh, master! And is it truly mine?"

"Take it!" he said. "It buys bread, and bread brings life."

So he lay down in the yard again, sick with relief at being alone again. For with the peasants he could be alone, but his own friends would never let him be alone. And in the safety of the yard, the young cock was dear to him, as it shouted in the helpless zest of life, and finished in the helpless humiliation of being tied by the leg. This day the ass stood swishing her tail under the shed. The man who had died lay down and turned utterly away from life, in the sickness of death in life.

But the woman brought wine and water, and sweetened cakes, and roused him, so that he ate a little, to please her. The day was hot, and as she crouched to serve him, he saw her breasts sway from her humble body, under her smock. He knew she wished he would desire her, and she was youngish, and not unpleasant. And he, who had never known a woman, would have desired her if he could. But he could not want her, though he felt gently towards her soft, crouching, humble body. But it was her thoughts, her consciousness, he could not mingle with. She was pleased with the money, and now she wanted to take more from him. She wanted the embrace of his body. But her little soul was hard, and short-sighted, and grasping, her body had its little greed, and no gentle reverence of the return gift. So he spoke a quiet, pleasant word to her and turned away. He could not touch the little, personal body, the little, personal life of this woman, nor in any other. He turned away from it without hesitation.

Risen from the dead, he had realised at last that the body, too, has its little life, and beyond that, the greater life. He was virgin, in recoil from the little, greedy life of the body. But now he knew that virginity is a form of greed; and that the body rises again to give and to take, to take and to give, ungreedily.

Now he knew that he had risen for the woman, or women, who knew the greater life of the body, not greedy to give, not greedy to take, and with whom he could mingle his body. But having died, he was patient, knowing there was time, an eternity of time. And he was driven by no greedy desire, either to give himself to others, or to grasp anything for himself. For he had died.

The peasant came home from work and said:

"Master, I thank you for the money. But we did not want it. And all I have is yours."

But the man who had died was sad, because the peasant stood there in the little, personal body, and his eyes were cunning and sparkling with the hope of greater rewards in money later on. True, the peasant had taken him in free, and had risked getting no reward. But the hope was cunning in him. Yet even this was as men are made. So when the peasant would have helped him to rise, for night had fallen, the man who had died said:

"Don't touch me, brother. I am not yet risen to the Father."

The sun burned with greater splendour, and burnished the young cock brighter. But the peasant kept the string renewed, and the bird was a prisoner. Yet the flame of life burned up to a sharp point in the cock, so that it eyed askance and haughtily the man who had died. And the man smiled and held the bird dear, and he said to it:

"Surely thou art risen to the Father, among birds." And the young cock, answering, crowed.

When at dawn on the third morning the man went to the garden, he was absorbed, thinking of the greater life of the body, beyond the little, narrow, personal life. So he came through the thick screen of laurel and myrtle bushes, near the rock, suddenly, and he saw three women near the tomb. One was Madeleine, and one was the woman who had been his mother, and the third was a woman he knew, called Joan. He looked up, and saw them all, and they saw him, and they were all afraid.

He stood arrested in the distance, knowing they were there to claim him back, bodily. But he would in no wise return to them. Pallid, in the shadow of a grey morning that was blowing to rain, he saw them, and turned away. But Madeleine hastened towards him.

"I did not bring them," she said. "They have come of themselves. See, I have brought you money!...Will you not speak to them?"

She offered him some gold pieces, and he took them, saying:

"May I have this money? I shall need it. I cannot speak to them, for I am not yet ascended to the Father. And I must leave you now."

"Ah! Where will you go?" she cried.

He looked at her, and saw she was clutching for the man in him who had died and was dead, the man of his youth and his mission, of his chastity and his fear, of his little life, his giving without taking.

"I must go to my Father!" he said.

"And you will leave us? There is your mother!" she cried, turning round with the old anguish, which yet was sweet to her.

"But now I must ascend to my Father," he said, and he drew back into the bushes, and so turned quickly, and went away, saying to himself:

"Now I belong to no one and have no connection, and mission or gospel is gone from me. Lo! I cannot make even my own life, and what have I to save?...I can learn to be alone."

So he went back to the peasants' house, to the yard where the young cock was tied by the leg with a string. And he wanted no one, for it was best to be alone; for the presence of people made him lonely. The sun and the subtle salve of spring healed his wounds, even the gaping wound of disillusion through his bowels was closing up. And his need of men and women, his fever to have them and to be saved by them, this too was healing in him. Whatever came of touch between himself and the race of men, henceforth, should come without trespass or compulsion. For he said to himself:

"I tried to compel them to live, so they compelled me to die. It is always so, with compulsion. The recoil kills the advance. Now is my time to be alone."

Therefore he went no more to the garden, but lay still and

saw the sun, or walked at dusk across the olive slopes, among the green wheat, that rose a palm-breadth higher every sunny day. And always he thought to himself:

'How good it is to have fulfilled my mission, and to be beyond it. Now I can be alone, and leave all things to themselves, and the fig tree may be barren if it will, and the rich may be rich. My way is my own alone.'

So the green jets of leaves unspread on the fig tree, with the bright, translucent, green blood of the tree. And the young cock grew brighter, more lustrous with the sun's burnishing; yet always tied by the leg with a string. And the sun went down more and more in pomp, out of the gold and red-flushed air. The man who had died was aware of it all, and he thought:

'The Word is but the midge that bites at evening. Man is tormented with words like midges, and they follow him right into the tomb. But beyond the tomb they cannot go. Now I have passed the place where words can bite no more and the air is clear, and there is nothing to say, and I am alone within my own skin, which is the walls of all my domain.'

So he healed of his wounds, and enjoyed his immortality of being alive without fret. For in the tomb he had slipped that noose which we call care. For in the tomb he had left his striving self, which cares and asserts itself. Now his uncaring self healed and became whole within his skin, and he smiled to himself with pure aloneness, which is one sort of immortality.

Then he said to himself: "I will wander the earth, and say nothing. For nothing is so marvellous as to be alone in the phenomenal world, which is raging, and yet apart. And I have not seen it, I was too much blinded by my confusion within it. Now I will wander among the stirring of the phenomenal world, for it is the stirring of all things among themselves which leaves me purely alone."

So he communed with himself, and decided to be a physician. Because the power was still in him to heal any man or child who touched his compassion. Therefore he cut his hair and his beard after the right fashion, and smiled to himself. And he bought himself shoes, and the right mantle, and put the right cloth over his head, hiding all the little scars. And the peasant said:

"Master, will you go forth from us?"

"Yes, for the time is come for me to return to men."

So he gave the peasant a piece of money, and said to him:

"Give me the cock that escaped and is now tied by the leg. For he shall go forth with me."

So for a piece of money the peasant gave the cock to the man who had died, and at dawn the man who had died set out into the phenomenal world, to be fulfilled in his own loneliness in the midst of it. For previously he had been too much mixed up in it. Then he had died. Now he must come back, to be alone in the midst. Yet even now he did not go quite alone, for under his arm, as he went, he carried the cock, whose tail fluttered gaily behind, and who craned his head excitedly, for he too was adventuring out for the first time into the wider phenomenal world, which is the stirring of the body of cocks also. And the peasant woman shed a few tears, but then went indoors, being a peasant, to look again at the pieces of money. And it seemed to her, a gleam came out of the pieces of money, wonderful.

The man who had died wandered on, and it was a sunny day. He looked around as he went, and stood aside as the pack-train passed by, towards the city. And he said to himself:

"Strange is the phenomenal world, dirty and clean together! And I am the same. Yet I am apart! And life bubbles variously. Why should I have wanted it to bubble all alike? What a pity I preached to them! A sermon is so much more likely to cake into mud, and to close the fountains, than is a psalm or a song. I made a mistake. I understand that they executed me for preaching to them. Yet they could not finally execute me, for now I am risen in my own aloneness, and inherit the earth, since I lay no claim on it. And I will be alone in the seethe of all things; first and foremost, for ever, I shall be alone. But I must toss this bird into the seethe of phenomena, for he must ride his wave. How hot he is with life! Soon, in some place, I shall leave him among the hens. And perhaps one evening I shall meet a woman who can lure my risen body, yet leave me my aloneness. For the body of my desire has died, and I am not in touch anywhere. Yet how do I know! All at least is life. And this cock gleams with bright aloneness, though he answers the lure of hens. And I shall hasten on to that village on the hill ahead of me; already I am tired and weak, and want to close my eyes to everything."

Hastening a little with the desire to have finished going, he overtook two men going slowly, and talking. And being soft-footed, he heard they were speaking of himself. And he remembered them, for he had known them in his life, the life of his mission. So he greeted them, but did not disclose himself in the dusk, and they did not know him. He said to them:

"What then of him who would be king, and was put to death for it?"

They answered suspiciously: "Why ask you of him?"

"I have known him, and thought much about him," he said.

So they replied: "He has risen."

"Yea! And where is he, and how does he live?"

"We know not, for it is not revealed. Yet he is risen, and in a little while will ascend unto the Father."

"Yea! And where then is his Father?"

"Know ye not? You are then of the Gentiles! The Father is in Heaven, above the cloud and the firmament."

"Truly? Then how will he ascend?"

"As Elijah the Prophet, he shall go up in a glory."

"Even into the sky."

"Into the sky."

"Then is he not risen in the flesh?"

"He is risen in the flesh."

"And will he take flesh up into the sky?"

"The Father in Heaven will take him up."

The man who had died said no more, for his say was over, and words beget words, even as gnats. But the man asked him: "Why do you carry a cock?"

"I am a healer," he said, "and the bird hath virtue."

"You are not a believer?"

"Yea! I believe the bird is full of life and virtue."

They walked on in silence after this, and he felt they disliked his answer. So he smiled to himself, for a dangerous phenomenon in the world is a man of narrow belief, who denies the right of his neighbour to be alone. And as they came to the outskirts of the village, the man who had died stood still in the gloaming and said in his old voice:

"Know ye me not?"

And they cried in fear: "Master!"

"Yea!" he said, laughing softly. And he turned suddenly away, down a side lane, and was gone under the wall before they knew.

So he came to an inn where the asses stood in the yard. And he called for fritters, and they were made for him. So he slept under a shed. But in the morning he was wakened by a loud crowing, and his cock's voice ringing in his ears. So he saw the rooster of the inn walking forth to battle, with his hens, a goodly number, behind him. Then the cock of the man who had died sprang forth, and a battle began between the birds. The man of the inn ran to save his rooster, but the man who had died said:

"If my bird wins I will give him thee. And if he lose, thou shalt eat him."

So the birds fought savagely, and the cock of the man who had died killed the common cock of the yard. Then the man who had died said to his young cock:

"Thou at least hast found thy kingdom, and the females to thy body. Thy aloneness can take on splendour, polished by the lure of thy hens."

And he left his bird there, and went on deeper into the phenomenal world, which is a vast complexity of entanglements and allurements. And he asked himself a last question:

"From what, and to what, could this infinite whirl be saved?"

So he went his way, and was alone. But the way of the world was past belief, as he saw the strange entanglement of passions and circumstance and compulsion everywhere, but always the dread insomnia of compulsion. It was fear, the ultimate fear of death, that made men mad. So always he must move on, for if he stayed, his neighbours wound the strangling of their fear and bullying round him. There was nothing he could touch, for all, in a mad assertion of the ego, wanted to put a compulsion on him, and violate his intrinsic solitude. It was the mania of cities and societies and hosts, to lay a compulsion upon a man, upon all men. For men and women alike were mad with the egoistic fear of their own nothingness. And he thought of his own mission, how he had tried to lay the compulsion of love on all men. And the old nausea came back on him. For there was no contact without a subtle attempt to inflict a compulsion. And already he had been compelled even into death. The nausea of the old wound broke out afresh, and he looked again on the world with repulsion, dreading its mean contacts.

2

The wind came cold and strong from inland, from the invisible snows of Lebanon. But the temple, facing south and west, towards Egypt, faced the splendid sun of winter as he curved down towards the sea, the warmth and radiance flooded in between the pillars of painted wood. But the sea was invisible, because of the trees, though its dashing sounded among the hum of pines. The air was turning golden to afternoon. The woman who served Isis stood in her yellow robe, and looked up at the steep slopes coming down to the sea, where the olive trees silvered under the wind like water splashing. She was alone save for the goddess. And in the winter afternoon the light stood erect and magnificent off the invisible sea, filling the hills of the coast. She went towards the sun, through the grove of Mediterranean pine trees and evergreen oaks, in the midst of which the temple stood, on a little, tree-covered tongue of land between two bays.

It was only a very little way, and then she stood among the dry trunks of the outermost pines, on the rocks under which the sea smote and sucked, facing the open where the bright sun gloried in winter. The sea was dark, almost indigo, running away from the land, and crested with white. The hand of the wind brushed it strangely with shadow, as it brushed the olives of the slopes with silver. And there was no boat out.

The three boats were drawn high up on the steep shingle of the little bay, by the small grey tower. Along the edge of the shingle ran a high wall, inside which was a garden occupying the brief flat of the bay, then rising in terraces up the steep slope of the coast. And there, some little way up, within another wall, stood the low white villa, white and alone as the coast, overlooking the sea. But higher, much higher up, where the olives had given way to pine trees again, ran the coast road, keeping to the height to be above the gullies that came down to the bays.

Upon it all poured the royal sunshine of the January afternoon. Or rather, all was part of the great sun, glow and substance and immaculate loneliness of the sea, and pure brightness.

Crouching in the rocks above the dark water, which only swung up and down, two slaves, half naked, were dressing pigeons for the evening meal. They pierced the throat of a blue, live bird, and let the drops of blood fall into the heaving sea, with curious concentration. They were performing some sacrifice, or working some incantation. The woman of the temple, yellow and white and alone like a winter narcissus stood between the pines of the small, humped peninsula where the temple secretly hid, and watched.

A black-and-white pigeon, vividly white, like a ghost escaped over the low dark sea, sped out, caught the wind, tilted, rode, soared and swept over the pine trees, and wheeled away, a speck, inland. It had escaped. The priestess heard the cry of the boy slave, a garden slave of about seventeen. He raised his arms to heaven in anger as the pigeon wheeled away, naked and angry and young he held out his arms. Then he turned and seized the girl in an access of rage, and beat her with his fist that was stained with pigeon's blood. And she lay down with her face hidden, passive and quivering. The woman who owned them watched. And as she watched, she saw another onlooker, a stranger, in a low, broad hat, and a cloak of grey homespun, a dark bearded man standing on the little causeway of a rock that was the neck of her temple peninsula. By the blowing of his dark-grey cloak she saw him. And he saw her, on the rocks like a white-and-yellow narcissus, because of the flutter of her white linen tunic, below the yellow mantle of wool. And both of them watched the two slaves.

The boy suddenly left off beating the girl. He crouched over her, touching her, trying to make her speak. But she lay quite inert, face down on the smoothed rock. And he put his arms round her and lifted her, but she slipped back to earth like one dead, yet far too quickly for anything dead. The boy, desperate, caught her by the hips and hugged her to him, turning her over there. There she seemed inert, all her fight was in her shoulders. He twisted her over, intent and unconscious, and pushed his hands between her thighs, to push them apart. And in an instant he was covering her in the blind, frightened frenzy of a boy's first passion. Quick and frenzied his young body quivered naked on hers, blind, for a minute. Then it lay quite still, as if dead.

And then, in terror, he peeped up. He peeped round, and drew slowly to his feet, adjusting his loin-rag. He saw the stranger, and then he saw, on the rocks beyond, the lady of Isis, his mistress. And as he saw her, his whole body shrank and cowed, and with a strange cringing motion he scuttled lamely towards the door in the wall.

The girl sat up and looked after him. When she had seen him disappear, she too looked round. And she saw the stranger and the priestess. Then with a sullen movement she turned away, as if she had seen nothing, to the four dead pigeons and the knife, which lay there on the rock. And she began to strip the small feathers, so that they rose on the wind like dust.

The priestess turned away. Slaves! Let the overseer watch them. She was not interested. She went slowly through the pines again, back to the temple, which stood in the sun in a small clearing at the centre of the tongue of land. It was a small temple of wood, painted all pink and white and blue, having at the front four wooden pillars rising like stems to the swollen lotus-bud of Egypt at the top, supporting the roof and open, spiky lotus-flowers of the outer frieze, which went round under the eaves. Two low steps of stone led up to the platform before the pillars, and the chamber behind the pillars was open. There a low stone altar stood, with a few embers in its hollow, and the dark stain of blood in its end groove.

She knew her temple so well, for she had built it at her own expense, and tended it for seven years. There it stood, pink and white, like a flower in the little clearing, backed by blackish evergreen oaks; and the shadow of afternoon was already washing over its pillar bases.

She entered slowly, passing through to the dark inner chamber, lighted by a perfumed oil-flame. And once more she pushed shut the door, and once more she threw a few grains of incense on a brazier before the goddess, and once more she sat down before her goddess, in the almost-darkness, to muse, to go away into the dreams of the goddess.

It was Isis; but not Isis, Mother of Horus. It was Isis Bereaved, Isis in Search. The goddess, in painted marble, lifted her face and strode, one thigh forward, through the frail fluting of her robe, in the anguish of bereavement and of search. She was looking for the fragments of the dead Osiris, dead and scattered asunder, dead, torn apart, and thrown in fragments over the wide world. And she must find his hands and his feet, his heart, his thighs, his head, his belly, she must gather him together and fold her arms round the re-assembled body till it became warm again, and roused to life, and could embrace her, and could fecundate her womb. And the strange rapture and anguish of search went on through the years, as she lifted her throat and her hollowed eyes looked inward, in the tormented ecstasy of seeking, and the delicate navel of her bud-like belly showed through the frail, girdled robe with the eternal asking, asking, of her search. And through the years she found him bit by bit, heart and head and limbs and body. And yet she had not found the last reality, the final clue to him, that alone could bring him really back to her. For she was Isis of the subtle lotus, the womb which waits submerged and in bud, waits for the touch of that other inward sun that streams its rays from the loins of the male Osiris.

This was the mystery the woman had served alone for seven years, since she was twenty, till now she was twenty-seven. Before, when she was young, she had lived in the world, in Rome, in Ephesus, in Egypt. For her father had been one of Anthony's captains and comrades, had fought with Anthony and had stood with him when Caesar was murdered, and through to the days of shame. Then he had come again across to Asia, out of favour with Rome, and had been killed in the mountains beyond Lebanon. The widow, having no favour to hope for from Octavius, had retired to her small property on the coast under Lebanon, taking her daughter from the world, a girl of nineteen, beautiful but unmarried.

When she was young the girl had known Caesar, and had shrunk from his eagle-like rapacity. The golden Anthony had sat with her many a half-hour, in the splendour of his great limbs and glowing manhood, and talked with her of the philosophies and the gods. For he was fascinated as a child by the gods, though he mocked at them, and forgot them in his own vanity. But he said to her:

"I have sacrificed two doves for you, to Venus, for I am afraid you make no offering to the sweet goddess. Beware you will offend her. Come, why is the flower of you so cool within? Does never a ray nor a glance find its way through? Ah, come, a maid should open to the sun, when the sun leans towards her to caress her."

And the big, bright eyes of Anthony laughed down on her, bathing her in his glow. And she felt the lovely glow of his male beauty and his amorousness bathe all her limbs and her body. But it was as he said: the very flower of her womb was cool, was almost cold, like a bud in shadow of frost, for all the flooding of his sunshine. So Anthony, respecting her father, who loved her, had left her.

And it had always been the same. She saw many men, young and old. And on the whole, she liked the old ones best, for they talked to her still and sincere, and did not expect her to open like a flower to the sun of their maleness. Once she asked a philosopher: "Are all women born to be given to men?" To which the old man answered slowly:

"Rare women wait for the re-born man. For the lotus, as you know, will not answer to all the bright heat of the sun. But she curves her dark, hidden head in the depths, and stirs not. Till, in the night, one of these rare, invisible suns that have been killed and shine no more, rises among the stars in unseen purple, and like the violet, sends its rare purple rays out into the night. To these the lotus stirs as to a caress, and rises upwards through the flood, and lifts up her bent head, and opens with an expansion such as no other flower knows, and spreads her sharp rays of bliss, and offers her soft, gold depths such as no other flower possesses, to the penetration of the flooding, violet-dark sun that has died and risen and makes no show. But for the golden brief day-suns of show such as Anthony, and for the hard winter suns of power, such as Caesar, the lotus stirs not, nor will ever stir. Those will only tear open the bud. Ah, I tell you, wait for the re-born and wait for the bud to stir."

So she had waited. For all the men were soldiers or politicians in the Roman spell, assertive, manly, splendid apparently but of an inward meanness, an inadequacy. And Rome and Egypt alike had left her alone, unroused. And she was a woman to herself, she would not give herself for a surface glow, nor marry for reasons. She would wait for the lotus to stir.

And then, in Egypt, she had found Isis, in whom she spelled her mystery. She had brought Isis to the shores of Sidon, and lived with her in the mystery of search; whilst her mother, who loved affairs, controlled the small estate and the slaves with a free hand.

When the woman had roused from her muse and risen to perform the last brief ritual to Isis, she replenished the lamp and left the sanctuary, locking the door. In the outer world, the sun had already set, and twilight was chill among the humming trees, which hummed still, though the wind was abating.

A stranger in a dark, broad hat rose from the corner of the temple steps, holding his hat in the wind. He was dark-faced, with a black pointed beard. "Oh, madam, whose shelter may I implore?" he said to the woman, who stood in her yellow mantle on a step above him, beside a pink-and-white painted pillar. Her face was rather long and pale, her dusky blonde hair was held under a thin gold net. She looked down on the vagabond with indifference. It was the same she had seen watching the slaves.

"Why come you down from the road?" she asked.

"I saw the temple like a pale flower on the coast, and would rest among the trees of the precincts, if the lady of the goddess permits."

"It is Isis in Search," she said, answering his first question.

"The goddess is great," he replied.

She looked at him still with mistrust. There was a faint, remote smile in the dark eyes lifted to her, though the face was hollow with suffering. The vagabond divined her hesitation, and was mocking her.

"Stay here upon the steps," she said. "A slave will show you the shelter."

"The lady of Egypt is gracious."

She went down the rocky path of the humped peninsula in her gilded sandals. Beautiful were her ivory feet, beneath the white tunic, and above the saffron mantle her dusky-blonde head bent as with endless musings. A woman entangled in her own dream. The man smiled a little, half bitterly, and sat again on the step to wait, drawing his mantle round him, in the cold twilight.

At length a slave appeared, also in hodden grey.

"Seek ye the shelter of our lady?" he said insolently. "Even so."

"Then come."

With the brusque insolence of a slave waiting on a vagabond, the young fellow led through the trees and down into a little gully in the rock, where, almost in darkness, was a small cave, with a litter of the tall heaths that grew on the waste places of the coast, under the stone-pines. The place was dark, but absolutely silent from the wind. There was still a faint odour of goats.

"Here sleep!" said the slave. "For the goats come no more on this half-island. And there is water." He pointed to a little basin of rock where the maidenhair fern fringed a dripping mouthful of water.

Having scornfully bestowed his patronage, the slave departed. The man who had died climbed out to the tip of the peninsula, where the wave thrashed. It was rapidly getting dark, and the stars were coming out. The wind was abating for the night. Inland, the steep grooved up-slope was dark to the long wavering outline of the crest against the translucent sky. Only now and then a lantern flickered towards the villa.

The man who had died went back to the shelter. There he took bread from his leather pouch, dipped it in the water of the tiny spring, and slowly ate. Having eaten and washed his mouth, he looked once more at the bright stars in the pure windy sky, then settled the heath for his bed. Having laid his hat and his sandals aside, and put his pouch under his cheek for a pillow, he slept, for he was very tired. Yet during the night the cold woke him pinching wearily through his weariness. Outside was brilliantly starry, and still windy. He sat and hugged himself in a sort of coma, and towards dawn went to sleep again.

In the morning the coast was still chill in shadow, though the sun was up behind the hills, when the woman came down from the villa towards the goddess. The sea was fair and pale blue, lovely in newness, and at last the wind was still. Yet the waves broke white in the many rocks, and tore in the shingle of the little bay. The woman came slowly towards her dream. Yet she was aware of an interruption.

As she followed the little neck of rock on to her peninsula, and climbed the slope between the trees to the temple, a slave came down and stood, making his obeisance. There was a faint insolence in his humility. "Speak!" she said.

"Lady, the man is there, he still sleeps. Lady, may I speak?"

"Speak!" she said, repelled by the fellow.

"Lady, the man is an escaped malefactor."

The slave seemed to triumph in imparting the unpleasant news.

"By what sign?"

"Behold his hands and feet! Will the lady look on him?"

"Lead on!"

The slave led quickly over the mound of the hill down to the tiny ravine. There he stood aside, and the woman went into the crack towards the cave. Her heart beat a little. Above all, she must preserve her temple inviolate.

The vagabond was asleep with his cheek on his scrip, his

mantle wrapped round him, but his bare, soiled feet curling side by side, to keep each other warm, and his hand lying clenched in sleep. And in the pale skin of his feet usually covered by sandal-straps, she saw the scars, and in the palm of the loose hand.

She had no interest in men, particularly in the servile class. Yet she looked at the sleeping face. It was worn, hollow, and rather ugly. But, 'a true priestess, she saw the other kind of beauty in it, the sheer stillness of the deeper life. There was even a sort of majesty in the dark brows, over the still, hollow cheeks. She saw that his black hair, left long, in contrast to the Roman fashion, was touched with grey at the temples, and the black pointed beard had threads of grey. But that must be suffering or mis-fortune, for the man was young. His dusky skin had the silvery glisten of youth still.

There was a beauty of much suffering, and the strange calm candour of finer life in the whole delicate ugliness of the face. For the first time, she was touched on the quick at the sight of a man, as if the tip of a fine flame of living had touched her. It was the first time. Men had roused all kinds of feeling in her, but never had touched her with the flame-tip of life.

She went back under the rock to where the slave waited.

"Know!" she said. "This is no malefactor, but a free citizen of the east. Do not disturb him. But when he comes forth, bring him to me; tell him I would speak with him."

She spoke coldly, for she found slaves invariably repellent, a little repulsive. They were so embedded in the lesser life, and their appetites and their small consciousness were a little dis-gusting. So she wrapped her dream round her and went to the temple, where a slave girl brought winter roses and jasmine for the altar. But to-day, even in her ministrations, she was disturbed.

The sun rose over the hill, sparkling, the light fell trium-phantly on the little pine-covered peninsula of the coast, and on the pink temple, in the pristine newness. The man who had died woke up, and put on his sandals. He put on his hat too, slung his scrip under his mantle, and went out, to see the morning in all its blue and its new gold. He glanced at the little yellow-and-white narcissus sparkling gaily in the rocks. And he saw the slave waiting for him like a menace.

"Master!" said the slave. "Our lady would speak with you at the house of Isis."

"It is well," said the wanderer.

He went slowly, staying to look at the pale blue sea like a flower in unruffled bloom, and the white fringes among the rocks, like white rock-flowers, the hollow slopes sheering up high from the shore, grey with olive trees and green with bright young wheat, and set with the white, small villa. All fair and pure in the January morning.

The sun fell on the corner of the temple, he sat down on the step in the sunshine, in the infinite patience of waiting. He had come back to life, but not the same life that he had left, the life of little people and the little day. Re-born, he was in the other life, the greater day of the human consciousness. And he was alone and apart from the little day, and out of contact with the daily people. Not yet had he accepted the irrevocable *noli me tangere* which separates the re-born from the vulgar. The separation was absolute, as yet here at the temple he felt peace, the hard, bright pagan peace with hostility of slaves beneath.

The woman came into the dark inner doorway of the temple from the shrine, and stood there, hesitating. She could see the dark figure of the man, sitting in that terrible stillness that was portentous to her, had something almost menacing in its patience.

She advanced across the outer chamber of the temple, and the man, becoming aware of her, stood up. She addressed him in Greek, but he said:

"Madam, my Greek is limited. Allow me to speak vulgar Syrian."

"Whence come you? Whither go you?" she asked, with a hurried preoccupation of a priestess.

"From the east beyond Damascus—and I go west as the road goes," he replied slowly.

She glanced at him with sudden anxiety and shyness.

"But why do you have the marks of a malefactor?" she asked abruptly.

"Did the Lady of Isis spy upon me in my sleep?" he asked, with a grey weariness.

"The slave warned me—your hands and feet—" she said. He looked at her. Then he said:

"Will the Lady of Isis allow me to bid her farewell, and go up to the road?"

The wind came in a sudden puff, lifting his mantle and his hat. He put up his hand to hold the brim, and she saw again the thin brown hand with its scar.

"See! The scar!" she said, pointing.

"Even so!" he said. "But farewell, and to Isis my homage and my thanks for sleep."

He was going. But she looked up at him with her wondering blue eyes.

"Will you not look at Isis?" she said, with sudden impulse. And something stirred in him, like pain.

"Where then?" he said.

"Come!"

He followed her into the inner shrine, into the almost-darkness. When his eyes got used to the faint glow of the lamp, he saw the goddess striding like a ship, eager in the swirl of her gown, and he made his obeisance.

"Great is Isis!" he said. "In her search she is greater than death. Wonderful is such walking in a woman, wonderful the goal. All men praise thee, Isis, thou greater than the mother unto man."

The woman of Isis heard, and threw incense on the brazier. Then she looked at the man.

"Is it well with thee here?" she asked him. "Has Isis brought thee home to herself?"

He looked at the priestess in wonder and trouble. "I know not," he said.

But the woman was pondering that this was the lost Osiris. She felt it in the quick of her soul. And her agitation was intense.

He would not stay in the close, dark, perfumed shrine. He went out again to the morning, to the cold air. He felt something approaching to touch him, and all his flesh was still woven with pain and the wild commandment: *Noli me tangere!* Touch me not! Oh, don't touch me!

The woman followed into the open with timid eagerness. He was moving away.

"Oh, stranger, do not go! Oh, stay a while with Isis!"

He looked at her, at her face open like a flower, as if a sun had risen in her soul. And again his loins stirred.

"Would you detain me, girl of Isis?" he said.

"Stay! I am sure you are Osiris!" she said.

He laughed suddenly. "Not yet!" he said. Then he looked at her wistful face. "But I will sleep another night in the cave of the goats, if Isis wills it," he added.

She put her hands together with a priestess's childish happiness.

"Ah! Isis will be glad!" she said.

So he went down to the shore in great trouble, saying to himself: "Shall I give myself into this touch? Shall I give myself into this touch Men have tortured me to death with their touch. Yet this girl of Isis is a tender flame of healing. I am a physician, yet I have no healing like the flame of this tender girl. The flame of this tender girl! Like the first pale crocus of the spring. How could I have been blind to the healing and the bliss in the crocus-like body of a tender woman! Ah, tenderness! More terrible and lovely than the death I died—"

He pried small shell-fish from the rocks, and ate them with relish and wonder for the simple taste of the sea. And inwardly he was tremulous, thinking: "Dare I come into touch? For this is farther than death. I have dared to let them lay hands on me and put me to death. But dare I come into this tender touch of life? Oh, this is harder—"

But the woman went into the shrine again, and sat rapt in pure muse, through the long hours, watching the swirling stride of the yearning goddess, and the navel of the bud-like belly, like a seal on the virgin urge of the search. And she gave herself to the woman-flow and to the urge of Isis in Search.

Towards sundown she went on the peninsula to look for him. And she found him gone towards the sun, as she had gone the day before, and sitting on the pine-needles at the foot of the tree, where she had stood when first she saw him. Now she approached tremulously and slowly, afraid, lest he did not want her. She stood near him unseen, till suddenly he glanced up at her from under his broad hat, and saw the westering sun on her netted hair. He was startled, yet he expected her.

"Is that your home?" he said, pointing to the white, low villa on the slope of olives.

"It is my mother's house. She is a widow, and I am her only child."

"And are these all her slaves?"

"Except those that are mine."

Their eyes met for a moment.

"Will you too sit to see the sun go down?" he said.

He had not risen to speak to her. He had known too much pain. So she sat on the dry brown pine-needles, gathering her saffron mantle round her knees. A boat was coming in, out of the open glow into the shadow of the bay, and slaves were lifting small nets, their babble coming off the surface of the water.

"And this is home to you," he said.

"But I serve Isis in Search," she replied.

He looked at her. She was like a soft, musing cloud, somehow remote. His soul smote him with passion and compassion.

"Mayst thou find thy desire, maiden," he said, with sudden earnestness.

"And art thou not Osiris?" she asked.

He flushed suddenly.

"Yes, if thou wilt heal me!" he said. "For the death aloofness is still upon me, and I cannot escape it."

She looked at him for a moment in fear from the soft blue sun of her eyes. Then she lowered her head, and they sat in silence in the warmth and glow of the western sun: the man who had died, and the woman of the pure search.

The sun was curving down to the sea, in grand winter splendour. It fell on the twinkling, naked bodies of the slaves, with their ruddy broad hams and their small black heads, as they ran spreading the nets on the pebble beach. The all-tolerant Pan watched over them. All-tolerant Pan should be their god for ever.

The woman rose as the sun's rim dipped, saying:

"If you will stay, I shall send down victual and covering."

"The lady your mother, what will she say?"

The woman of Isis looked at him strangely, but with a tinge of misgiving.

"It is my own," she said.

"It is good," he said, smiling faintly and foreseeing difficulties.

He watched her go, with her absorbed, strange motion of the self-dedicate. Her dun head was a little bent, the white linen swung about her ivory ankles. And he saw the naked slaves stand to look at her, with a certain wonder, and even a certain mischief. But she passed intent through the door in the wall, on the bay.

The man who had died sat on at the foot of the tree overlooking the strand, for on the little shore everything happened. At the small stream which ran in round the corner of the property wall, women slaves were still washing linen, and now and again came the hollow chock! chock! chock! as they beat it against the smooth stones in the dark little hollow of the pool. There was a smell of olive refuse on the air; and sometimes still the faint rumble of the grindstone that was milling the olives, inside the garden, and the sound of the slave calling to the ass at the mill. Then through the doorway a woman stepped, a grey-haired woman in a mantle of whitish wool, and there followed her a bare-headed man in a toga, a Roman: probably her steward or overseer. They stood on the high shingle above the sea, and cast round a rapid glance. The broad-hammed, ruddy-bodied slaves bent absorbed and abject over the nets, picking them clean, the women washing linen thrust their palms with energy down on the wash, the old slave bent absorbed at the water's edge, washing the fish and the polyps of the catch. And the woman and the overseer saw it all in one glance. They also saw, seated at the foot of the tree on the rocks of the peninsula, the strange man silent and alone. And the man who had died saw that they spoke of him. Out of the little sacred world of the peninsula he looked on the common world, and saw it still hostile.

The sun was touching the sea, across the tiny bay stretched the shadow of the opposite humped headland. Over the shingle, now blue and cold in shadow, the elderly woman trod heavily, in shadow too, to look at the fish spread in the flat basket of the old man crouching at the water's edge: a naked old slave with fat hips and shoulders, on whose soft, fairish-orange body the last sun twinkled, then died. The old slave continued cleaning the fish absorbedly, not looking up: as if the lady were the shadow of twilight falling on him.

Then from the gateway stepped two slave-girls with flat baskets on their heads, and from one basket the terra-cotta wine-jar and the oil-jar poked up, leaning slightly. Over the massive shingle, under the wall, came the girls, and the woman of Isis in her saffron mantle stepped in twilight after them. Out at sea, the sun still shone. Here was shadow. The mother with grey head stood at the sea's edge and watched the daughter, all yellow and white, with dun blonde head, swinging unseeing and unheeding after the slave-girls, towards the neck of rock of the peninsula; the daughter, travelling in her absorbed other-world. And not moving from her place, the elderly mother watched that procession of three file up the rise of the head-land, between the trees, and disappear, shut in by trees. No slave had lifted a head to look. The grey-haired woman still watched the trees where her daughter had disappeared. Then she glanced again at the foot of the tree, where the man who had died was still sitting, inconspicuous now, for the sun had left him; and only the far blade of the sea shone bright. It was evening. Patience! Let destiny move!

The mother plodded with a stamping stride up the shingle: not long and swinging and rapt, like the daughter, but short and determined. Then down the rocks opposite came two na-ked slaves trotting with huge bundles of dark green on their shoulders, so their broad, naked legs twinkled underneath like insects' legs, and their heads were hidden. They came trotting across the shingle, heedless and intent on their way, when sud-denly the man, the Roman-looking overseer, addressed them, and they stopped dead. They stood invisible under their loads, as if they might disappear altogether, now they were arrested. Then a hand came out and pointed to the peninsula. Then the two green-heaped slaves trotted on, towards the temple pre-cincts. The grey-haired woman joined the man, and slowly the two passed through the door again, from the shingle of the sea to the property of the villa. Then the old, fat-shouldered slave rose, pallid in the shadow, with his tray of fish from the sea, and the woman rose from the pool, dusky and alive, piling the wet linen in a heap on to the flat baskets, and the slaves who had cleaned the net gathered its whitish folds together. And the old slave with the fish-basket on his shoulder, and the women slaves with the heaped baskets of wet linen on their heads, and the two slaves with the folded net, and the slave with oars on his shoulders, and the boy with the folded sail on his arm, gathered in a naked group near the door, and the man who had died heard the low buzz of their chatter. Then as the wind wafted cold; they began to pass through the door.

It was the life of the little day, the life of little people. And the man who had died said to himself: "Unless we encompass it in the greater day, and set the little life in the circle of the greater life, all is disaster."

Even the tops of the hills were in shadow. Only the sky was still upwardly radiant. The sea was a vast milky shadow. The man who had died rose a little stiffly and turned into the grove.

There was no one at the temple. He went on to his lair in the rock. There, the slave-men had carried out the old heath of the bedding, swept the rock floor, and were spreading with nice art the myrtle, then the rougher heath, then the soft, bushy heath-tips on top, for a bed. Over it all they put a well-tanned white ox-skin. The maids had laid folded woollen covers at the head of the cave, and the wine-jar, the oil-jar, a terra-cotta drinking-cup and a basket containing bread, salt, cheese, dried figs and eggs stood neatly arranged. There was also a little brazier of charcoal. The cave was suddenly full, and a dwelling-place.

The woman of Isis stood in the hollow by the tiny spring.

Only one slave at a time could pass. The girl-slaves waited at the entrance to the narrow place. When the man who had died appeared, the woman sent the girls away. The men-slaves still arranged the bed, making the job as long as possible. But the woman of Isis dismissed them too. And the man who had died came to look at his house.

"Is it well?" the woman asked him.

"It is very well," the man replied. "But the lady, your mother, and he who is no doubt the steward, watched while the slaves brought the goods. Will they not oppose you?"

"I have my own portion! Can I not give of my own? Who is going to oppose me and the gods?" she said, with a certain soft fury, touched with exasperation. So that he knew that her mother would oppose her, and that the spirit of the little life would fight against the spirit of the greater. And he thought: 'Why did the woman of Isis relinquish her portion in the daily world? She should have kept her goods fiercely!'

"Will you eat and drink?" she said. "On the ashes are warm eggs. And I will go up to the meal at the villa. But in the second hour of the night I shall come down to the temple. O, then, will you come too to Isis?" She looked at him, and a queer glow dilated her eyes. This was her dream, and it was greater than herself. He could not bear to thwart her or hurt her in the least thing now. She was in the full glow of her woman's mystery.

"Shall I wait at the temple?" he said.

"O, wait at the second hour and I shall come." He heard the humming supplication in her voice and his fibres quivered. "But the lady, your mother?" he said gently.

The woman looked at him, startled.

"She will not thwart me!" she said.

So he knew that the mother would thwart the daughter, for the daughter had left her goods in the hands of her mother, who would hold fast to this power.

But she went, and the man who had died lay reclining on his couch, and ate the eggs from the ashes, and dipped his bread in oil, and ate it, for his flesh was dry: and he mixed wine and water, and drank. And so he lay still, and the lamp made a small bud of light.

He was absorbed and enmeshed in new sensations. The woman of Isis was lovely to him, not so much in form as in the wonderful womanly glow of her. Suns beyond suns had dipped her in mysterious fire, the mysterious fire of a potent woman, and to touch her was like touching the sun. Best of all was her tender desire for him, like sunshine, so soft and still.

"She is like sunshine upon me," he said to himself, stretching his limbs. "I have never before stretched my limbs in such sunshine, as her desire for me. The greatest of all gods granted me this."

At the same time he was haunted by the fear of the outer world. "If they can, they will kill us," he said to himself. "But there is a law of the sun which protects us."

And again he said to himself: "I have risen naked and branded. But if I am naked enough for this contact, I have not died in vain. Before I was clogged."

He rose and went out. The night was chill and starry, and of a great wintry splendour. "There are destinies of splendour," he said to the night, "after all our doom of littleness and meanness and pain."

So he went up silently to the temple, and waited in darkness against the inner wall, looking out on a grey darkness, stars, and rims of trees. And he said again to himself: "There are destinies of splendour, and there is a greater power."

So at last he saw the light of her silk lanthorn swinging, coming intermittent between the trees, yet coming swiftly. She was alone, and near, the light softly swishing on her mantle-hem. And he trembled with fear and with joy, saying to himself: "I am almost more afraid of this touch than I was of death. For I am more nakedly exposed to it."

"I am here, Lady of Isis," he said softly out of the dark. "Ah!" she cried, in fear also, yet in rapture. For she was given to her dream.

She unlocked the door of the shrine, and he followed after her. Then she latched the door shut again. The air inside was warm and close and perfumed. The man who had died stood by the closed door and watched the woman. She had come first to the goddess. And dim-lit, the goddess-statue stood surging forward, a little fearsome like a great woman-presence urging.

The priestess did not look at him. She took off her saffron

mantle and laid it on a low couch. In the dim light she was bare-armed, in her girdled white tunic. But she was still hiding herself away from him. He stood back in shadow and watched her softly fan the brazier and fling on incense. Faint clouds of sweet aroma arose on the air. She turned to the statue in the ritual of approach, softly swaying forward with a slight lurch, like a moored boat, tipping towards the goddess.

He watched the strange rapt woman, and he said to himself: "I must leave her alone in her rapture, her female mysteries." So she tipped in her strange forward-swaying rhythm before the goddess. Then she broke into a murmur of Greek, which he could not understand. And, as she murmured, her swaying softly subsided, like a boat on a sea that grows still. And as he watched her, he saw her soul in its aloneness, and its female difference. He said to himself: "How different she is from me, how strangely different! She is afraid of me, and my male difference. She is getting herself naked and clear of her fear. How sensitive and softly alive she is, with a life so different from mine! How beautiful with a soft, strange courage, of life, so different from my courage of death! What a beautiful thing, like the heart of a rose, like the core of a flame. She is making herself completely penetrable. Ah! how terrible to fail her, or to trespass on her!"

She turned to him, her face glowing from the goddess. "You are Osiris, aren't you?" she said naively.

"If you will," he said.

"Will you let Isis discover you? Will you not take off your things?"

He looked at the woman, and lost his breath. And his wounds, and especially the death-wound through his belly, began to cry again.

"It has hurt so much!" he said. "You must forgive me if I am still held back."

But he took off his cloak and his tunic and went naked towards the idol, his breast panting with the sudden terror of overwhelming pain, memory of overwhelming pain, and grief too bitter.

"They did me to death!" he said in excuse of himself, turning his face to her for a moment.

And she saw the ghost of the death in him as he stood there thin and stark before her, and suddenly she was terrified, and she felt robbed. She felt the shadow of the grey, grisly wing of death triumphant.

"Ah, Goddess," he said to the idol in the vernacular. "I would be so glad to live, if you would give me my clue again."

For her again he felt desperate, faced by the demand of life, and burdened still by his death.

"Let me anoint you!" the woman said to him softly. "Let me anoint the scars! Show me, and let me anoint them!"

He forgot his nakedness in this re-evoked old pain. He sat on the edge of the couch, and she poured a little ointment into the palm of his hand. And as she chafed his hand, it all came back, the nails, the holes, the cruelty, the unjust cruelty against him who had offered only kindness. The agony of injustice and cruelty came over him again, as in his death-hour. But she chafed the palm, murmuring: "What was torn becomes a new flesh, what was a wound is full of fresh life; this scar is the eye of the violet."

And he could not help smiling at her, in her naïve priestess's absorption. This was her dream, and he was only a dream-object to her. She would never know or understand what he was. Especially she would never know the death that was gone before in him. But what did it matter? She was different. She was woman: her life and her death were different from him. Only she was good to him.

When she chafed his feet with oil and tender, tender healing, he could not refrain from saying to her:

"Once a woman washed my feet with tears, and wiped them with her hair, and poured on precious ointment."

The woman of Isis looked up at him from her earnest work, interrupted again.

"Were they hurt then?" she said. "Your feet?"

"No, no! It was while they were whole."

"And did you love her?"

"Love had passed in her. She only warned to serve," he replied. "She had been a prostitute."

"And did you let her serve you?" she asked.

"Yea."

"Did you let her serve you with the corpse of her love?"

"Ay!"

Suddenly it dawned on him: I asked them all to serve me with the corpse of their love. And in the end I offered them only the corpse of my love. This is my body—take and eat—my corpse—

A vivid shame went through him. 'After all,' he thought, 'I wanted them to love with dead bodies. If I had kissed Judas with live love, perhaps he would never have kissed me with death. Perhaps he loved me in the flesh, and I willed that he should love me bodilessly, with the corpse of love—'

There dawned on him the reality of the soft, warm love which is in touch, and which is full of delight. "And I told them, blessed are they that mourn," he said to himself. "Alas, if I mourned even this woman here, now I am in death, I should have to remain dead, and I want so much to live. Life has brought me to this woman with warm hands. And her touch is more to me now than all my words. For I want to live—"

"Go then to the goddess!" she said softly, gently pushing him towards Isis. And as he stood there dazed and naked as an unborn thing, he heard the woman murmuring to the goddess, murmuring, murmuring with a plaintive appeal. She was stooping now, looking at the scar in the soft flesh of the socket of his side, a scar deep and like an eye sore with endless weeping, just in the soft socket above the hip. It was here that his blood had left him, and his essential seed. The woman was trembling softly and murmuring in Greek. And he in the recurring dismay of having died, and in the anguished perplexity of having tried to force life, felt his wounds crying aloud, and the deep places of the body howling again: "I have been murdered, and I lent myself to murder. They murdered me, but I lent myself to murder—"

The woman, silent now, but quivering, laid oil in her hand and put her palm over the wound in his right side. He winced, and the wound absorbed his life again, as thousands of times before. And in the dark, wild pain and panic of his consciousness rang only one cry: "Oh, how can she take this death out of me? She can never know! She can never understand! She can never equal it!..."

135

In silence, she softly rhythmically chafed the scar with oil. Absorbed now in her priestess's task, softly, softly gathering power, while the vitals of the man howled in panic. But as she gradually gathered power, and passed in a girdle round him to the opposite scar, gradually warmth began to take the place of the cold terror, and he felt: 'I am going to be Warm again, and I am going to be whole! I shall be warm like the morning. I shall be a man. It doesn't need understanding. It needs newness. She brings me newness—'

And he listened to the faint, ceaseless wail of distress of his wounds, sounding as if for ever under the horizons of his consciousness. But the wail was growing dim, more dim.

He thought of the woman toiling over him: 'She does not know! She does not realise the death in me. But she has another consciousness. She comes to me from the opposite end of the night.'

Having chafed all his lower body with oil, having worked with her slow intensity of a priestess, so that the sound of his wounds grew dimmer and dimmer, suddenly she put her breast against the wound in his left side, and her arms round him, folding over the wound in his right side, and she pressed him to her, in a power of living warmth, like the folds of a river. And the wailing died out altogether, and there was a stillness, and darkness in his soul, unbroken, dark stillness, wholeness.

Then slowly, slowly, in the perfect darkness of his inner man, he felt the stir of something coming. A dawn, a new sun. A new sun was coming up in him, in the perfect inner darkness of himself. He waited for it breathless, quivering with a fearful hope..."Now I am not myself. I am something new..."

And as it rose, he felt, with a cold breath of disappointment, the girdle of the living woman slip down from him, the warmth and the glow slipped from him, leaving him stark. She crouched, spent, at the feet of the goddess, hiding her face.

Stooping, he laid his hand softly on her warm, bright shoulder, and the shock of desire went through him, shock after shock, so that he wondered if it were another sort of death: but full of magnificence.

Now all his consciousness was there in the crouching, hidden woman. He stooped beside her and caressed her softly, blindly, murmuring inarticulate things. And his death and his passion of sacrifice were all as nothing to him now, he knew only the crouching fullness of the woman there, the soft white rock of life..."On this rock I built my life." The deep-folded, penetrable rock of the living woman! The woman, hiding her face. Himself bending over, powerful and new like dawn.

He crouched to her, and he felt the blaze of his manhood and his power rise up in his loins, magnificent.

"I am risen!"

Magnificent, blazing indomitable in the depths of his loins, his own sun dawned, and sent its fire running along his limbs, so that his face shone unconsciously.

He untied the string on the linen tunic and slipped the garment down, till he saw the white glow of her white-gold breasts. And he touched them, and he felt his life go molten. "Father!" he said, "why did you hide this from me?" And he touched her with the poignancy of wonder, and the marvellous piercing transcendence of desire. "Lo!" he said, "this is beyond prayer." It was the deep, interfolded warmth, warmth living and penetrable, the woman, the heart of the rose! My mansion is the intricate warm rose, my joy is this blossom!

She looked up at him suddenly, her face like a lifted light, wistful, tender, her eyes like many wet flowers. And he drew her to his breast with a passion of tenderness and consuming desire, and the last thought: 'My hour is upon me, I am taken unawares—'

So he knew her, and was one with her.

Afterwards, with a dim wonder, she touched the great scars in his sides with her finger-tips, and said:

"But they no longer hurt?"

"They are suns!" he said. "They shine from your torch. They are my atonement with you."

And when they left the temple, it was the coldness before dawn. As he closed the door, he looked again at the goddess, and he said: "Lo, Isis is a kindly goddess; and full of tenderness. Great gods are warm-hearted, and have tender goddesses."

The woman wrapped herself in her mantle and went home in silence, sightless, brooding like the lotus softly shutting again, with its gold core full of fresh life. She saw nothing, for her own petals were a sheath to her. Only she thought: 'I am full of Osiris. I am full of the risen Osiris!

But the man looked at the vivid stars before dawn, as they rained down to the sea, and the dog-star green towards the sea's rim. And he thought: 'How plastic it is, how full of curves and folds like an invisible rose of dark-petalled openness that shows where the dew touches its darkness! How full it is, and great beyond all gods. How it leans around me, and I am part of it, the great rose of Space. I am like a grain of its perfume, and the woman is a grain of its beauty. Now the world is one flower of many petalled darknesses, and I am in its perfume as in a touch.'

So, in the absolute stillness and fullness of touch, he slept in his cave while the dawn came. And after the dawn, the wind rose and brought a storm, with cold rain. So he stayed in his cave in the peace and the delight of being in touch, delighting to hear the sea, and the rain on the earth, and to see one white-and-gold narcissus bowing wet, and still wet. And he said: "This is the great atonement, the being in touch. The grey sea and the rain, the wet narcissus and the woman I wait for, the invisible Isis and the unseen sun are all in touch, and at one."

He waited at the temple for the woman, and she came in the rain. But she said to him:

"Let me sit awhile with Isis. And come to me, will you come to me, in the second hour of night?"

So he went back to the cave and lay in stillness and in the joy of being in touch, waiting for the woman who would come with the night, and consummate again the contact. Then when night came the woman came, and came gladly, for her great yearning, too, was upon her, to be in touch, to be in touch with him, nearer.

So the days came, and the nights came, and days came again, and the contact was perfected and fulfilled. And he said: "I will ask her nothing, not even her name, for a name would set her apart."

And she said to herself: "He is Osiris. I wish to know no more."

Plum blossom blew from the trees, the time of the narcissus was past, anemones lit up the ground and were gone, the perfume of bean-field was in the air. All changed, the blossom of the universe changed its petals and swung round to look another way. The spring was fulfilled, a contact was established, the man and the woman were fulfilled of one another, and departure was in the air.

One day he met her under the trees, when the morning sun was hot, and the pines smelled sweet, and on the hills the last pear blossom was scattering. She came slowly towards him, and in her gentle lingering, her tender hanging back from him, he knew a change in her.

"Hast thou conceived?" he asked her.

"Why?" she said.

"Thou art like a tree whose green leaves follow the blossom, full of sap. And there is a withdrawing about thee."

"It is so," she said. "I am with young by thee. Is it good?"

"Yea!" he said. "How should it not be good? So the nightingale calls no more from the valley-bed. But where wilt thou bear the child, for I am naked of all but life?"

"We will stay here," she said.

"But the lady, your mother?"

A shadow crossed her brow. She did not answer.

"What when she knows?" he said.

"She begins to know."

"And would she hurt you?"

"Ah, not me! What I have is all my own. And I shall be big with Osiris...But thou, do you watch her slaves."

She looked at him, and the peace of her maternity was troubled by anxiety.

"Let not your heart be troubled!" he said. "I have died the death once."

So he knew the time was come again for him to depart. He would go alone, with his destiny. Yet not alone, for the touch would be upon him, even as he left his touch on her. And invisible suns would go with him.

Yet he must go. For here on the bay the little life of jealousy and property was resuming sway again, as the suns of passionate fecundity relaxed their sway. In the name of property, the widow and her slaves would seek to be revenged on him for the bread he had eaten, and the living touch he had established, the woman he had delighted in. But he said: "Not twice! They shall not now profane the touch in me. My wits against theirs."

So he watched. And he knew they plotted. So he moved from the little cave and found another shelter, a tiny cove of sand by the sea, dry and secret under the rocks.

He said to the woman:

"I must go now soon. Trouble is coming to me from the slaves. But I am a man, and the world is open. But what is between us is good, and is established. Be at peace. And when the nightingale calls again from your valley-bed, I shall come again, sure as spring."

She said: "O, don't go! Stay with me on half the island, and I will build a house for you and me under the pine trees by the temple, where we can live apart."

Yet she knew that he would go. And even she wanted the coolness of her own air around her, and the release from anxiety.

"If I stay," he said, "they will betray me to the Romans and to their justice. But I will never be betrayed again. So when I am gone, live in peace with the growing child. And I shall come again: all is good between us, near or apart. The suns come back in their seasons: and I shall come again."

"Do not go yet," she said. "I have set a slave to watch at the neck of the peninsula. Do not go yet, till the harm shows."

But as he lay in his little cove, on a calm, still night, he heard the soft knock of oars, and the bump of a boat against the rock. So he crept out to listen. And he heard the Roman overseer say:

"Lead softly to the goat's den. And Lysippus shall throw the net over the malefactor while he sleeps, and we will bring him before justice, and the Lady of Isis shall know nothing of it..."

The man who had died caught a whiff of flesh from the oiled and naked slaves as they crept up, then the faint perfume of the Roman. He crept nearer to the sea. The slave who sat in the boat sat motionless, holding the oars, for the sea was quite still. And the man who had died knew him.

So out of the deep cleft of a rock he said, in a clear voice:

"Art thou not that slave who possessed the maiden under the eyes of Isis? Art thou not the youth? Speak!"

The youth stood up in the boat in terror. His movement sent the boat bumping against the rock. The slave sprang out in wild fear, and fled up the rocks. The man who had died quickly seized the boat and stepped in, and pushed off. The oars were yet warm with the unpleasant warmth of the hands of the slaves. But the man pulled slowly out, to get into the current which set down the coast, and would carry him in silence. The high coast was utterly dark against the starry night. There was no glimmer from the peninsula: the priestess came no more at night. The man who had died rowed slowly on, with the current, and laughed to himself: "I have sowed the seed of my life and my resurrection, and put my touch forever upon the choice woman of this day, and I carry her perfume in my flesh like essence of roses. She is dear to me in the middle of my being. But the gold and flowing serpent is coiling up again, to sleep at the root of my tree."

"So let the boat carry me. To-morrow is another day."

The Border Line

Katherine Farquhar was a handsome woman of forty, no longer slim, but attractive in her soft, full, feminine way. The French porters ran round her, getting a voluptuous pleasure from merely carrying her bags. And she gave them ridiculously high tips, because, in the first place, she had never really known the value of money, and secondly, she had a morbid fear of underpaying anyone, but particularly a man who was eager to serve her.

It was really a joke to her, how eagerly these Frenchmen—all sorts of Frenchmen—ran round her and *Madamed* her. Their voluptuous obsequiousness. Because, after all, she was *Boche*. Fifteen years of marriage to an Englishman—or rather to two Englishmen—had not altered her racially. Daughter of a German Baron she was, and remained, in her own mind and body, although England had become her life-home. And surely she looked German, with her fresh complexion and her strong, full figure. But like most people in the world, she was a mixture, with Russian blood and French blood also in her veins. And she had lived in one country and another, till she was somewhat indifferent to her surroundings. So that perhaps the Parisian men might be excused for running round her so eagerly, and getting a voluptuous pleasure from calling a taxi for her, or giving up a place in the omnibus to her, or carrying her bags, or holding the menu card before her. Nevertheless, it amused her. And she had to confess she liked them, these Parisians. They had their own kind of manliness, even if it wasn't an English sort; and if a woman looked pleasant and soft-fleshed, and a wee bit helpless, they were ardent and generous. Katherine understood so well that Frenchmen were rude to the dry, hard-seeming, competent Englishwoman or American. She sympathized with the Frenchman's point of view: too much obvious capacity to help herself is a disagreeable trait in a woman.

At the Gare de l'Est, of course, everybody was expected to be *Boche*, and it was almost a convention, with the porters, to assume a certain small-boyish superciliousness. Nevertheless, there was the same voluptuous scramble to escort Katherine Farquhar to her seat in the first-class carriage. *Madame* was travelling alone.

She was going to Germany via Strasburg, meeting her sister in Baden-Baden. Philip, her husband, was in Germany collecting some sort of evidence for his newspaper. Katherine felt a little weary of newspapers, and of the sort of "evidence" that is extracted out of nowhere to feed them. However, Philip was quite clever, he was a little somebody in the world.

Her world, she had realized, consisted almost entirely of little somebodies. She was outside the sphere of the nobodies, always had been. And the Somebodies with a capital S, were all safely dead. She knew enough of the world to-day to know that it is not going to put up with any great Somebody: but many little nobodies and a sufficient number of little somebodies. Which, after all, is as it should be, she felt.

Sometimes she had vague misgivings.

Paris, for example, with its Louvre and its Luxembourg and its cathedral, seemed intended for Somebody. In a ghostly way it called for some supreme Somebody. But all its little men, nobodies and somebodies, were as sparrows twittering for crumbs, and dropping their little droppings on the palace cornices.

To Katherine, Paris brought back again her first husband, Alan Anstruther, that red-haired fighting Celt, father of her two grown-up children. Alan had had a weird innate conviction that he was beyond ordinary judgment. Katherine could never quite see where it came in. Son of a Scottish baronet, and captain in a Highland regiment did not seem to her stupendous. As for Alan himself, he was handsome in uniform, with his kilt swinging and his blue eye glaring. Even stark naked and without any trimmings, he had a bony, dauntless, overbearing manliness of his own. The one thing Katherine could *not quite* appreciate was his silent, indomitable assumption that he was actually firstborn, a born lord. He was a clever man too, ready to assume that General This or Colonel That might really be his superior. Until he actually came into contact with General This or Colonel That. Whereupon his overweening blue eye arched in his bony face, and a faint tinge of contempt infused itself into his homage.

Lordly or not, he wasn't much of a success in the worldly sense. Katherine had loved him, and he had loved her: that was indisputable. But when it came to innate conviction of lordliness, it was a question which of them was worse. For she, in her amiable, queen-bee self thought that ultimately hers was the right to the last homage.

Alan had been too unyielding and haughty to say much. But sometimes he would stand and look at her in silent rage, wonder, and indignation. The wondering indignation had been *almost* too much for her. What did the man think he was?

He was one of the hard, clever Scotsmen, with a philosophic tendency, but without sentimentality. His contempt of Nietzsche, whom she adored, was intolerable. Alan just asserted himself like a pillar of rock, and expected the tides of the modern world to recede around him. They didn't.

So he concerned himself with astronomy, gazing through a telescope and watching the worlds beyond worlds. Which seemed to give him relief.

After ten years, they had ceased to live together, passionate as they both were. They were too proud and unforgiving to yield to one another, and much too haughty to yield to any outsider.

Alan had a friend, Philip, also a Scotsman, and a university friend. Philip, trained for the bar, had gone into journalism, and had made himself a name. He was a little black Highlander, of the insidious sort, clever, and *knowing*. This look of knowing in his dark eyes, and the feeling of secrecy that went with his dark little body, made him interesting to women. Another thing he could do was to give off a great sense of warmth and offering, like a dog when it loves you. He seemed to be able to do this at will. And Katherine, after feeling cool about him and rather despising him for years, at last fell under the spell of the dark, insidious fellow.

"You!" she said to Alan, whose overweening masterfulness drove her wild. "You don't even know that a woman exists. And that's where Philip Farquhar is more than you are. He *does* know something of what a woman *is*."

"Bah! the little—" said Alan, using an obscene word of contempt.

Nevertheless, the friendship endured, kept up by Philip, who had an almost uncanny love for Alan. Alan was mostly indifferent. But he was used to Philip, and habit meant a great deal to him.

"Alan really is an amazing man!" Philip would say to Katherine. "He is the only real man, what I call a real man, that I have ever met."

"But why is he the only real man?" she asked. "Don't you call *yourself* a real man?"

"Oh, *I*—I'm different! My strength lies in giving in—and then recovering myself. I do let myself be swept away. But so far, I've always managed to get myself back again. Alan—" and Philip even had a half-reverential, half-envious way of uttering the word—"Alan *never* lets himself be swept away. And he's the only man I know who doesn't."

"Yah!" she said. "He is fooled by plenty of things. You can fool him through his vanity."

"No," said Philip. "Never altogether. You *can't* deceive him right through. When a thing really touches Alan, it is tested once and for all. You know if it's false or not. He's the only man I ever met who *can't help* being real."

"Ha! You overrate his reality," said Katherine, rather scornfully.

And later, when Alan shrugged his shoulders with that mere indifferent tolerance, at the mention of Philip, she got angry.

"You are a poor friend," she said.

"Friend!" he answered. "I never was Farquhar's friend! If he asserts that he's mine, that's his side of the question. I never positively cared for the man. He's too much over the wrong side of the border for me."

"Then," she answered, "you've no business to let him *consider* he is your friend. You've no right to let him think so much of you. You should tell him you don't like him."

"I've told him a dozen times. He seems to enjoy it. It seems part of his game."

And he went away to his astronomy.

Came the war, and the departure of Alan's regiment for France.

"There!" he said. "Now you have to pay the penalty of having married a soldier. You find him fighting your own people. So it is."

She was too much struck by this blow even to weep.

"Good-bye!" he said, kissing her gently, lingeringly. After all, he had been a husband to her.

And as he looked back at her, with the gentle, protective husband-knowledge in his blue eyes, and at the same time that other quiet realization of destiny, her consciousness fluttered into incoherence. She only wanted to alter everything, to alter the past, to alter all the flow of history—the terrible flow of history. Secretly somewhere inside herself she felt that with her queen-bee love, and queen-bee will, she *could* divert the whole flow of history—nay, even reverse it.

But in the remote, realizing look that lay at the back of his eyes, back of all his changeless husband-care, she saw that it could never be so. That the whole of her womanly, motherly concentration could never put back the great flow of human destiny. That, as he said, only the cold strength of a man, accepting the destiny of destruction, could see the human flow through the chaos and beyond to a new outlet. But the chaos first, and the long rage of destruction.

For an instant her will broke. Almost her soul seemed broken. And then he was gone. And as soon as he was gone she recovered the core of her assurance.

Philip was a great consolation to her. He asserted that the war was monstrous, that it should never have been, and that men should refuse to consider it as anything but a colossal, disgraceful accident.

She, in her German soul, knew that it was no accident. It was inevitable, and even necessary. But Philip's attitude soothed her enormously, restored her to herself.

Alan never came back. In the spring of 1915 he was missing. She had never mourned for him. She had never really considered him dead. In a certain sense she had triumphed. The queen-bee had recovered her sway, as queen of the earth; the woman, the mother, the female with the ear of corn in her hand, as against the man with the sword.

Philip had gone through the war as a journalist, always throwing his weight on the side of humanity, and human truth and peace. He had been an inexpressible consolation. And in 1921 she had married him.

The thread of fate might be spun, it might even be measured out, but the hand of Lachesis had been stayed from cutting it through.

At first it was wonderfully pleasant and restful and voluptuous, especially for a woman of thirty-eight, to be married to Philip. Katherine felt he caressed her senses, and soothed her, and gave her what she wanted.

Then, gradually, a curious sense of degradation started in her spirit. She felt unsure, uncertain. It was almost like having a disease. Life became dull and unreal to her, as it had never been before. She did not even struggle and suffer. In the numbness of her flesh she could feel no reactions. Everything was turning into mud.

Then again, she would recover, and *enjoy* herself wonderfully. And after a while, the suffocating sense of nullity and degradation once more. Why, why, why did she feel degraded, in her secret soul? *Never,* of course, outwardly.

The memory of Alan came back into her. She still thought of him and his relentlessness with an arrested heart, but without the angry hostility she used to feel. A little awe of him, of his memory, stole back into her spirit. She resisted it. She was not used to feeling awe.

She realized, however, the difference between being married to a soldier, a ceaseless born fighter, a sword not to be sheathed, and this other man, this cunning civilian, this subtle equivocator, this adjuster of the scales of truth.

Philip was cleverer than she was. He set her up, the queen-bee, the mother, the woman, the female judgment, and he served her with subtle, cunning homage. He put the scales, the balance in her hand. But also, cunningly, he blindfolded her, and manipulated the scales when she was sightless.

Dimly she realized all this. But only dimly, confusedly, because she was blindfolded. Philip had the subtle, fawning power that could keep her always blindfolded.

Sometimes she gasped and gasped from her oppressed lungs. And sometimes the bony, hard, masterful, but honest face of Alan would come back, and suddenly it would seem to her that she was all right again, that the strange, voluptuous suffocation, which left her soul in mud, was gone, and she could breathe air of the open heavens once more. Even fighting air.

It came to her on the boat crossing the Channel. Suddenly she seemed to feel Alan at her side again, as if Philip had never existed. As if Philip had never meant anything more to her than the shop-assistant measuring off her orders. And, escaping, as it were, by herself across the cold, wintry Channel, she suddenly deluded herself into feeling as if Philip had never existed, only Alan had ever been her husband. He was her husband still. And she was going to meet him.

This gave her her blitheness in Paris, and made the Frenchman so nice to her. For the Latins love to feel a woman is really enveloped in the spell of some man. Beyond all race is the problem of man and woman.

Katherine now sat dimly, vaguely excited and almost happy in the railway-carriage on the Est railroad. It was like the old days when she was going home to Germany. Or even more like the old days when she was coming back to Alan. Because, in the past, when he was her husband, feel as she might towards him, she could never get over the sensation that the wheels of the railway-carriage had wings, when they were taking her back to him. Even when she knew that he was going to be awful to her, hard and relentless and destructive, still the motion went on wings.

Whereas towards Philip she moved with a strange, disintegrating reluctance. She decided not to think of him.

As she looked unseeing out of the carriage window, suddenly, with a jolt, the wintry landscape realized itself in her consciousness. The flat, grey, wintry landscape, ploughed fields of greyish earth that looked as if they were compound of the clay of dead men. Pallid, stark, thin trees stood like wire beside straight, abstract roads. A ruined farm between a few more wire trees. And a dismal village filed past, with smashed houses like rotten teeth between the straight rows of the village street.

With sudden horror she realized that she must be in the Marne country, the ghastly Marne country, century after century digging the corpses of frustrated men into its soil. The border country, where the Latin races and the Germanic neutralize one another into horrid ash.

Perhaps even the corpse of her own man among that grey clay.

It was too much for her. She sat ashy herself with horror, wanting to escape.

"If I had only known," she said. "If only I had known, I would have gone by Basle."

The train drew up at Soissons; name ghastly to her. She simply tried to make herself unreceptive to everything. And mercifully luncheon was served, she went down to the restaurant car, and sat opposite to a little French officer in horizon-blue uniform, who suggested anything but war. He looked so naïve, rather childlike and nice, with the certain innocence that so many French people preserve under their so-called wickedness, that she felt really relieved. He bowed to her with an odd, shy little bow when she returned him his half-bottle of red wine, which had slowly jigged its way the length of the table, owing to the motion of the train. How nice he was! And how he would give himself to a woman, if she would only find real pleasure in the male that he was.

Nevertheless, she herself felt very remote from this business of male and female, and giving and taking.

After luncheon, in the heat of the train and the flush of her half-bottle of white wine, she went to sleep again, her feet grilling uncomfortably on the iron plate of the carriage floor. And as she slept, life, as she had known it, seemed all to turn artificial to her, the sunshine of the world an artificial light, with smoke above, like the light of torches, and things artificially growing, in a night that was lit up artificially with such intensity that it gave the illusion of day. It had been an illusion, her life-day, as a ballroom evening is an illusion. Her love and her emotions, her very panic of love, had been an illusion. She realized how love had become panic-stricken inside her, during the war.

And now even this panic of love was an illusion. She had run to Philip to be saved. And now, both her panic-love and Philip's salvation were an illusion.

What remained then? Even panic-stricken love, the intensest thing, perhaps, she had ever felt, was only an illusion. What was left? The grey shadows of death?

When she looked out again it was growing dark, and they were at Nancy. She used to know this country as a girl. At half-past seven she was in Strasburg, where she must stay the night as there was no train over the Rhine till morning.

The porter, a blond, hefty fellow, addressed her at once in Alsatian German. He insisted on escorting her safely to her hotel—a German hotel—keeping guard over her like an appointed sentinel, very faithful and competent, so different from Frenchmen.

It was a cold, wintry night, but she wanted to go out after dinner to see the minster. She remembered it all so well, in that other life.

The wind blew icily in the street. The town seemed empty, as if its spirit had left it. The few squat, hefty foot-passengers were all talking the harsh Alsatian German. Shop-signs were in French, often with a little concession to German underneath. And the shops were full of goods, glutted with goods from the once-German factories of Mulhausen and other cities.

She crossed the night-dark river, where the washhouses of the washerwomen were anchored along the stream, a few odd women still kneeling over the water's edge, in the dim electric light, rinsing their clothes in the grim, cold water. In the big square the icy wind was blowing, and the place seemed a desert. A city once more conquered.

After all she could not remember her way to the cathedral.

She saw a French policeman in his blue cape and peaked cap, looking a lonely, vulnerable, silky specimen in this harsh Alsatian city. Crossing over to him she asked him in French where was the cathedral.

He pointed out to her, the first turning on the left. He did not seem hostile: nobody seemed really hostile. Only the great frozen weariness of winter in a conquered city, on a weary everlasting border-line.

And the Frenchmen seemed far more weary, and also, more sensitive than the crude Alsatians.

She remembered the little street, the old, overhanging houses with black timbers and high gables. And like a great ghost, a reddish flush in its darkness, the uncanny cathedral breasting the oncomer, standing gigantic, looking down in darkness out of darkness, on the pigmy humanness of the city. It was built of reddish stone, that had a flush in the night, like dark flesh. And vast, an incomprehensibly tall, strange thing, it looked down out of the night. The great rose window, poised high, seemed like the breast of the vast Thing, and prisms and needles of stone shot up, as if it were plumage, dimly, half-visible in heaven.

There it was, in the upper darkness of the ponderous winter night, like a menace. She remembered, her spirit used in the past to soar aloft with it. But now, looming with a faint rust of blood out of the upper black heavens, the Thing stood suspended, looking down with vast, demonish menace, calm and implacable.

Mystery and dim, ancient fear came over the woman's soul. The cathedral looked so strange and demonish-heathen. And an ancient, indomitable blood seemed to stir in it. It stood there like some vast silent beast with teeth of stone, waiting, and wondering when to stoop against this pallid humanity.

And dimly she realized that behind all the ashy pallor and sulphur of our civilization, lurks the great blood-creature waiting, implacable and eternal, ready at last to crush our white brittleness and let the shadowy blood move erect once more, in a new implacable pride and strength. Even out of the lower heavens looms the great blood-dusky Thing, blotting out the Cross it was supposed to exalt.

The scroll of the night sky seemed to roll back, showing a huge, blood-dusky presence looming enormous, stooping, looking down, awaiting its moment.

As she turned to go away, to move away from the closed wings of the minster, she noticed a man standing on the pavement, in the direction of the post-office, which functions obscurely in the Cathedral Square. Immediately, she knew that that man, standing dark and motionless, was Alan. He was alone, motionless, remote.

He did not move towards her. She hesitated, then went in his direction, as if going to the post-office. He stood perfectly motionless, and her heart died as she drew near. Then, as she passed, he turned suddenly, looking down on her.

It was he, though she could hardly see his face, it was so dark, with a dusky glow in the shadow.

"Alan!" she said.

He did not speak, but laid his hand detainingly on her arm, as he used in the early days, with strange silent authority. And turning her with a faint pressure on her arm, he went along with her, leisurely, through the main street of the city, under the arcade where the shops were still lighted up.

She glanced at his face: it seemed much more dusky, and duskily ruddy, than she had known him. He was a stranger: and yet it was he, no other. He said nothing at all. But that was also in keeping. His mouth was closed, his watchful eyes seemed changeless, and there was a shadow of silence around him, impenetrable, but not cold. Rather aloof and gentle, like the silence that surrounds a wild animal.

She knew that she was walking with his spirit. But that even did not trouble her. It seemed natural. And there came over her again the feeling she had forgotten, the restful, thoughtless pleasure of a woman who moves in the aura of the man to whom she belongs. As a young woman she had had this unremarkable, yet very precious feeling, when she was with her husband. It had been a full contentment; and perhaps the fullness of it had made her unconscious of it. Later, it seemed to her she had almost wilfully destroyed it, this soft flow of contentment which she, a woman, had from him as a man.

Now, afterwards, she realized it. And as she walked at his side through the conquered city, she realized that it was the one enduring thing a woman can have, the intangible soft flood of contentment that carries her along at the side of the man she is married to. It is her perfection and her highest attainment.

Now, in the afterwards, she knew it. Now the strife was gone. And dimly she wondered why, why, why she had ever fought against it. No matter what the man does or is, as a person, if a woman can move at his side in this dim, full flood of contentment, she has the highest of him, and her scratching efforts at getting more than this, are her ignominious efforts at self-nullity.

Now, she knew it, and she submitted. Now that she was walking with a man who came from the halls of death, to her, for her relief. The strong, silent kindliness of him towards her, even now, was able to wipe out the ashy, nervous horror of the world from her body. She went at his side still and released, like one newly unbound, walking in the dimness of her own contentment.

At the bridge-head he came to a standstill, and drew his hand from her arm. She knew he was going to leave her. But he looked at her from under his peaked cap, darkly but kindly, and he waved his hand with a slight, kindly gesture of farewell and of promise, as if in the farewell he promised never to leave her, never to let the kindliness go out in his heart, to let it stay hers always.

She hurried over the bridge with tears running down her cheeks, and on to her hotel. Hastily she climbed to her room. And as she undressed, she avoided the sight of her own face in the mirror. She must not rupture the spell of his presence.

Now, in the afterwards she realized *how* careful she must be, not to break the mystery that enveloped her. Now that she knew he had come back to her from the dead, she was aware how precious and how fragile the coming was. He had come back with his heart dark and kind, wanting her even in the afterwards. And not in any sense must she go against him. The warm, powerful, silent ghost had come back to her. It was he. She must not even try to think about him definitely, not to realize him or to understand. Only in her own woman's soul could she silently ponder him, darkly, and know him present in her, without ever staring at him or trying to find him out. Once she tried to lay hands on him, to *have* him, to *realize* him, he would be gone for ever, and gone for ever this last precious flood of her woman's peace.

"Ah, no!" she said to herself. "If he leaves his peace with me, I must ask no questions whatsoever."

And she repented, silently, of the way she had questioned and demanded answers, in the past. What were the answers, when she had got them? Terrible ash in the mouth.

She now knew the supreme modern terror, of a world all ashy and nerve-dead. If a man could come back out of death to save her from this, she would not ask questions of him, but be humble, and beyond tears grateful.

In the morning, she went out into the icy wind, under the grey sky, to see if he would be there again. Not that she *needed* him: his presence was still about her. But he might be waiting.

The town was stony and cold. The people looked pale, chilled through, and doomed in some way. Very far from her they were. She felt a sort of pity for them, but knew she could do nothing, nothing in time or eternity. And they looked at her, and looked quickly away again, as if they were uneasy in themselves.

The cathedral reared its great reddish-grey façade in the stark light; but it did not loom as in the night. The cathedral square was hard and cold. Inside, the church was cold and repellent, in spite of the glow of stained glass. And he was nowhere to be found.

So she hastened away to her hotel and to the station, to catch the 10.30 train into Germany.

It was a lonely, dismal train, with a few forlorn souls waiting to cross the Rhine. Her Alsatian porter looked after her with the same dogged care as before. She got into the first-class carriage that was going through to Prague—she was the only passenger travelling first. A real French porter, in blouse and moustache, and swagger, tried to say something a bit jeering to her, in his few words of German. But she only looked at him, and he subsided. He didn't really want to be rude. There was a certain hopelessness even about that.

The train crept slowly, disheartened, out of town. She saw the weird humped-up creature of the cathedral in the distance, pointing its one finger above the city. Why, oh, why, had the old Germanic races put it there, like that!

Slowly the country disintegrated into the Rhine flats and marshes, the canals, the willow trees, the overflow streams, the wet places frozen but not flooded. Weary the place all seemed. And old Father Rhine flowing in greenish volume, implacable, separating the races now weary of race struggle, but locked in the toils as in the coils of a great snake, unable to escape. Cold, full, green, and utterly disheartening the river came along under the wintry sky, passing beneath the bridge of iron.

There was a long wait in Kehl, where the German officials and the French observed a numb, dreary kind of neutrality. Passport and customs examination was soon over. But the train waited and waited, as if unable to get away from that one point of pure negation, where the two races neutralized one another, and no polarity was felt, no life—no principle dominated.

Katherine Farquhar just sat still, in the suspended silence of her husband's return. She heeded neither French nor German, spoke one language or the other at need, hardly knowing. She waited, while the hot train steamed and hissed, arrested at the perfect neutral point of the new border line, just across the Rhine.

And at last a little sun came out, and the train silently drew away, nervously, from the neutrality.

In the great flat field, of the Rhine plain, the shallow flood water was frozen, the furrows ran straight towards nowhere, the air seemed frozen too, but the earth felt strong and barbaric, it seemed to vibrate, with its straight furrows, in a deep, savage undertone. There was the frozen, savage thrill in the air also, something wild and unsubdued, pre-Roman. This part of the Rhine valley, even on the right bank in Germany, was occupied by the French; hence the curious vacancy, the suspense, as if no men lived there, but some spirit was watching, watching over the vast, empty, straight-furrowed fields and the water-meadows. Stillness, emptiness, suspense, and a sense of something still impending.

A long wait in the station of Appenweier, on the main line of the Right-bank Railway. The station was empty. Katherine remembered its excited, thrilling bustle in pre-war days.

"Yes," said the German guard to the station-master. "What do they hurry us out of Strasburg for, if they are only going to keep us so long here?"

The heavy Badisch German! The sense of resentful impotence in the Germans! Katherine smiled to herself. She realized that here the train left the occupied territory.

At last they set off, northwards, free for the moment, in Germany. It was the land beyond the Rhine, Germany of the pine forests. The very earth seemed strong and unsubdued, bristling with a few reeds and bushes, like savage hair. There was the same silence, and waiting, and the old barbaric undertone of the white-skinned north, under the waning civilization. The audible overtone of our civilization seemed to be wearing thin, the old, low, pine-forest hum and roar of the ancient north seemed to be sounding through. At least, in Katherine's inner ear.

And there were the ponderous hills of the Black Forest, heaped and waiting sullenly, as if guarding the inner Germany. Black round hills, black with forest, save where white snow-patches of field had been cut out. Black and white, waiting there in the near distance, in sullen guard.

She knew the country so well. But not in this present mood, the emptiness, the sullenness, the heavy, recoiled waiting.

Steinbach! Then she was nearly there! She would have to change in Oos, for Baden-Baden, her destination. Probably Philip would be there to meet her in Oos; he would have come down from Heidelberg.

Yes, there he was! And at once she thought he looked ill, yellowish. His figure hollow and defeated.

"Aren't you well?" she asked, as she stepped out of the train on to the empty station.

"I'm so frightfully cold," he said. "I can't get warm."

"And the train was so hot," she said.

At last a porter came to carry her bags across to the little connecting train.

"How are you?" he said, looking at her with a certain pinched look in his face, and fear in his eyes.

"All right! It all feels very queer," she said.

"I don't know how it is," he said, "but Germany freezes my inside, and does something to my chest."

"We needn't stay long," she said easily.

He was watching the bright look in her face. And she was thinking how queer and *chétif* he looked! Extraordinary! As she looked at him she felt for the first time, with curious clarity, that it was humiliating to be married to him, even in name. She was humiliated even by the fact that her name was Katherine Farquhar. Yet she used to think it a nice name!

"Just think of me married to that little man!" she thought to herself. "Think of my having his name!"

It didn't fit. She thought of her own name: Katherine von Todtnau; or of her married name: Katherine Anstruther. The first seemed most fitting. But the second was her second nature. The third, Katherine Farquhar, wasn't her at all.

"Have you seen Marianne?" she asked.

"Oh, yes!"

He was very brief. What was the matter with him?

"You'll have to be careful, with your cold," she said politely.

"I *am* careful!" he cried petulantly.

Marianne, her sister, was at the station, and in two minutes they were rattling away in German and laughing and crying and exploding with laughter again, Philip quite ignored. In these days of frozen economy, there was no taxi. A porter would wheel up the luggage on a trolley, the new arrivals walked to their little hotel, through the half-deserted town.

"But the little one is quite nice!" said Marianne deprecatingly.

"Isn't he!" cried Katherine in the same tone.

And both sisters stood still and laughed in the middle of the street. "The little one" was Philip.

"The other was more a man," said Marianne. "But I'm sure this one is easier. *The little one!* Yes, he *should* be easier," and she laughed in her mocking way.

"The stand-up-mannikin!" said Katherine, referring to those little toy men weighted at the base with lead, that always stand up again.

"Yes! Yes!" cried Marianne. "I'm sure he *always* comes up

again! *Prumm!*" She made a gesture of knocking him over. "And there he rises once more!" She slowly raised her hand, as if the mannikin were elevating himself.

The two sisters stood in the street laughing consumedly.

Marianne also had lost her husband in the war. But she seemed only more reckless and ruthless.

"Ah, Katy!" she said, after dinner. "You are always such a good child! But you are different. Harder! No, you are not the same good Katy, the same kind Katy. You are no longer kind."

"And you?" said Katy.

"Ah, me! I don't matter. I watch what the end will be."

Marianne was six years older than Katherine, and she had now ceased to struggle for anything at all. She was a woman who had lived her life. So at last, life seemed endlessly quaint and amusing to her. She accepted everything, wondering over the powerful primitiveness of it all, at the root-pulse.

"I don't care any more at all what people do or don't do," she said. "Life is a great big tree, and the dead leaves fall. But very wonderful is the pulse in the roots! So strong, and so pitiless."

It was as if she found a final relief in the radical pitilessness of the Tree of Life.

Philip was very unhappy in this atmosphere. At the core of him a Scotch sentimentalist, he had calculated, very cannily, that the emotional, sentimental values would hold good as long as he lived, which was long enough for him. The old male pride and power were doomed. They had finally fallen in the war. Alan with them. But the emotional, sentimental values still held good.

Only not here in Germany. Here the very emotions had become exhausted. "Give us pitilessness. Give us the Tree of Life in winter, dehumanized and ruthless." So everything seemed to say. And it was too much for him.

He wanted to be soft and sweet and loving, at evening, to Katherine. But there came Marianne's hollow, reckless laugh at the door; he was frustrated. And—

"Ach! Is it possible that anybody forty years old should still be in love? Ach! I had thought it impossible any more; after the war! Even a little indecent, shall I say!" laughed Marianne, seeing the frustrated languishing look on his face.

"If *love* isn't left, what is?" he said petulantly.

"Ach! I don't know! Really I don't. Can't you tell me?" she asked with a weird naïveté of the *afterwards*.

He gathered himself together, the little stand-up-mannikin, waiting till Marianne was gone and he could be softly alone with Katherine.

When the two were alone he said:

"I'm most frightfully glad you've come, Kathy. I could hardly have held out another day without you. I feel you're the only thing on earth that remains real."

"You don't seem very real to me," she said.

"I'm not real! I'm *not!*—not when I'm alone. But when I am with you I am the most real man alive. I know it!"

He asserted this with vehemence and a weird, personal sort of passion that used to thrill her, but now repelled her.

"Why should you need me?" she said. "I am real without you."

She was thinking of Alan.

This was a blow to Philip. He considered for a moment. Then he said:

"Yes. You are! You are always real. But that's because you are a woman. A man without a woman *can't* be real."

He twisted his face and shook his hand with a sort of false vehemence.

She looked at him, was repelled. After all, Alan could wander alone in the lonely places of the dead, and still be the ultimate real thing, to her.

She had given her allegiance elsewhere. Strange, how unspeakably cold she felt towards this little equivocal civilian.

"Don't let us talk to-night," she said. "I am *so* sleepy. I want to go to sleep this very minute. You don't mind, do you? Good-night!"

She went to her room, with the green glazed stove. Outside she could see the trees of Seufzer Allee, and the intense winter night. Curiously dark and wolfish the nights came on, with the little town obscurely lighted, for economy's sake, and no tram-cars running, for economy's sake, and the whole place, strangely, slipping back from our civilization, people moving in the dark like in a barbarian village, with the thrill of fear and menace in the wolfish air.

She slept soundly, none the less. But the raw air scraped her chest.

In the morning Philip was looking yellower, and coughing a good deal. She urged him to stay in bed. She wanted, really, to be free of him. And she also wanted him to be safe, too. He insisted, however, on staying about.

She could tell he had something on his mind. At last it came out.

"Do you dream much here?" he said.

"I think I did dream," she said. "But I can't remember what about."

"I dream terribly," he said.

"What sort of dreams?"

"All sorts!" He gave a rueful laugh. "But nearly always about Alan." He glanced at her quickly to see how she took it. She gave no sign.

"And what about him?" she said calmly.

"Oh!—" he gave a desperate little gesture. "Why last night I dreamed that I woke up, and someone was lying on my bed, *outside* the bedclothes. I thought at first it was you, so I wanted to speak to you. But I couldn't. Then I knew it was Alan, lying there in the cold. And he was terribly heavy. He was so heavy I couldn't move, because the bed-clothes—you know I don't have that bolster thing—they were so tight on me, I could hardly breathe, they were like tight lead round me. It was so awful, they were like a lead coffin-shell. And he was lying outside with that terrible weight. When I woke at last, I thought I *was* dead."

"It's because you've got a cold on your chest," she said. "Why won't you stay in bed and see a doctor?"

"I don't *want* a doctor," he said.

"You're so obstinate! At least you should drink the waters here. They'd be good for you."

During the day she walked in the woods with Marianne. It was sunny, and there was thin snow. But the cold in the air was heavy, stormy, unbreakable, and the woods seemed black, black. In a hollow open space, like a bowl, were little tortured bare vines. Never had she seen the pale vine-stocks look so tortured. And the black trees seemed to grow out of unutterably cold depths, and they seemed to be drinking away what warmth of life there was, while the vines in the clearing writhed with cold as leaves writhe in a fire.

After sunset, before dinner-time, she wanted to go to drink the hot waters from the spring at the big bath-hall under the New Castle. Philip insisted on going with her, though she urged him to stay indoors. They went down the dark hill and between the dark buildings of reddish stone, like the stone of Strasburg Cathedral.

At the obscure fountain in the alcove of the courtyard a little group of people were waiting, dark and silent, like dark spirits round a source of steam. Some had come to drink. Some had come for a pail of hot water. Some had come merely to warm their fingers and get something hot inside them. Some had come furtively, with hot-water bottles, to warm their icy beds a little. Everybody was bed-rock poor and silent, but well-clad, respectable, unbeaten.

Katherine and Philip waited a while. Then, in a far corner of the dark rocky grotto, where the fountain of hot water came out of the wall, Katherine saw Alan standing. He was standing as if waiting his turn to drink, behind the other people. Philip apparently did not see him.

She pressed forward in the silent sombre group of people, and held her glass under the tap, above the pail which a man was filling. The hot water ran over her fingers gratefully. She rinsed her glass down the fountain bowl.

"Na!" said the man of the pail, in his rough, but reckless, good-humoured Badisch: "Throw it in the bucket. It's only wash-water."

She laughed, and lifted her pocket-glass to drink. It was something of an ordeal among the group of silent people there in the almost dark. There was a feeble lamp outside in the courtyard; inside the grotto was deep shadow.

Nevertheless, Alan was watching her, and she drank to him, in the hot, queer, hellish-tasting water. She drank a second small glassful. Then she filled the glass again, in front of all the waiting people and handed it to Philip.

She did not look at Alan, but away in the courtyard, where more people were approaching, and where the steam of the springs rose from the grating in the ground, ghostly on the night air.

Philip drew back a little to drink. But at the first mouthful he choked, and began to cough. He coughed and coughed, in a convulsed spasm as if choking. She went to him anxiously. And then she saw that Alan also had come forward, and stood beside her, behind the coughing little Philip.

"What is it?" she said to the coughing man. "Did some of the water go the wrong way?"

He shook his head, but could not answer. At length, exhausted, but quiet, he handed her the glass, and they moved away from the silent group of watchful dark people.

And Alan was walking on her other side holding her hand.

When they came into the hall of the hotel she saw with horror that there was a red smear of blood on Philip's chin, and red blotches on his overcoat.

"What have you done?" she cried.

He looked down at his breast, then up at her with haunted eyes. Fear, an agony and a horror of fear in his face. He went ghastly pale. Thinking he would swoon, she put her arm round him. But she felt someone silently but firmly, and with strange, cold power, pulling her arm away. She knew it was Alan.

The hotel porter helped Philip up to his room, and she assisted her husband to undress and get to bed. But each time her hand touched the sick man's body, to sustain him, she felt it drawn silently, coldly, powerfully away, with complete relentlessness.

The doctor came and made his examination. He said it was not serious: only the rupture of a superficial blood-vessel. The patient must lie quite still and warm, and take light food. Avoid all excitement or agitation.

Philip's face had a haunted, martyred, guilty look. She soothed him as much as possible, but dared hardly touch him.

"Won't you sleep with me to-night, in case I dream?" he said to her, with big, excruciating eyes full of fear.

"You'll be better alone," she said softly. "You'll be better alone. I'll tuck you up warm, and sit with you a while. Keep yourself all covered up!"

She tucked him close, and sat by the bed. On the other side of the bed sat Alan, bare-headed, with his silent, expressionless, reddish face. The closed line of his lips, under the small reddish moustache, never changed, and he kept his eyelids half lowered. But there was a wonderful changeless dignity in his pose, as if he could sit thus, silent, and waiting, through the centuries. And through the warm air of the room he radiated this strange, stony coldness, that seemed heavy as the hand of death. It did not hurt Katherine. But Philip's face seemed chilled and bluish.

Katherine went to her room, when the sick man slept. Alan did not follow her. And she did not question. It was for the two men to work out destiny between them.

In the night, towards morning she heard a hoarse, horrible cry. She ran to Philip's room. He was sitting up in bed, blood running down his chin, his face livid, and his eyes rolling delirious.

"What is it?" she said in panic.

"He lay on top of me!" cried Philip, rolling his eyes inwards in horror. "He lay on top of me, and turned my heart cold and burst my blood-vessel in my chest."

Katherine stood petrified. There was blood all over the sheets. She rang the bell violently. Across the bed stood Alan, looking at her with his unmoving blue eyes, just watching her. She could feel the strange stone-coldness of his presence touching even her heart. And she looked back at him humbly, she knew he had power over her too. That strange, cold, stony touch on her heart.

The servants came, and the doctor. And Alan went away. Philip was washed and changed, and went peacefully to sleep, looking like a corpse.

The day passed slowly. Alan did not appear. Even now, Katherine wanted him to come. Awful though he was, she wanted him to be there, to give her her surety, even though it was only the surety of dread; and her contentment, though it were the contentment of death.

At night she had a sofa-bed brought for her into Philip's room. He seemed quieter, better. She had not left him all day. And Alan had not appeared. At half-past nine, Philip sleeping quietly, she too lay down to sleep.

She woke in the night feeling the same stone-coldness in the air. Had the stove gone out? Then she heard Philip's whispering call of terror: *"Katherine! Katherine!"* She went over quickly, and slipped into his bed, putting her arms round him. He was shuddering, and stony cold. She drew him to her.

But immediately two hands cold and strong as iron seized her arms and pulled them away. She was pushed out of the bed, and pushed on to the floor of the bedroom. For an instant, the rage came into her heart, she wanted to get up and fight for the dying man. But a greater power, the knowledge of the uselessness and the fatal dishonourableness of her womanly interference made her desist. She lay for a time helpless and powerless on the floor, in her nightdress.

Then she felt herself lifted. In the dimness of coming dawn, she knew it was Alan. She could see the breast of his uniform—the old uniform she had known long before the war. And his face bending over her, cool and fresh.

He was still cold. But the stoniness had gone out of him, she did not mind his coldness. He pressed her firm hand hard to his own hard body. He was hard and cold like a tree, and alive. And the prickling of his moustache was the cold prickling of fir-needles.

He held her fast and hard, and seemed to possess her through every pore of her body. Not now the old, procreative way of possession. He held her fast, and possessed her through every pore in her body. Then he laid her in her own bed, to sleep.

When she awoke, the sun was shining, and Philip lay dead in a pool of blood.

Somehow she did not mind. She was only thinking of Alan. After all, she belonged to the man who could keep her. To the only man who knew how to keep her, and could only possess her through all the pores of her body, so that there was no recoil from him. Not just through one act, one function holding her. But as a cloud holds a shower.

The men that were just functional men: let them pass and perish. She wanted her contentment like life itself, through every pore, through every bit of her. The man who could hold her as the wind held her, as the air held her, all surrounded. The man whose aura permeated into every vein, through all her pores, as the scent of a pine-tree when one stands beneath it. A man, not like a faun or a satyr or an angel or a demon, but like the Tree of Life itself, implacable and unquestionable and permeating, voiceless, abiding.

In the afternoon she went to walk by herself. She climbed uphill, steep, past the New Castle, and up through the pine-woods, climbing upwards to the Old Castle. There it stood, among dense trees, its old, rose-red stone walls broken and silent. Two men, queer, wild ruffians with bundles on their backs, stood in the broken, roofless hall, looking round.

"Yes," the elder one, with the round beard, was saying, "There are no more Dukes of Baden, and counts and barons and peers of the realm are as much in ruin as this place. Soon we shall be all alike, *Lumpen*, tramps."

"Also no more ladies," said the younger one, in a lower voice. "Every tramp can have his lady."

Katherine heard him, with a pang of fear. Knowing the castle, she climbed the stairs and round the balustrade above the great hall, looking out far over the country. The sun was sinking. The Rhine was a dim magnesium ribbon, away on the plain. Across was the Russian Chapel; below, on the left, the town, and the Lichtenthal. No more gamblers, no more cosmopolitan play. Evening and the dark round hills going lonely, snow on the Merkur hill.

Mercury! Hermes! The messenger! Even as she thought it, standing there on the wall, Alan came along and stood beside her, and she felt at ease. The two men down below were looking up at her. They watched in silence, not knowing the way up. They were in the cold shadow of the hall below. A little, lingering sun, reddish, caught her where she was, above.

Again, for the last time, she looked over the land: the sun sinking below the Rhine, the hills of Germany this side, and the frozen stillness of the winter afternoon. "Yes, let us go," she heard the elder man's voice. "We are hardly men or women any more. We are more like the men and women who have drunk in this hall, living after our day."

"Only we eat and smile still, and the men want the women still."

"No! No! A man forgets his trouser-lining when he sees the ghost and the woman together."

The two tramps turned and departed, heavy-shod, up the hill.

Katherine felt Alan's touch on her arm, and she climbed down from the old, broken castle. He led her through the woods, past the red rocks. The sun had sunk, the trees were blue. He lingered again under a great pine-tree, in the shadow. And again, as he pressed her fast, and pressed his cold face against her, it was as if the wood of the tree itself were growing round her, the hard, live wood compressing and almost devouring her, the sharp needles brushing her face, the limbs of the living tree enveloping her, crushing her in the last, final ecstasy of submission, squeezing from her the last drop of her passion, like the cold, white berries of the mistletoe on the Tree of Life.

Sun

1

"Take her away, into the sun," the doctor said. She herself was sceptical of the sun, but she permitted herself to be carried away, with her child, and a nurse, and her mother, over the sea.

The ship sailed at midnight. And for two hours her husband stayed with her, while the child was put to bed, and the passengers came on board. It was a black night, the Hudson swayed with heaving blackness, shaken over with spilled dribbles of light. She leaned over the rail, and looking down thought: this is the sea; it is deeper than one imagines, and fuller of memories. At that moment the sea seemed to heave like the serpent of chaos that has lived for ever.

"These partings are no good, you know," her husband was saying, at her side. "They're no good. I don't like them."

His tone was full of apprehension, misgiving, and there was a certain clinging to the last straw of hope.

"No, neither do I," she responded in a flat voice. She remembered how bitterly they wanted to get away from one another, he and she. The emotion of parting gave a slight tug at her emotions, but only caused the iron that had gone into her soul to gore deeper.

So, they looked at their sleeping son, and the father's eyes were wet. But it is not the wetting of the eyes that counts, it is the deep iron rhythm of habit, the year-long, life-habits; the deep-set stroke of power. And in their two lives, the stroke of power was hostile, his and hers. Like two engines running at variance, they shattered one another.

"All ashore! All ashore!"

"Maurice, you must go."

And she thought to herself: For him it is All Ashore! For me it is Out to Sea!

Well, he waved his hanky on the midnight dreariness of the pier, as the boat inched away; one among a crowd. One among a crowd! *C'est ça!*

The ferry-boats, like great dishes piled with rows of lights, were still slanting across the Hudson. That black mouth must be the Lackawanna Station.

The ship ebbed on between the lights, the Hudson seemed interminable. But at last they were round the bend, and there was the poor harvest of lights at the Battery. Liberty flung up her torch in a tantrum. There was the wash of the sea.

And though the Atlantic was grey as lava, they did come at last into the sun. Even she had a house above the bluest of seas, with a vast garden, or vineyard, all vines and olives, dropping steeply in terrace after terrace, to the strip of coast plain; and the garden full of secret places, deep groves of lemon far down in the cleft of earth, and hidden, pure green reservoirs of water; then a spring issuing out of a little cavern, where the old Sicules had drunk before the Greeks came; and a grey goat bleating, stabled in an ancient tomb with the niches empty. There was the scent of mimosa, and beyond, the snow of the volcano.

She saw it all, and in a measure it was soothing. But it was all external. She didn't really care about it. She was herself just the same, with all her anger and frustration inside her, and her incapacity to feel anything real. The child imitated her, and preyed on her peace of mind. She felt so horribly, ghastly responsible for him: as if she must be responsible for every breath he drew. And that was torture to her, to the child, and to everybody else concerned.

"You know, Juliet, the doctor told you to lie in the sun, without your clothes. Why don't you?" said her mother.

"When I am fit to do so, I will. Do you want to kill me?" Juliet flew at her.

"To kill you, no! Only to do you good."

"For God's sake, leave off wanting to do me good."

The mother at last was so hurt and incensed, she departed.

The sea went white, and then invisible. Pouring rain fell. It was cold, in the house built for the sun.

Again a morning when the sun lifted himself molten and sparkling, naked over the sea's rim. The house faced south-east, Juliet lay in her bed and watched him rise. It was as if she had never seen the sun rise before. She had never seen the naked sun stand up pure upon the sea-line, shaking the night off himself, like wetness. And he was full and naked. And she wanted to come to him.

So the desire sprang secretly in her, to be naked to the sun. She cherished her desire like a secret. She wanted to come together with the sun.

But she would have to go away from the house—away from people. And it is not easy, in a country where every olive tree has eyes, and every slope is seen from afar, to go hidden, and have intercourse with the sun.

But she found a place: a rocky bluff shoved out to the sea and sun, and overgrown with the large cactus called prickly pear. Out of this thicket of cactus rose one cypress tree, with a pallid, thick trunk, and a tip that leaned over, flexible, in the blue. It stood like a guardian looking to sea; or a candle whose huge flame was darkness against light: the long tongue of darkness licking up at the sky.

Juliet sat down by the cypress tree, and took off her clothes. The contorted cactus made a forest, hideous yet fascinating, about her. She sat and offered her bosom to the sun, sighing, even now, with a certain hard pain, against the cruelty of having to give herself: but exulting that at last it was no human lover.

But the sun marched in blue heaven and sent down his rays as he went. She felt the soft air of the sea on her breasts, that seemed as if they would never ripen. But she hardly felt the sun. Fruits that would wither and not mature, her breasts.

Soon, however, she felt the sun inside them, warmer than ever love had been, warmer than milk or the hands of her baby. At last, her breasts were like long white grapes in the hot sun.

She slid off all her clothes, and lay naked in the sun, and as she lay she looked up through her fingers at the central sun, his blue pulsing roundness, whose outer edges streamed brilliance. Pulsing with marvellous blue, and alive, and streaming white fire from his edges, the Sun! He faced down to her with blue body of fire, and enveloped her breasts and her face, her throat, her tired belly, her knees, her thighs and her feet.

She lay with shut eyes, the colour of rosy flame through her lids. It was too much. She reached and put leaves over her eyes. Then she lay again, like a long gourd in the sun, green that must ripen to gold.

She could feel the sun penetrating into her bones; nay, further, even into her emotions and thoughts. The dark tensions of her emotion began to give way, the cold dark clots of her thoughts began to dissolve. She was beginning to be warm right through. Turning over, she let her shoulders lie in the sun, her loins, the backs of her thighs, even her heels. And she lay half stunned with the strangeness of the thing that was happening to her. Her weary, chilled heart was melting, and in melting, evaporating. Only her womb remained tense and resistant, the eternal resistance. It would resist even the sun.

When she was dressed again she lay once more and looked up at the cypress tree, whose crest, a filament, fell this way and that in the breeze. Meanwhile, she was conscious of the great sun roaming in heaven, and of her own resistance.

So, dazed, she went home, only half-seeing, sun-blinded and sun-dazed. And her blindness was like a richness to her, and her dim, warm, heavy half-consciousness was like wealth.

"Mummy! Mummy!" her child came running towards her, calling in that peculiar bird-like little anguish of want, always wanting her. She was surprised that her drowsed heart for once felt none of the anxious love-tension in return. She caught the child up in her arms, but she thought: He should not be such a lump! If he had any sun in him, he would spring up.—And she felt again the unyielding resistance of her womb, against him and everything.

She resented, rather, his little hands clutching at her, espe-

cially her neck. She pulled her throat away. She did not want
him getting hold of it. She put the child down.

"Run!" she said. "Run in the sun!"

And there and then she took off his clothes and set him naked on the warm terrace.

"Play in the sun!" she said.

He was frightened and wanted to cry. But she, in the warm
indolence of her body, and the complete indifference of her
heart, and the resistance of her womb, rolled him an orange
across the red tiles, and with his soft, unformed little body he
toddled after it. Then, immediately he had it, he dropped it because it felt strange against his flesh. And he looked back at her,
wrinkling his face to cry, frightened because he was stark.

"Bring me the orange," she said, amazed at her own deep
indifference to his trepidation. "Bring Mummy the orange."

"He shall not grow up like his father," she said to herself.
"Like a worm that the sun has never seen."

2

She had had the child so much on her mind, in a torment of
responsibility, as if, having borne him, she had to answer for his
whole existence. Even if his nose were running, it had been repulsive and a goad in her vitals, as if she must say to herself: Look
at the thing you brought forth! Now a change took place. She
was no longer vitally consumed about the child, she took the
strain of her anxiety and her will from off him. And he thrived
all the more for it. She was thinking inside herself, of the sun
in his splendour, and his entering into her. Her life was now a
secret ritual. She always lay awake, before dawn, watching for the
grey to colour to pale gold, to know if clouds lay on the sea's
edge. Her joy was when he rose all molten in his nakedness, and
threw off blue-white fire, into the tender heaven.

But sometimes he came ruddy, like a big, shy creature. And
sometimes slow and crimson red, with a look of anger, slowly
pushing and shouldering. Sometimes again she could not see
him, only the level cloud threw down gold and scarlet from
above, as he moved behind the wall.

She was fortunate. Weeks went by, and though the dawn was sometimes clouded, and afternoon was sometimes grey, never a day passed sunless, and most days, winter though it was, streamed radiant. The thin little wild crocuses came up mauve and striped, the wild narcissus hung their winter stars.

Every day, she went down to the cypress tree, among the cactus grove on the knoll with yellowish cliffs at the foot. She was wiser and subtler now, wearing only a dove-grey wrapper, and sandals. So that in an instant, in any hidden niche, she was naked to the sun. And the moment she was covered again she was grey and invisible.

Every day, in the morning towards noon, she lay at the foot of the powerful, silver-pawed cypress tree, while the sun strode jovial in heaven. By now she knew the sun in every thread of her body. Her heart of anxiety, that anxious, straining heart, had disappeared altogether, like a flower that falls in the sun, and leaves only a little ripening fruit. And her tense womb, though still closed, was slowly unfolding, slowly, slowly, like a lily bud under water, as the sun mysteriously touched it. Like a lily bud under water it was slowly rising to the sun, to expand at last, to the sun, only to the sun.

She knew the sun in all her body, the blue-molten with his white fire edges, throwing off fire. And, though he shone on all the world, when she lay unclothed he focussed on her. It was one of the wonders of the sun, he could shine on a million people, and still be the radiant, splendid, unique sun, focussed on her alone.

With her knowledge of the sun, and her conviction that the sun was gradually penetrating her to know her, in the cosmic carnal sense of the word, came over her a feeling of a detachment from people, and a certain contemptuous tolerance for human beings altogether. They were so un-elemental, so un-sunned. They were so like graveyard worms.

Even the peasants passing up the rocky, ancient little road with their donkeys, sun-blackened as they were, were not sunned right through. There was a little soft white core of fear, like a snail in a shell, where the soul of the man cowered in fear of the natural blaze of life. He dared not quite see the sun: always innerly cowed. All men were like that.

Why admit men!

With her indifference to people, to men, she was not now so cautious about being seen. She had told Marinina, who went shopping for her in the village, that the doctor had ordered sun-baths. Let that suffice.

Marinina was a woman of sixty or more, tall, thin, erect, with curling dark-grey hair, and dark-grey eyes that had the shrewd-ness of thousands of years in them, with the laugh, half mockery, that underlies all long experience. Tragedy is lack of experience.

"It must be beautiful to go naked in the sun," said Marinina, with a shrewd laugh in her eyes as she looked keenly at the other woman. Juliet's fair, bobbed hair curled in a little cloud at her temples. Marinina was a woman of Magna Graecia, and had far memories. She looked again at Juliet.

"But when a woman is beautiful, she can show herself to the sun? eh? isn't it true?" she added, with that queer, breathless little laugh of the women of the past.

"Who knows if I am beautiful!" said Juliet.

But beautiful or not, she felt that by the sun she was appreci-ated. Which is the same.

When, out of the sun at noon, sometimes she stole down over the rocks and past the cliff-edge, down to the deep gully where the lemons hung in cool eternal shadow; and in the silence slipped off her wrapper to wash herself quickly at one of the deep, clear green basins, she would notice, in the bare green twilight under the lemon leaves, that all her body was rosy, rosy, and turning to gold. She was like another person. She was another person.

So she remembered that the Greeks had said a white un-sunned body was unhealthy, and fishy.

And she would rub a little olive oil into her skin, and wander a moment in the dark underworld of the lemons, balancing a lemon-flower in her navel, laughing to herself. There was just a chance some peasant might see her. But if he did, he would be more afraid of her than she of him. She knew of the white core of fear in the clothed bodies of men.

She knew it even in her little son. How he mistrusted her, now that she laughed at him, with the sun in her face! She insisted on his toddling naked in the sunshine, every day. And now his little body was pink too, his blond hair was pushed thick from his brow, his cheeks had a pomegranate scarlet, in the delicate gold of the sunny skin. He was bonny and healthy, and the servants, loving his gold and red and blue, called him an angel from heaven.

But he mistrusted his mother: she laughed at him. And she saw, in his wide blue eyes, under the little frown, that centre of fear, misgiving, which she believed was at the centre of all male eyes, now. She called it fear of the sun. And her womb stayed shut against all men, sun-fearers.

"He fears the sun," she would say to herself, looking down into the eyes of the child.

And as she watched him toddling, swaying, tumbling in the sunshine, making his little bird-like noises, she saw that he held himself tight and hidden from the sun, inside himself, and his balance was clumsy, his movements a little gross. His spirit was like a snail in a shell, in a damp, cold crevice inside himself. It made her think of his father. And she wished she could make him come forth, break out in a gesture of recklessness, a salutation to the sun.

She determined to take him with her, down to the cypress tree among the cactus. She would have to watch him, because of the thorns. But surely in that place he would come forth from the little shell, deep inside him. That little civilised tension would disappear off his brow.

She spread a rug for him and sat down. Then she slid off her wrapper and lay down herself, watching a hawk high in the blue, and the tip of the cypress hanging over.

The boy played with stones on the rug. When he got up to toddle away, she got up too. He turned and looked at her. Almost, from his blue eyes, it was the challenging, warm look of the true male. And he was handsome, with the scarlet in the golden blond of his skin. He was not really white. His skin was gold-dusky.

"Mind the thorns, darling," she said.

"Thorns!" re-echoed the child, in a birdy chirp, still looking at her over his shoulder, like some naked *putto* in a picture, doubtful.

"Nasty prickly thorns."

"Ickly thorns!"

He staggered in his little sandals over the stones, pulling at the dry mint. She was quick as a serpent, leaping to him, when he was going to fall against the prickles. It surprised even herself. "What a wild cat I am, really!" she said to herself.

She brought him every day, when the sun shone, to the cypress tree.

"Come!" she said, "Let us go to the cypress tree."

And if there was a cloudy day, with the *tramontana* blowing, so that she could not go down, the child would chirp incessantly: "Cypress tree! Cypress tree!"

He missed it as much as she did.

It was not just taking sun-baths. It was much more than that. Something deep inside her unfolded and relaxed, and she was given to a cosmic influence. By some mysterious will inside her, deeper than her known consciousness and her known will, she was put into connection with the sun, and the stream of the sun flowed through her, round her womb. She herself, her conscious self, was secondary, a secondary person, almost an onlooker. The true Juliet lived in the dark flow of the sun within her deep body, like a river of dark rays circling, circling dark and violet round the sweet, shut bud of her womb.

She had always been mistress of herself, aware of what she was doing, and held tense in her own command. Now she felt inside her quite another sort of power, something greater than herself, darker and more savage, the element flowing upon her. Now she was vague, in the spell of a power beyond herself.

3

The end of February was suddenly very hot. Almond blossom was falling like pink snow, in the touch of the smallest breeze. The mauve, silky little anemones were out, the asphodels tall in bud, and the sea was corn-flower blue.

Juliet had ceased to care about anything. Now, most of the day, she and the child were naked in the sun, and it was all she wanted. Sometimes she went down to the sea to bathe: often she wandered in the gullies where the sun shone in, and she was out of sight. Sometimes she saw a peasant with an ass, and he saw her. But she went so simply and quietly with her child; and the fame of the sun's healing power, for the soul as well as for the body, had already spread among the people; so that there was no excitement.

The child and she were now both tanned with a rosy-golden tan, all over. "I am another being," she said to herself, as she looked at her red-gold breasts and thighs.

The child, too, was another creature, with a peculiar, quiet, sun-darkened absorption. Now he played by himself in silence, and she need hardly notice him. He seemed no longer to notice when he was alone.

There was not a breeze, and the sea was ultramarine. She sat by the great silver paw of the cypress tree, drowsed in the sun, but her breasts alert, full of sap. She was becoming aware of an activity rousing in her, an activity which would bring another self awake in her. She still did not want to be aware. The new rousing would mean a new contact, and this she did not want. She knew well enough the vast cold apparatus of civilisation, and what contact with it meant; and how difficult it was to evade.

The child had gone a few yards down the rocky path, round the great sprawling of a cactus. She had seen him, a real gold-brown infant of the winds, with burnt gold hair and red cheeks, collecting the speckled pitcher-flowers and laying them in rows. He could balance now, and was quick for his own emergencies, like an absorbed young animal playing.

Suddenly she heard him speaking: *Look, Mummy! Mummy look!* A note in his bird-like voice made her lean forward sharply.

Her heart stood still. He was looking over his naked little shoulder at her, and pointing with a loose little hand at a snake which had reared itself up a yard away from him, and was opening its mouth so that its forked, soft tongue flickered black like a shadow, uttering a short hiss.

"Look! Mummy!"

"Yes, darling, it's a snake!" came the slow deep voice. He looked at her, his wide blue eyes uncertain whether to be afraid or not. Some stillness of the sun in her reassured him.

"Snake!" he chirped.

"Yes, darling! Don't touch it, it can bite."

The snake had sunk down, and was reaching away from the coils in which it had been basking asleep, and slowly easing its long, gold-brown body into the rocks, with slow curves. The boy turned and watched it in silence. Then he said:

"Snake going!"

"Yes! Let it go. It likes to be alone."

He still watched the slow, easing length as the creature drew itself apathetic out of sight.

"Snake gone back," he said.

"Yes, it is gone back. Come to Mummy a moment."

He came and sat with his plump, naked little body on her naked lap, and she smoothed his burnt, bright hair. She said nothing, feeling that everything was past. The curious careless power of the sun filled her, filled the whole place like a charm, and the snake was part of the place, along with her and the child.

Another day, in the dry stone wall of one of the olive terraces, she saw a black snake horizontally creeping.

"Marinina," she said, "I saw a black snake. Are they harmful?"

"Ah, the black snakes, no! But the yellow ones, yes! If the yellow ones bite you, you die. But they frighten me, they frighten me, even the black ones, when I see one."

Juliet still went to the cypress tree with the child. But she always looked carefully round, before she sat down, examining everywhere the child might go. Then she would lie and turn to the sun again, her tanned, pear-shaped breasts pointing up. She would take no thought for the morrow. She refused to think outside the garden, and she could not write letters. She would tell the nurse to write. So she lay in the sun, but not for long, for it was getting strong, fierce. And in spite of herself, the bud that had been tight and deep immersed in the innermost gloom of her, was rearing, rearing and straightening its curved stem, to open its dark tips and show a gleam of rose. Her womb was coming open wide with rosy ecstasy, like a lotus flower.

4

Spring was becoming summer, in the south of the sun, and the rays were very powerful. In the hot hours she would lie in the shade of trees, or she would even go down to the depths of the cool lemon grove. Or sometimes she went in the shadowy deeps of the gullies, at the bottom of the little ravine, towards home. The child fluttered around in silence, like a young animal absorbed in life.

Going slowly home in her nakedness down among the bushes of the dark ravine, one noon, she came round a rock suddenly upon the peasant of the next *podere,* who was stooping binding up a bundle of brush-wood he had cut, his ass standing near. He was wearing summer cotton trousers, and stooping his buttocks towards her. It was utterly still and private down in the dark bed of the little ravine. A weakness came over her, for a moment she could not move. The man lifted the bundle of wood with power-ful shoulders, and turned to the ass. He started and stood trans-fixed as he saw her, as if it were a vision. Then his eyes met hers, and she felt the blue fire running through her limbs to her womb, which was spreading in the helpless ecstasy. Still they looked into each other's eyes, and the fire flowed between them, like the blue, streaming fire from the heart of the sun. And she saw the phallus rise under his clothing, and knew he would come towards her.

"Mummy, a man! Mummy!" The child had put a hand against her thigh. "Mummy, a man!"

She heard the note of fear and swung round.

"It's all right, boy!" she said, and taking him by the hand, she led him back round the rock again, while the peasant watched her naked, retreating buttocks lift and fall.

She put on her wrap, and taking the boy in her arms, began to stagger up a steep goat-track through the yellow-flowering tangle of shrubs, up to the level of day, and the olive trees below the house. There she sat down to collect herself.

The sea was blue, very blue and soft and still-looking, and her womb inside her was wide open, wide open like a lotus flower, or a cactus flower, in a radiant sort of eagerness. She could feel it, and it dominated her consciousness. And a biting chagrin burned in her breast, against the child, against the complication of frustration.

She knew the peasant by sight: a man something over thirty, broad and very powerfully set. She had many times watched him from the terrace of her house: watched him come with his ass, watched him trimming the olive trees, working alone, always alone and physically powerful, with a broad red face and a quiet self-possession. She had spoken to him once or twice, and met his big blue eyes, dark and southern hot. And she knew his sudden gestures, a little violent and over-generous. But she had never thought of him. Save she had noticed that he was always very clean and well-cared for: and then she had seen his wife one day, when the latter had brought the man's meal, and they sat in the shade of a carob tree, on either side the spread white cloth. And then Juliet had seen that the man's wife was older than he, a dark, proud, gloomy woman. And then a young woman had come with a child, and the man had danced with the child, so young and passionate. But it was not his own child: he had no children. It was when he danced with the child, in such a sprightly way, as if full of suppressed passion, that Juliet had first really noticed him. But even then, she had never thought of him. Such a broad red face, such a great chest, and rather short legs. Too much a crude beast for her to think of, a peasant.

But now the strange challenge of his eyes had held her, blue and overwhelming like the blue sun's heart. And she had seen the fierce stirring of the phallus under his thin trousers: for her. And with his red face, and with his broad body, he was like the sun to her, the sun in its broad heat.

She felt him so powerfully, that she could not go further from him.

She continued to sit there under the tree. Then she heard nurse tinkling a bell at the house and calling. And the child called back. She had to rise and go home.

In the afternoon she sat on the terrace of her house, that looked over the olive slopes to the sea. The man came and went, came and went to the little hut on his *podere,* on the edge of the cactus grove. And he glanced again at her house, at her sitting on the terrace. And her womb was open to him.

Yet she had not the courage to go down to him. She was paralysed. She had tea, and still sat there on the terrace. And the man came and went, and glanced, and glanced again. Till the evening bell had jangled from the capuchin church at the village gate, and the darkness came on. And still she sat on the terrace. Till at last in the moonlight she saw him load his ass and drive it sadly along the path to the little road. She heard him pass on the stones of the road behind her house. He was gone—gone home to the village, to sleep, to sleep with his wife, who would want to know why he was so late. He was gone in dejection.

Juliet sat late on into the night, watching the moon on the sea. The sun had opened her womb, and she was no longer free. The trouble of the open lotus blossom had come upon her, and now it was she who had not the courage to take the steps across the gully.

But at last she slept. And in the morning she felt better. Her womb seemed to have closed again: the lotus flower seemed back in bud again. She wanted so much that it should be so. Only the immersed bud, and the sun! She would never think of that man.

She bathed in one of the great tanks away down in the lemon-grove, down in the far ravine, far as possible from the other wild gully, and cool. Below, under the lemons, the child was wading among the yellow oxalis flowers of the shadow, gathering fallen lemons, passing with his tanned little body into flecks of light, moving all dappled. She sat in the sun on the steep bank in the gully, feeling almost free again, the flower drooping in shadowy bud, safe inside her.

Suddenly, high over the land's edge, against the full-lit pale blue sky, Marinina appeared, a black cloth tied round her head, calling quietly: *Signora! Signora Giulietta!*

Juliet faced round, standing up. Marinina paused a moment,

seeing the naked woman standing alert, her sun-faded hair in a little cloud. Then the swift old woman came down the slant of the steep, sun-blazed track.

She stood a few steps, erect, in front of the sun-coloured woman, and eyed her shrewdly.

"But how beautiful you are, you!" she said coolly, almost cynically. "Your husband has come."

"What husband?" cried Juliet.

The old woman gave a shrewd bark of a little laugh, the mockery of the woman of the past.

"Haven't you got one, a husband, you?" she said, taunting.

"How? Where? In America," said Juliet.

The old woman glanced over her shoulder, with another noiseless laugh.

"No America at all. He was following me here. He will have missed the path." And she threw back her head in the noiseless laugh of women.

The paths were all grown high with grass and flowers and *nepitella*, till they were like bird-tracks in an eternally wild place. Strange, the vivid wildness of the old classic places, that have known men so long.

Juliet looked at the Sicilian woman with meditating eyes.

"Oh very well," she said at last. "Let him come."

And a little flame leaped in her. It was the opening flower. At least he was a man.

"Bring him here? Now?" asked Marinina, her mocking, smoke-grey eyes looking with laughter into Juliet's eyes. Then she gave a little jerk of her shoulders.

"All right! As you wish! But for him it is a rare one!" She opened her mouth with a noiseless laugh of amusement then she pointed down to the child, who was heaping lemons against his little chest. "Look how beautiful the child is! An angel from heaven! That certainly will please him, poor thing. Then I shall bring him?"

"Bring him," said Juliet.

The old woman scrambled rapidly up the track again, and found Maurice at a loss among the vine terraces, standing there in his grey felt hat and dark-grey city suit. He looked pathetically out of place, in that resplendent sunshine and the grace of the old Greek world; like a blot of ink on the pale, sun-glowing slope.

"Come!" said Marinina to him. "She is down here."

And swiftly she led the way, striding with a long stride, marking the way through the grasses. Suddenly she stopped on the brow of the slope. The tops of the lemon trees were dark, away below.

"You, you go down here," she said to him, and he thanked her, glancing up at her swiftly.

He was a man of forty, clean-shaven, grey-faced, very quiet and really shy. He managed his own business carefully without startling success, but efficiently. And he confided in nobody. The old woman of Magna Graecia saw him at a glance: he is good, she said to herself, but not a man, poor thing.

"Down there is the *Signora*," said Marinina, pointing like one of the Fates.

And again he said, "Thank you! Thank you!" without a twinkle, and stepped carefully into the track. Marinina lifted her chin with a joyful wickedness. Then she strode off towards the house.

Maurice was watching his step, through the tangle of Mediterranean herbage, so he did not catch sight of his wife till he came round a little bend, quite near her. She was standing erect and nude by the jutting rock, glistening with the sun and with warm life. Her breasts seemed to be lifting up, alert, to listen, her thighs looked brown and fleet. Inside her, the lotus of her womb was wide open, spread almost gaping in the violet rays of the sun, like a great lotus flower. And she thrilled helplessly: a man was coming. Her glance on him, as he came gingerly, like ink on blotting-paper, was swift and nervous.

Maurice, poor fellow, hesitated and glanced away from her, turning his face aside.

"Hello, Julie!" he said, with a little nervous cough. "Splendid! Splendid!"

He advanced with his face averted, shooting further glances

at her, furtively, as she stood with the peculiar satiny gleam of the sun on her tanned skin. Somehow she did not seem so terribly naked. It was the golden-rose of the sun that clothed her.

"Hello Maurice!" she said, hanging back from him, and a cold shadow falling on the open flower of her womb. "I wasn't expecting you so soon."

"No," he said. "No! I managed to slip away a little earlier."

And again he coughed unawares. Furtively, purposely he had taken her by surprise. They stood several yards away from one another, and there was silence. But this was a new Julie to him, with the suntanned, wind-stroked thighs: not that nervous New York woman.

"Well!" he said, "er—this is splendid—splendid! You are—er—splendid!—Where is the boy?"

He felt, in his far-off depths, the desire stirring in him for the limbs and sun-wrapped flesh of the woman: the woman of flesh. It was a new desire in his life, and it hurt him. He wanted to side-track.

"There he is," she said, pointing down to where a naked urchin in the deep shade was piling fallen lemons together.

The father gave an odd little laugh, almost neighing.

"Ah! yes! There he is! So there's the little man! Fine!" His nervous, suppressed soul was thrilling with violent thrills, he clung to the straw of his upper consciousness. "Hello, Johnny!" he called, and it sounded rather feeble. "Hello Johnny!"

The child looked up, spilling lemons from his chubby arms, but did not respond.

"I guess we'll go down to him," said Juliet, as she turned and went striding down the path. In spite of herself, the cold shadow was lifting off the open flower of her womb, and every petal was thrilling again. Her husband followed, watching the rosy, fleet-looking lifting and sinking of her quick hips, as she swayed a little in the socket of her waist. He was dazed with admiration, but also at a deadly loss. He was used to her as a person. And this was no longer a person, but a fleet sun-strong body, soulless and alluring as a nymph, twinkling its haunches. What would he do with himself? He was utterly out of the picture, in his dark grey suit and pale grey hat, and his grey, monastic face of a shy business man, and his grey mercantile mentality. Strange thrills shot through his loins and his legs. He was terrified, and he felt he might give a wild whoop of triumph, and jump towards that woman of tanned flesh.

"He looks all right, doesn't he," said Juliet, as they came through the deep sea of yellow-flowering oxalis, under the lemon-trees.

"Ah!—yes! yes! Splendid! Splendid!—Hello Johnny! Do you know Daddy? Do you know Daddy, Johnny?"

He squatted down, forgetting his trouser-crease, and held out his hands.

"Lemons!" said the child, birdily chirping. "Two lemons!"

"Two lemons!" replied the father. "Lots of lemons!"

The infant came and put a lemon in each of his father's open hands. Then he stood back to look.

"Two lemons!" repeated the father. "Come, Johnny! Come and say Hello! to Daddy."

"Daddy going back?" said the child.

"Going back? Well—well—not today."

And he took his son in his arms.

"Take a coat off! Daddy take a coat off!" said the boy, squirming debonair away from the cloth.

"All right, son! Daddy take a coat off."

He took off his coat and laid it carefully aside, then looked at the creases in his trousers, hitched them a little, and crouched down and took his son in his arms. The child's warm naked body against him made him feel faint. The naked woman looked down at the rosy infant in the arms of the man in his shirt-sleeves. The boy had pulled off his father's hat, and Juliet looked at the sleek black-and-grey hair of her husband, not a hair out of place. And utterly, utterly sunless! The cold shadow was over the flower of her womb again. She was silent for a long time, while the father talked to the child, who had been fond of his Daddy.

"What are you going to do about it, Maurice?" she said suddenly. He looked at her swiftly, sideways, hearing her abrupt American voice. He had forgotten her.

"Er—about what, Julie?"

"Oh, everything! About this! I can't go back into East Forty-Seventh."

"Er—" he hesitated, "no, I suppose not—Not just now, at least."

"Never!" she said abruptly, and there was a silence.

"Well—er—I don't know," he said.

"Do you think you can come out here?" she said savagely.

"Yes!—I can stay for a month. I think I can manage a month," he hesitated. Then he ventured a complicated, shy peep at her, and turned away his face again.

She looked down at him, her alert breasts lifted with a sigh, as if she would impatiently shake the cold shadow of sunlessness off her.

"I can't go back," she said slowly, "I can't go back on this sun. If you can't come here—"

She ended on an open note. But the voice of the abrupt, personal American woman had died out, and he heard the voice of the woman of flesh, the sun-ripe body. He glanced at her again and again, with growing desire and lessening fear.

"No!" he said. "This kind of thing suits you. You are splendid.—No, I don't think you can go back."

And at the caressive sound of his voice, in spite of her, her womb-flower began to open and thrill its petals.

He was thinking visionarily of her in the New York flat, pale, silent, oppressing him terribly. He was the soul of gentle timidity in his human relations, and her silent, awful hostility after the baby was born had frightened him deeply. Because he had realized that she could not help it. Women were like that. Their feelings took a reverse direction, even against their own selves, and it was awful—devastating. Awful, awful to live in the house with a woman like that, whose feelings were reversed even against herself. He had felt himself borne down under the stream of her heavy hostility. She had ground even herself down to the quick, and the child as well. No, anything rather than that. Thank God, that menacing ghost-woman seemed to be sunned out of her now.

"But what about you?" she asked.

"I? Oh, I!—I can carry on in the business, and—er come over here for long holidays—so long as you like to stay here. You stay as long as you wish—" He looked down a long time at the earth. He was so frightened of rousing that menacing, avenging spirit of womanhood in her, he did so hope she might stay as he had seen her now, like a naked, ripening strawberry, a female like a fruit. He glanced up at her with a touch of supplication in his uneasy eyes.

"Even for ever?" she said.

"Well—er—yes, if you like. For ever is a long time. One can't set a date."

"And can I do anything I like?" She looked him straight in the eyes, challenging. And he was powerless against her rosy, wind-hardened nakedness, in his fear of arousing that other woman in her, the personal American woman, spectral and vengeful.

"Er—yes!—I suppose so! So long as you don't make yourself unhappy—or the boy."

Again he looked up at her with a complicated, uneasy ap-peal—thinking of the child, but hoping for himself.

"I won't," she said quickly.

"No!" he said, "No! I don't think you will."

There was a pause. The bells of the village were hastily clang-ing mid-day. That meant lunch.

She slipped into her grey crêpe kimono, and fastened a broad green sash around her waist. Then she slipped a little blue shirt over the boy's head, and they went up to the house.

At table she watched her husband, his grey city face, his glued, grey-black hair, his very precise table manners, and his extreme moderation in eating and drinking. Sometimes he glanced at her furtively, from under his black lashes. He had the uneasy, gold-grey eyes of a creature that has been caught young, and reared entirely in captivity, strange and cold, knowing no warm hopes. Only his black eye-brows and eye-lashes were nice. She did not take him in. She did not realize him. Being so sunned, she could not see him, his sunlessness was like nonentity.

They went on to the balcony for coffee, under the rosy mass of the bougainvillea. Below, beyond, on the next *podere,* the peasant and his wife were sitting under the carob tree, near the tall green wheat, sitting facing one another across a little white cloth spread on the ground. There was still a huge piece of bread—but they had finished eating and sat with dark wine in their glasses.

The peasant looked up at the terrace, as soon as the American emerged. Juliet put her husband with his back to the scene. Then she sat down, and looked back at the peasant. Until she saw his dark-visaged wife turn to look too.

5

The man was hopelessly in love with her. She saw his broad, rather short red face gazing up at her fixedly: till his wife turned too to look, then he picked up his glass and tossed the wine down his throat. The wife stared long at the figures on the balcony. She was handsome and rather gloomy, and surely older than he, with that great difference that lies between a rather overwhelming, superior woman over forty, and her more irresponsible husband of thirty-five or so. It seemed like the difference of a whole generation. "He is my generation," thought Juliet, "and she is Maurice's generation." Juliet was not yet thirty.

The peasant in his white cotton trousers and pale pink shirt, and battered old straw hat, was attractive, so clean, and full of the cleanliness of health. He was stout and broad, and seemed short-ish, but his flesh was full of vitality, as if he were always about to spring up into movement, to work, even, as she had seen him with the child, to play. He was the type of Italian peasant that wants to make an offering of himself, passionately wants to make an offering of himself, of his powerful flesh and thudding blood-stroke. But he was also completely a peasant, in that he would wait for the woman to make the move. He would hang round in a long, consuming passivity of desire, hoping, hoping for the woman to come for him. But he would never try to advance to her: never. She would have to make the advance. Only he would hang round, within reach.

Feeling her look at him, he flung off his old straw hat, show-ing his round, close-cropped brown head, and reached out with

187

a large brown-red hand for the great loaf, from which he broke a piece and started chewing with bulging cheek. He knew she was looking at him. And she had such power over him, the hot inarticulate animal, with such a hot, massive blood-stream down his great veins! He was hot through with countless suns, and mindless as noon. And shy with a violent, farouche shyness, that would wait for her with consuming wanting, but would never, never move towards her.

With him, it would be like bathing in another kind of sunshine, heavy and big and perspiring: and afterwards one would forget. Personally, he would not exist. It would be just a bath of warm, powerful life—then separating and forgetting. Then again, the procreative bath, like sun.

But would that not be good! She was so tired of personal contacts, and having to talk with the man afterwards. With that healthy creature, one would just go satisfied away, afterwards. As she sat there, she felt the life streaming from him to her, and her to him. She knew by his movements he felt her even more than she felt him. It was almost a definite pain of consciousness in the body of each of them, and each sat as if distracted, watched by a keen-eyed spouse, possessor.

And Juliet thought: Why shouldn't I go to him! Why shouldn't I bear his child? It would be like bearing a child to the unconscious sun and the unconscious earth, a child like a fruit.—And the flower of her womb radiated. It did not care about sentiment or possession. It wanted man-dew only, utterly improvident. But her heart was clouded with fear. She dare not! She dare not! If only the man would find some way! But he would not. He would only hover and wait, hover in endless desire, waiting for her to cross the gully. And she dare not, she dare not. And he would hang round.

"You are not afraid of people seeing you when you take your sun-baths?" said her husband, turning round and looking across at the peasants. The saturnine wife over the gully, turned also to stare at the Villa. It was a kind of battle.

"No! One needn't be seen. Will you do it too? Will you take the sun-baths?" said Juliet to him.

"Why—er—yes! I think I should like to, while I am here."

There was a gleam in his eyes, a desperate kind of courage of desire to taste this new fruit, this woman with rosy, sun-ripening breasts tilting within her wrapper. And she thought of him with his blanched, etiolated little city figure, walking in the sun in the desperation of a husband's rights. And her mind swooned again. The strange, branded little fellow, the good citizen, branded like a criminal in the naked eye of the sun. How he would hate exposing himself!

And the flower of her womb went dizzy, dizzy. She knew she would take him. She knew she would bear his child. She knew it was for him, the branded little city man, that her womb was open radiating like a lotus, like the purple spread of a daisy anemone, dark at the core. She knew she would not go across to the peasant; she had not enough courage, she was not free enough. And she knew the peasant would never come for her, he had the dogged passivity of the earth, and would wait, wait, only putting himself in her sight, again and again, lingering across her vision, with the persistency of animal yearning.

She had seen the flushed blood in the peasant's burnt face, and felt the jetting, sudden blue heat pouring over her from his kindled eyes, and the rousing of his big penis against his body—for her, surging for her. Yet she would never come to him—she daren't, she daren't, so much was against her. And the little etiolated body of her husband, city-branded, would possess her, and his little, frantic penis would beget another child in her. She could not help it. She was bound to the vast, fixed wheel of circumstance, and there was no Perseus in the universe to cut the bonds.

The Rocking-Horse Winner

There was a woman who was beautiful, who started with all the advantages, yet she had no luck. She married for love, and the love turned to dust. She had bonny children, yet she felt they had been thrust upon her, and she could not love them. They looked at her coldly, as if they were finding fault with her. And hurriedly she felt she must cover up some fault in herself. Yet what it was that she must cover up she never knew. Nevertheless, when her children were present, she always felt the centre of her heart go hard. This troubled her, and in her manner she was all the more gentle and anxious for her children, as if she loved them very much. Only she herself knew that at the centre of her heart was a hard little place that could not feel love, no, not for anybody. Everybody else said of her: "She is such a good mother. She adores her children." Only she herself, and her children themselves, knew it was not so. They read it in each other's eyes.

There were a boy and two little girls. They lived in a pleasant house, with a garden, and they had discreet servants, and felt themselves superior to anyone in the neighbourhood.

Although they lived in style, they felt always an anxiety in the house. There was never enough money. The mother had a small income, and the father had a small income, but not nearly enough for the social position which they had to keep up. The father went in to town to some office. But though he had good prospects, these prospects never materialised. There was always the grinding sense of the shortage of money, though the style was always kept up.

At last the mother said, "I will see if *I* can't make something." But she did not know where to begin. She racked her brains, and tried this thing and the other, but could not find anything successful. The failure made deep lines come into her face. Her children were growing up, they would have to go to school. There must be more money, there must be more money. The father, who was always very handsome and expensive in his tastes, seemed as if he never *would* be able to do anything worth doing. And the mother, who had a great belief in herself, did not succeed any better, and her tastes were just as expensive.

And so the house came to be haunted by the unspoken phrase: There must be more money! There must be more money! The children could hear it all the time, though nobody said it aloud. They heard it at Christmas, when the expensive and splendid toys filled the nursery. Behind the shining modern rocking-horse, behind the smart doll's-house, a voice would start whispering: "There *must* be more money! There *must* be more money!" And the children would stop playing, to listen for a moment. They would look into each other's eyes, to see if they had all heard. And each one saw in the eyes of the other two that they too had heard. "There *must* be more money! There *must* be more money!"

It came whispering from the springs of the still-swaying rocking-horse, and even the horse, bending his wooden, champing head, heard it. The big doll, sitting so pink and smirking in her new pram, could hear it quite plainly, and seemed to be smirking all the more self-consciously because of it. The foolish puppy, too, that took the place of the teddy-bear, he was looking so extraordinarily foolish for no other reason but that he heard the secret whisper all over the house: "There *must* be more money."

Yet nobody ever said it aloud. The whisper was everywhere, and therefore no one spoke it. Just as no one ever says: "We are breathing!" in spite of the fact that breath is coming and going all the time.

"Mother!" said the boy Paul one day. "Why don't we keep a car of our own? Why do we always use uncle's, or else a taxi?"

"Because we're the poor members of the family," said the mother.

"But why *are* we, mother?"

"Well—I suppose," she said slowly and bitterly, "it's because your father has no luck."

The boy was silent for some time.

"Is luck money, mother?" he asked, rather timidly.

"No, Paul! Not quite. It's what causes you to have money."

"Oh!" said Paul vaguely. "I thought when Uncle Oscar said filthy lucker, it meant money."

"Filthy lucre does mean money," said the mother. "But it's lucre, not luck."

"Oh!" said the boy. "Then what *is* luck, mother?"

"It's what causes you to have money. If you're lucky you have money. That's why it's better to be born lucky than rich. If you're rich, you may lose your money. But if you're lucky, you will always get more money."

"Oh! Will you! And is father not lucky?"

"Very unlucky, I should say," she said bitterly.

The boy watched her with unsure eyes.

"Why?" he asked.

"I don't know. Nobody ever knows why one person is lucky and another unlucky."

"Don't they? Nobody at all? Does *nobody* know?"

"Perhaps God! But He never tells."

"He ought to, then. And aren't you lucky either, mother?"

"I can't be, if I married an unlucky husband."

"But by yourself, aren't you?"

"I used to think I was, before I married. Now I think I am very unlucky indeed."

"Why?"

"Well—never mind! Perhaps I'm not really," she said.

The child looked at her, to see if she meant it. But he saw, by the lines of her mouth, that she was only trying to hide something from him.

"Well, anyhow," he said stoutly, "I'm a lucky person."

"Why?" said his mother, with a sudden laugh.

He stared at her. He didn't even know why he had said it.

"God told me," he asserted, brazening it out.

"I hope He did, dear!" she said, again with a laugh, but rather bitter.

"He did, mother!"

"Excellent!" said the mother, using one of her husband's exclamations.

The boy saw she did not believe him; or rather, that she paid no attention to his assertion. This angered him somewhere, and made him want to compel her attention.

He went off by himself, vaguely, in a childish way, seeking for the clue to "luck". Absorbed, taking no heed of other people, he went about with a sort of stealth, seeking inwardly for luck. He wanted luck, he wanted it, he wanted it. When the two girls were playing dolls, in the nursery, he would sit on his big rocking-horse, charging madly into space, with a frenzy that made the little girls peer at him uneasily. Wildly the horse careered, the waving dark hair of the boy tossed, his eyes had a strange glare in them. The little girls dared not speak to him.

When he had ridden to the end of his mad little journey, he climbed down and stood in front of his rocking-horse, staring fixedly into its lowered face. Its red mouth was slightly open, its big eye was wide and glassy bright.

"Now!" he would silently command the snorting steed. "Now take me to where there is luck! Now take me!"

And he would slash the horse on the neck with the little whip he had asked Uncle Oscar for. He *knew* the horse could take him to where there was luck, if only he forced it. So he would mount again, and start on his furious ride, hoping at last to get there. He knew he could get there.

"You'll break your horse, Paul!" said the nurse.

"He's always riding like that! I wish he'd leave off!" said his elder sister Joan.

But he only glared down on them in silence. Nurse gave him up. She could make nothing of him. Anyhow he was growing beyond her.

One day his mother and his Uncle Oscar came in when he was on one of his furious rides. He did not speak to them.

"Hallo! you young jockey! Riding a winner?" said his uncle.

"Aren't you growing too big for a rocking-horse? You're not a very little boy any longer, you know," said his mother.

But Paul only gave a blue glare from his big, rather close-set eyes. He would speak to nobody when he was in full tilt. His mother watched him with an anxious expression on her face.

At last he suddenly stopped forcing his horse into the mechanical gallop, and slid down.

"Well, I got there!" he announced fiercely, his blue eyes still flaring, and his sturdy long legs straddling apart.

"Where did you get to?" asked his mother.

"Where I wanted to go to," he flared back at her.

"That's right, son!" said Uncle Oscar. "Don't you stop till you get there. What's the horse's name?"

"He doesn't have a name," said the boy.

"Gets on without all right?" asked the uncle.

"Well, he has different names. He was called Sansovino last week."

"Sansovino, eh? Won the Ascot. How did you know his name?"

"He always talks about horse-races with Bassett," said Joan.

The uncle was delighted to find that his small nephew was posted with all the racing news. Bassett, the young gardener who had been wounded in the left foot in the war, and had got his present job through Oscar Cresswell, whose batman he had been, was a perfect blade of the "turf". He lived in the racing events, and the small boy lived with him.

Oscar Cresswell got it all from Bassett.

"Master Paul comes and asks me, so I can't do more than tell him, sir," said Bassett, his face terribly serious, as if he were speaking of religious matters.

"And does he ever put anything on a horse he fancies?"

"Well—I don't want to give him away—he's a young sport, a fine sport, sir. Would you mind asking him himself? He sort of takes a pleasure in it, and perhaps he'd feel I was giving him away, sir, if you don't mind."

Bassett was serious as a church.

The uncle went back to his nephew, and took him off for a ride in the car.

"Say, Paul, old man, do you ever put anything on a horse?" the uncle asked.

The boy watched the handsome man closely.

"Why, do you think I oughtn't to?" he parried.

"Not a bit of it! I thought perhaps you might give me a tip for the Lincoln."

The car sped on into the country, going down to Uncle Oscar's place in Hampshire.

"Honour bright?" said the nephew.

"Honour bright, son!" said the uncle.

"Well, then, Daffodil."

"Daffodil! I doubt it, sonny. What about Mirza?"

"I only know the winner," said the boy. "That's Daffodil!"

"Daffodil, eh?" There was a pause. Daffodil was an obscure horse comparatively.

"Uncle!"

"Yes, son?"

"You won't let it go any further, will you? I promised Bassett."

"Bassett be damned, old man! What's he got to do with it?"

"We're partners! We've been partners from the first! Uncle, he lent me my first five shillings, which I lost. I promised him, honour bright, it was only between me and him: only you gave me that ten-shilling note I started winning with, so I thought you were lucky. You won't let it go any further, will you?"

The boy gazed at his uncle from those big, hot, blue eyes, set rather close together. The uncle stirred and laughed uneasily.

"Right you are, son! I'll keep your tip private. Daffodil, eh! How much are you putting on him?"

"All except twenty pounds," said the boy. "I keep that in reserve." The uncle thought it a good joke.

"You keep twenty pounds in reserve, do you, you young romancer? What are you betting, then?"

"I'm betting three hundred," said the boy gravely. "But it's between you and me, Uncle Oscar! Honour bright?"

The uncle burst into a roar of laughter.

"It's between you and me all right, you young Nat Gould," he said, laughing. "But where's your three hundred?"

"Bassett keeps it for me. We're partners."

"You are, are you! And what is Bassett putting on Daffodil?"

"He won't go quite as high as I do, I expect. Perhaps he'll go a hundred and fifty."

"What, pennies?" laughed the uncle.

"Pounds," said the child, with a surprised look at his uncle. "Bassett keeps a bigger reserve than I do."

Between wonder and amusement, Uncle Oscar was silent. He pursued the matter no further, but he determined to take his nephew with him to the Lincoln races.

"Now, son," he said, "I'm putting twenty on Mirza, and I'll put five for you on any horse you fancy. What's your pick?"

"Daffodil, uncle!"

"No, not the fiver on Daffodil!"

"I should if it was my own fiver," said the child.

"Good! Good! Right you are! A fiver for me and a fiver for you on Daffodil."

The child had never been to a race-meeting before, and his eyes were blue fire. He pursed his mouth tight, and watched. A Frenchman just in front had put his money on Lancelot. Wild with excitement, he flayed his arms up and down, yelling 'Lancelot! Lancelot/' in his French accent.

Daffodil came in first, Lancelot second, Mirza third. The child, flushed and with eyes blazing, was curiously serene. His uncle brought him five five-pound notes: four to one.

"What am I to do with these?" he cried, waving them before the boy's eyes.

"I suppose we'll talk to Bassett," said the boy. "I expect I have fifteen hundred now: and twenty in reserve: and this twenty."

His uncle studied him for some moments.

"Look here, son!" he said. "You're not serious about Bassett and that fifteen hundred, are you?"

"Yes, I am. But it's between you and me, uncle! Honour bright!"

"Honour bright all right, son! But I must talk to Bassett."

"If you'd like to be a partner, uncle, with Bassett and me, we could all be partners. Only you'd have to promise, honour bright, uncle, not to let it go beyond us three. Bassett and I are lucky, and you must be lucky, because it was your ten shillings I started winning with . . ."

Uncle Oscar took both Bassett and Paul into Richmond Park for an afternoon, and there they talked.

"It's like this, you see, sir," Bassett said. "Master Paul would get me talking about racing events, spinning yarns, you know, sir. And he was always keen on knowing if I'd made or if I'd lost. It's about a year since, now, that I put five shillings on Blush of Dawn for him: and we lost. Then the luck turned, with that ten shillings he had from you: that we put on Singhalese. And since that time, it's been pretty steady, all things considering. What do you say, Master Paul?"

"We're all right when we're *sure*," said Paul. "It's when we're not quite sure that we go down."

"Oh, but we're careful then," said Bassett.

"But when are you *sure*?" smiled Uncle Oscar.

"It's Master Paul, sir," said Bassett, in a secret, religious voice. "It's as if he had it from heaven. Like Daffodil now, for the Lincoln. That was as sure as eggs."

"Did you put anything on Daffodil?" asked Oscar Cresswell.

"Yes, sir. I made my bit."

"And my nephew?"

Bassett was obstinately silent, looking at Paul.

"I made twelve hundred, didn't I, Bassett? I told uncle I was putting three hundred on Daffodil."

"That's right," said Bassett, nodding.

"But where's the money?" asked the uncle.

"I keep it safe locked up, sir. Master Paul, he can have it any minute he likes to ask for it."

"What, fifteen hundred pounds?"

"And twenty! And *forty*, that is, with the twenty he made on the course."

"It's amazing!" said the uncle.

"If Master Paul offers you to be partners, sir, I would, if I were you: if you'll excuse me," said Bassett.

Oscar Cresswell thought about it.

"I'll see the money," he said.

They drove home again, and sure enough, Bassett came round to the garden-house with fifteen hundred pounds in notes. The twenty pounds reserve was left with Joe Glee, in the Turf Commission deposit.

"You see, it's all right, uncle, when I'm sure! Then we go strong, for all we're worth. Don't we, Bassett?"

"We do that, Master Paul."

"And when are you sure?" said the uncle, laughing.

"Oh, well, sometimes I'm *absolutely* sure, like about Daffodil," said the boy; "and sometimes I have an idea; and sometimes I haven't even an idea, have I, Bassett? Then we're careful, because we mostly go down."

"You do, do you! And when you're sure, like about Daffodil, what makes you sure, sonny?"

"Oh, well, I don't know," said the boy uneasily. "I'm sure, you know, uncle; that's all."

"It's as if he had it from heaven, sir," Bassett reiterated.

"I should say so!" said the uncle.

But he became a partner. And when the Leger was coming on, Paul was "sure" about Lively Spark, which was a quite inconsiderable horse. The boy insisted on putting a thousand on the horse, Bassett went for five hundred, and Oscar Cresswell two hundred. Lively Spark came in first, and the betting had been ten to one against him. Paul had made ten thousand.

"You see," he said, "I was absolutely sure of him."

Even Oscar Cresswell had cleared two thousand.

"Look here, son," he said, "this sort of thing makes me nervous."

"It needn't, uncle! Perhaps I shan't be sure again for a long time."

"But what are you going to do with your money?" asked the uncle.

"Of course," said the boy, "I started it for mother. She said she had no luck, because father is unlucky, so I thought if *I* was lucky, it might stop whispering."

"What might stop whispering?"

"Our house! I *hate* our house for whispering."

"What does it whisper?"

"Why—why"—the boy fidgeted—"why, I don't know! But it's always short of money, you know, uncle."

"I know it, son, I know it."

"You know people send mother writs, don't you, uncle?"

"I'm afraid I do," said the uncle.

"And then the house whispers like people laughing at you behind your back. It's awful, that is! I thought if I was lucky—"

"You might stop it," added the uncle.

The boy watched him with big blue eyes, that had an uncanny cold fire in them, and he said never a word.

"Well then!" said the uncle. "What are we doing?"

"I shouldn't like mother to know I was lucky," said the boy.

"Why not, son?"

"She'd stop me."

"I don't think she would."

"Oh!"—and the boy writhed in an odd way—"I *don't* want her to know, uncle."

"All right, son! We'll manage it without her knowing."

They managed it very easily. Paul, at the other's suggestion, handed over five thousand pounds to his uncle, who deposited it with the family lawyer, who was then to inform Paul's mother that a relative had put five thousand pounds into his hands, which sum was to be paid out a thousand pounds at a time, on the mother's birthday, for the next five years.

"So she'll have a birthday present of a thousand pounds for five successive years," said Uncle Oscar. "I hope it won't make it all the harder for her later."

Paul's mother had her birthday in November. The house had been "whispering" worse than ever lately, and even in spite of his luck, Paul could not bear up against it. He was very anxious to see the effect of the birthday letter, telling his mother about the thousand pounds.

When there were no visitors, Paul now took his meals with his parents, as he was beyond the nursery control. His mother went into town nearly every day. She had discovered that she had an odd knack of sketching furs and dress materials, so she worked secretly in the studio of a friend who was the chief "artist" for the leading drapers. She drew the figures of ladies in furs and ladies in silk and sequins for the newspaper advertisements. This young woman artist earned several thousand pounds a year, but Paul's mother only made several hundreds, and she was again dissatisfied. She so wanted to be first in something, and she did not succeed, even in making sketches for drapery advertisements.

She was down to breakfast on the morning of her birthday. Paul watched her face as she read her letters. He knew the lawyer's letter. As his mother read it, her face hardened and became more expressionless. Then a cold, determined look came on her mouth. She hid the letter under the pile of others, and said not a word about it.

"Didn't you have anything nice in the post for your birthday, mother?" said Paul.

"Quite moderately nice," she said, her voice cold and absent.

She went away to town without saying more.

But in the afternoon Uncle Oscar appeared. He said Paul's mother had had a long interview with the lawyer, asking if the whole five thousand could not be advanced at once, as she was in debt.

"What do you think, uncle?" said the boy.

"I leave it to you, son."

"Oh, let her have it, then! We can get some more with the other," said the boy.

"A bird in the hand is worth two in the bush, laddie!" said Uncle Oscar.

"But I'm sure to *know* for the Grand National; or the Lincolnshire; or else the Derby. I'm sure to know for *one* of them," said Paul.

So Uncle Oscar signed the agreement, and Paul's mother touched the whole five thousand. Then something very curious happened. The voices in the house suddenly went mad, like a chorus of frogs on a spring evening. There were certain new furnishings, and Paul had a tutor. He was *really* going to Eton, his father's school, in the following autumn. There were flowers in the winter, and a blossoming of the luxury Paul's mother had been used to. And yet the voices in the house, behind the sprays of mimosa and almond-blossom, and from under the piles of iridescent cushions, simply trilled and screamed in a sort of ecstasy: "There *must* be more money! Oh-h-h! There *must* be more money! Oh, now, now-w! now-w-w—there *must* be more money!—more than ever! More than ever!"

It frightened Paul terribly. He studied away at his Latin and Greek with his tutors. But his intense hours were spent with Bassett. The Grand National had gone by: he had not "known", and had lost a hundred pounds. Summer was at hand. He was in agony for the Lincoln. But even for the Lincoln he didn't "know", and he lost fifty pounds. He became wild-eyed and strange, as if something were going to explode in him.

"Let it alone, son! Don't you bother about it!" urged Uncle Oscar. But it was as if the boy couldn't really hear what his uncle was saying.

"I've got to know for the Derby! I've *got* to know for the Derby!" the child reiterated, his big blue eyes blazing with a sort of madness.

His mother noticed how overwrought he was.

"You'd better go to the seaside. Wouldn't you like to go now to the seaside, instead of waiting? I think you'd better," she said, looking down at him anxiously, her heart curiously heavy because of him.

But the child lifted his uncanny blue eyes.

"I couldn't possibly go before the Derby, mother!" he said. "I couldn't possibly!"

"Why not?" she said, her voice becoming heavy when she was opposed. "Why not? You can still go from the seaside to see the Derby with your Uncle Oscar, if that's what you wish. No need for you to wait here. Besides, I think you care too much about these races. It's a bad sign. My family has been a gambling family, and you won't know till you grow up how much damage it has done. But it has done damage. I shall have to send Bassett away, and ask Uncle Oscar not to talk racing to you, unless you promise to be reasonable about it: go away to the seaside and forget it. You're all nerves!"

"I'll do what you like, mother, so long as you don't send me away till after the Derby," the boy said.

"Send you away from where? Just from this house?"

"Yes," he said, gazing at her.

"Why, you curious child, what makes you care about this house so much, suddenly? I never knew you loved it!"

He gazed at her without speaking. He had a secret within a secret, something he had not divulged, even to Bassett or to his Uncle Oscar.

But his mother, after standing undecided and a little bit sullen for some moments, said:

"Very well, then! Don't go to the seaside till after the Derby, if you don't wish it. But promise me you won't let your nerves go to pieces! Promise you won't think so much about horse-racing and *events*, as you call them!"

"Oh no!" said the boy, casually. "I won't think much about them, mother. You needn't worry. I wouldn't worry, mother, if I were you."

"If you were me and I were you," said his mother, "I wonder what we *should* do!"

"But you know you needn't worry, mother, don't you?" the boy repeated.

"I should be awfully glad to know it," she said wearily.

"Oh, well, you *can*, you know. I mean you *ought* to know you needn't worry!" he insisted.

"Ought I? Then I'll see about it," she said.

Paul's secret of secrets was his wooden horse, that which had no name. Since he was emancipated from a nurse and a nursery governess, he had had his rocking-horse removed to his own bedroom at the top of the house.

"Surely you're too big for a rocking-horse!" his mother had remonstrated.

"Well, you see, mother, till I can have a *real* horse, I like to have *some* sort of animal about," had been his quaint answer.

"Do you feel he keeps you company?" she laughed.

"Oh yes! He's very good, he always keeps me company, when I'm there," said Paul.

So the horse, rather shabby, stood in an arrested prance in the boy's bedroom.

The Derby was drawing near, and the boy grew more and more tense. He hardly heard what was spoken to him, he was very frail, and his eyes were really uncanny. His mother had sudden strange seizures of uneasiness about him. Sometimes, for half an hour, she would feel a sudden anxiety about him that was almost anguish. She wanted to rush to him at once, and know he was safe.

Two nights before the Derby, she was at a big party in town, when one of her rushes of anxiety about her boy, her first-born, gripped her heart till she could hardly speak. She fought with the feeling, might and main, for she believed in commonsense. But it was too strong. She had to leave the dance and go downstairs to telephone to the country. The children's nursery governess was terribly surprised and startled at being rung up in the night.

"Are the children all right, Miss Wilmot?"

"Oh yes, they are quite all right."

"Master Paul? Is he all right?"

"He went to bed as right as a trivet. Shall I run up and look at him?"

"No!" said Paul's mother reluctantly. "No! Don't trouble. It's all right. Don't sit up. We shall be home fairly soon." She did not want her son's privacy intruded upon.

"Very good," said the governess.

It was about one o'clock when Paul's mother and father drove up to their house. All was still. Paul's mother went to her room and slipped off her white fur cloak. She had told her maid not to wait up for her. She heard her husband downstairs, mixing a whisky-and-soda.

And then, because of the strange anxiety at her heart, she stole upstairs to her son's room. Noiselessly she went along the upper corridor. Was there a faint noise? What was it?

She stood, with arrested muscles, outside his door, listening.

There was a strange, heavy, and yet not loud noise. Her heart stood still. It was a soundless noise, yet rushing and powerful. Something huge, in violent, hushed motion. What was it? What in God's Name was it? She ought to know. She felt that she *knew* the noise. She knew what it was.

Yet she could not place it. She couldn't say what it was. And on and on it went, like a madness.

Softly, frozen with anxiety and fear, she turned the door-handle.

The room was dark. Yet in the space near the window, she heard and saw something plunging to and fro. She gazed in fear and amazement. Then suddenly she switched on the light, and saw her son, in his green pyjamas, madly surging on his rocking-horse. The blaze of light suddenly lit him up, as he urged the wooden horse, and lit her up, as she stood, blonde, in her dress of pale green and crystal, in the doorway.

"Paul!" she cried. "Whatever are you doing?"

"It's Malabar!" he screamed, in a powerful, strange voice. "It's Malabar!"

His eyes blazed at her for one strange and senseless second, as he ceased urging his wooden horse. Then he fell with a crash to the ground, and she, all her tormented motherhood flooding upon her, rushed to gather him up.

But he was unconscious, and unconscious he remained, with some brain-fever. He talked and tossed, and his mother sat stonily by his side.

"Malabar! It's Malabar! Bassett, Bassett, I *know*: it's Malabar!"

So the child cried, trying to get up and urge the rocking-horse that gave him his inspiration.

"What does he mean by Malabar?" asked the heart-frozen mother.

"I don't know," said the father, stonily.

"What does he mean by Malabar?" she asked her brother Oscar.

"It's one of the horses running for the Derby," was the answer.

And, in spite of himself, Oscar Cresswell spoke to Bassett, and himself put a thousand on Malabar: at fourteen to one.

The third day of the illness was critical: they were watching for a change. The boy, with his rather long, curly hair, was tossing ceaselessly on the pillow. He neither slept nor regained consciousness, and his eyes were like blue stones. His mother sat, feeling her heart had gone, turned actually into a stone.

In the evening, Oscar Cresswell did not come, but Bassett sent a message, saying could he come up for one moment, just one moment? Paul's mother was very angry at the intrusion, but on second thoughts she agreed. The boy was the same. Perhaps Bassett might bring him to consciousness.

The gardener, a shortish fellow with a little brown moustache and sharp little brown eyes, tiptoed into the room, touched his imaginary cap to Paul's mother, and stole to the bedside, staring with glittering, smallish eyes at the tossing, dying child.

"Master Paul!" he whispered. "Master Paul! Malabar came in first all right, a clean win. I did as you told me. You've made over seventy thousand pounds, you have; you've got over eighty thousand. Malabar came in all right, Master Paul."

"Malabar! Malabar! Did I say Malabar, mother? Did I say Malabar? Do you think I'm lucky, mother? I knew Malabar, didn't I? Over eighty thousand pounds! I call that lucky, don't you, mother? Over eighty thousand pounds! I knew, didn't I know I knew? Malabar came in all right. If I ride my horse till I'm sure, then I tell you, Basset, you can go as high as you like. Did you go for all you were worth, Bassett?"

"I went a thousand on it, Master Paul."

"I never told you, mother, that if I can ride my horse, and *get there*, then I'm absolutely sure—oh, absolutely! Mother, did I ever tell you? I *am* lucky!"

"No, you never did," said the mother.

But the boy died in the night.

And even as he lay dead, his mother heard her brother's voice saying to her: "My God, Hester, you're eighty-odd thousand to the good, and a poor devil of a son to the bad. But, poor devil, poor devil, he's best gone out of a life where he rides his rocking-horse to find a winner."

The Woman Who Rode Away

1

She had thought that this marriage, of all marriages, would be an adventure. Not that the man himself was exactly magical to her. A little, wiry, twisted fellow, twenty years older than herself, with brown eyes and greying hair, who had come to America a scrap of a wastrel, from Holland, years ago, as a tiny boy, and from the gold-mines of the west had been kicked south into Mexico, and now was more or less rich, owning silver-mines in the wilds of the Sierra Madre: it was obvious that the adventure lay in his circumstances, rather than his person. But he was still a little dynamo of energy, in spite of accidents survived, and what he had accomplished he had accomplished alone. One of those human oddments there is no accounting for.

When she actually *saw* what he had accomplished, her heart quailed. Great green-covered, unbroken mountain-hills, and in the midst of the lifeless isolation, the sharp pinkish mounds of the dried mud from the silver-works. Under the nakedness of the works, the walled-in, one-storey adobe house, with its garden inside, and its deep inner veranda with tropical climbers on the sides. And when you looked up from this shut-in flowered patio, you saw the huge pink cone of the silver-mud refuse, and the machinery of the extracting plant against heaven above. No more.

To be sure, the great wooden doors were often open. And then she could stand outside, in the vast open world. And see great, void, tree-clad hills piling behind one another, from nowhere into nowhere. They were green in autumn time. For the rest, pinkish, stark dry, and abstract.

And in his battered Ford car her husband would take her into the dead, thrice-dead little Spanish town forgotten among the mountains. The great, sundried dead church, the dead *por-tales*, the hopeless covered market-place, where, the first time she went, she saw a dead dog lying between the meat stalls and the vegetable array, stretched out as if for ever, nobody troubling to throw it away. Deadness within deadness.

Everybody feebly talking silver, and showing bits of ore. But silver was at a standstill. The great war came and went. Silver was a dead market. Her husband's mines were closed down. But she and he lived on in the adobe house under the works, among the flowers that were never very flowery to her.

She had two children, a boy and a girl. And her eldest, the boy, was nearly ten years old before she aroused from her stupor of subjected amazement. She was now thirty-three, a large, blue-eyed, dazed woman, beginning to grow stout. Her little, wiry, tough, twisted, brown-eyed husband was fifty-three, a man as tough as wire, tenacious as wire, still full of energy, but dimmed by the lapse of silver from the market, and by some curious inaccessibility on his wife's part.

He was a man of principles, and a good husband. In a way, he doted on her. He never quite got over his dazzled admiration of her. But essentially, he was still a bachelor. He had been thrown out on the world, a little bachelor, at the age of ten. When he married he was over forty, and had enough money to marry on. But his capital was all a bachelor's. He was boss of his own works, and marriage was the last and most intimate bit of his own works.

He admired his wife to extinction, he admired her body, all her points. And she was to him always the rather dazzling Californian girl from Berkeley, whom he had first known. Like any sheik, he kept her guarded among those mountains of Chihuahua. He was jealous of her as he was of his silver-mine: and that is saying a lot.

At thirty-three she really was still the girl from Berkeley, in all but physique. Her conscious development had stopped mysteriously with her marriage, completely arrested. Her husband had never become real to her, neither mentally nor physically. In spite of his late sort of passion for her, he never meant anything to her, physically. Only morally he swayed her, downed her, kept her in an invincible slavery.

So the years went by, in the adobe house strung round the sunny patio, with the silver-works overhead. Her husband was never still. When the silver went dead, he ran a ranch lower down, some twenty miles away, and raised pure-bred hogs, splendid creatures. At the same time, he hated pigs. He was a squeamish waif of an idealist, and really hated the physical side of life. He loved work, work, work, and making things. His marriage, his children, were something he was making, part of his business, but with a sentimental income this time.

Gradually her nerves began to go wrong: she must get out. She must get out. So he took her to El Paso for three months. And at least it was the United States.

But he kept his spell over her. The three months ended: back she was, just the same, in her adobe house among those eternal green or pinky-brown hills, void as only the undiscovered is void. She taught her children, she supervised the Mexican boys who were her servants. And sometimes her husband brought visitors, Spaniards or Mexicans or occasionally white men.

He really loved to have white men staying on the place. Yet he had not a moment's peace when they were there. It was as if his wife were some peculiar secret vein of ore in his mines, which no one must be aware of except himself. And she was fascinated by the young gentlemen, mining engineers, who were his guests at times. He, too, was fascinated by a real gentleman. But he was an old-timer miner with a wife, and if a gentleman looked at his wife, he felt as if his mine were being looted, the secrets of it pried out.

It was one of these young gentlemen who put the idea into her mind. They were all standing outside the great wooden doors of the patio, looking at the outer world. The eternal, motionless hills were all green, it was September, after the rains. There was no sign of anything, save the deserted mine, the deserted works, and a bunch of half-deserted miner's dwellings.

"I wonder," said the young man, "what there is behind those great blank hills."

"More hills," said Lederman. "If you go that way, Sonora and the coast. This way is the desert—you came from there—And the other way, hills and mountains."

"Yes, but what *lives* in the hills and mountains? *Surely* there is something wonderful? It looks *so* like nowhere on earth: like being on the moon."

"There's plenty of game, if you want to shoot. And Indians, if you call *them* wonderful."

"Wild ones?"

"Wild enough."

"But friendly?"

"It depends. Some of them are quite wild, and they don't let anybody near. They kill a missionary at sight. And where a missionary can't get, nobody can."

"But what does the government say?"

"They're so far from everywhere, the government leaves 'em alone. And they're wily; if they think there'll be trouble, they send a delegation to Chihuahua and make a formal submission. The government is glad to leave it at that."

"And do they live quite wild, with their own savage customs and religion?"

"Oh, yes. They use nothing but bows and arrows. I've seen them in town, in the Plaza, with funny sort of hats with flowers round them, and a bow in one hand, quite naked except for a sort of shirt, even in cold weather—striding round with their savage's bare legs."

"But don't you suppose it's wonderful, up there in their secret villages?"

"No. What would there be wonderful about it? Savages are savages, and all savages behave more or less alike: rather low-down and dirty, unsanitary, with a few cunning tricks, and struggling to get enough to eat."

"But surely they have old, old religions and mysteries—it *must* be wonderful, surely it must."

"I don't know about mysteries—howling and heathen practices, more or less indecent. No, I see nothing wonderful in that kind of stuff. And I wonder that you should, when you have lived in London or Paris or New York—"

"Ah, *everybody* lives in London or Paris or New York"—said the young man, as if this were an argument.

And his peculiar vague enthusiasm for unknown Indians found a full echo in the woman's heart. She was overcome by a foolish romanticism more unreal than a girl's. She felt it was her destiny to wander into the secret haunts of these timeless, mysterious, marvellous Indians of the mountains.

She kept her secret. The young man was departing, her husband was going with him down to Torreon, on business:—would be away for some days. But before the departure, she made her husband talk about the Indians: about the wandering tribes, resembling the Navajo, who were still wandering free; and the Yaquis of Sonora: and the different groups in the different valleys of Chihuahua State.

There was supposed to be one tribe, the Chilchuis, living in a high valley to the south, who were the sacred tribe of all the Indians. The descendants of Montezuma and of the old Aztec or Totonac kings still lived among them, and the old priests still kept up the ancient religion, and offered human sacrifices—so it was said. Some scientists had been to the Chilchui country, and had come back gaunt and exhausted with hunger and bitter privation, bringing various curious, barbaric objects of worship, but having seen nothing extraordinary in the hungry, stark village of savages.

Though Lederman talked in this off-hand way, it was obvious he felt some of the vulgar excitement at the idea of ancient and mysterious savages.

"How far away are they?" she asked.

"Oh—three days on horseback—past Cuchitee and a little lake there is up there."

Her husband and the young man departed. The woman made her crazy plans. Of late, to break the monotony of her life, she had harassed her husband into letting her go riding with him, occasionally, on horseback. She was never allowed to go out alone. The country truly was not safe, lawless and crude.

But she had her own horse, and she dreamed of being free as she had been as a girl, among the hills of California.

Her daughter, nine years old, was now in a tiny convent in the little half-deserted Spanish mining-town five miles away.

"Manuel," said the woman to her house-servant, "I'm going to ride to the convent to see Margarita, and take her a few things. Perhaps I shall stay the night in the convent. You look after Freddy and see everything is all right till I come back."

"Shall I ride with you on the master's horse, or shall Juan?" asked the servant.

"Neither of you. I shall go alone."

The young man looked her in the eyes, in protest. Absolutely impossible that the woman should ride alone!

"I shall go alone," repeated the large, placid-seeming, fair-complexioned woman, with peculiar overbearing emphasis. And the man silently, unhappily yielded.

"Why are you going alone, mother?" asked her son, as she made up parcels of food.

"Am I *never* to be let alone? Not one moment of my life?" she cried, with sudden explosion of energy. And the child, like the servant, shrank into silence.

She set off without a qualm, riding astride on her strong roan horse, and wearing a riding suit of coarse linen, a riding skirt over her linen breeches, a scarlet neck-tie over her white blouse, and a black felt hat on her head. She had food in her saddle-bags, an army canteen with water, and a large, native blanket tied on behind the saddle. Peering into the distance, she set off from her home. Manuel and the little boy stood in the gateway to watch her go. She did not even turn to wave them farewell.

But when she had ridden about a mile, she left the wild road and took a small trail to the right, that led into another valley, over steep places and past great trees, and through another deserted mining-settlement. It was September, the water was running freely in the little stream that had fed the now-abandoned mine. She got down to drink, and let the horse drink too.

She saw natives coming through the trees, away up the slope. They had seen her, and were watching her closely. She watched in turn. The three people, two women and a youth, were making a wide detour, so as not to come too close to her. She did not care. Mounting, she trotted ahead up the silent valley, beyond the silver-works, beyond any trace of mining. There was still a rough trail, that led over rocks and loose stones into the valley beyond. This trail she had already ridden, with her husband. Beyond that she knew she must go south.

Curiously she was not afraid, although it was a frightening country, the silent, fatal-seeming mountain-slopes, the occasional distant, suspicious, elusive natives among the trees, the great carrion birds occasionally hovering, like great flies, in the distance, over some carrion or some ranch house or some group of huts.

As she climbed, the trees shrank and the trail ran through a thorny scrub, that was trailed over with blue convolvulus and an occasional pink creeper. Then these flowers lapsed. She was nearing the pine-trees.

She was over the crest, and before her another silent, void, green-clad valley. It was past midday. Her horse turned to a little runlet of water, so she got down to eat her midday meal. She sat in silence looking at the motionless unliving valley, and at the sharp-peaked hills, rising higher to rock and pine-trees, southwards. She rested two hours in the heat of the day, while the horse cropped around her.

Curious that she was neither afraid nor lonely. Indeed, the loneliness was like a drink of cold water to one who is very thirsty. And a strange elation sustained her from within.

She travelled on, and camped at night in a valley beside a stream, deep among the bushes. She had seen cattle and had crossed several trails. There must be a ranch not far off. She heard the strange wailing shriek of a mountain-lion, and the answer of dogs. But she sat by her small camp fire in a secret hollow place and was not really afraid. She was buoyed up always by the curious, bubbling elation within her.

It was very cold before dawn. She lay wrapped in her blanket looking at the stars, listening to her horse shivering, and feeling like a woman who has died and passed beyond. She was not sure that she had not heard, during the night, a great crash at the centre of herself, which was the crash of her own death. Or else it was a crash at the centre of the earth, and meant something big and mysterious.

With the first peep of light she got up, numb with cold, and made a fire. She ate hastily, gave her horse some pieces of oil-seed cake, and set off again. She avoided any meeting—and since she met nobody, it was evident that she in turn was avoided. She came at last in sight of the village of Cuchitee, with its black houses with their reddish roofs, a sombre, dreary little cluster below another silent, long-abandoned mine. And beyond, a long, great mountain-side, rising up green and light to the darker, shaggier green of pine trees. And beyond the pine trees stretches of naked rock against the sky, rock slashed already and brindled with white stripes of snow. High up, the new snow had already begun to fall.

And now, as she neared, more or less, her destination, she began to go vague and disheartened. She had passed the little lake among yellowing aspen trees whose white trunks were round and suave like the white round arms of some woman. What a lovely place! In California she would have raved about it. But here she looked and saw that it was lovely, but she didn't care. She was weary and spent with her two nights in the open, and afraid of the coming night. She didn't know where she was going, or what she was going for. Her horse plodded dejectedly on, towards that immense and forbidding mountain-slope, following a stony little trail. And if she had had any will of her own left, she would have turned back, to the village, to be protected and sent home to her husband.

But she had no will of her own. Her horse splashed through a brook, and turned up a valley, under immense yellowing cotton-wood trees. She must have been near nine thousand feet above sea-level, and her head was light with the altitude and with weariness. Beyond the cotton-wood trees she could see, on each side, the steep sides of mountain-slopes hemming her in, sharp-plumaged with overlapping aspen, and, higher up, with sprouting, pointed spruce and pine tree. Her horse went on automatically. In this tight valley, on this slight trail, there was nowhere to go but ahead, climbing.

Suddenly her horse jumped, and three men in dark blankets were on the trail before her.

"*Adios!*" came the greeting, in the full, restrained Indian voice.

"*Adios!*" she replied, in her assured, American woman's voice.

"Where are you going?" came the quiet question, in Spanish.

The men in the dark *sarapes* had come closer, and were looking up at her.

"On ahead," she replied coolly, in her hard, Saxon Spanish.

These were just natives to her: dark-faced, strongly-built men in dark *sarapes* and straw hats. They would have been the same as the men who worked for her husband, except, strangely, for the long black hair that fell over their shoulders. She noted this long black hair with a certain distaste. These must be the wild Indians she had come to see.

"Where do you come from?" the same man asked. It was always the one man who spoke. He was young, with quick, large, bright black eyes that glanced sideways at her. He had a soft black moustache on his dark face, and a sparse tuft of beard, loose hairs on his chin. His long black hair, full of life, hung unrestrained on his shoulders. Dark as he was, he did not look as if he had washed lately.

His two companions were the same, but older men, powerful and silent. One had a thin black line of moustache, but was beardless. The other had the smooth cheeks and the sparse dark hairs marking the lines of his chin with the beard characteristic of the Indians.

"I come from far away," she replied, with half-jocular evasion.

This was received in silence.

"But where do you live?" asked the young man, with that same quiet insistence.

"In the north," she replied airily.

Again there was a moment's silence. The young man conversed quietly, in Indian, with his two companions.

"Where do you want to go, up this way?" he asked suddenly, with challenge and authority, pointing briefly up the trail.

"To the Chilchui Indians," answered the woman laconically.

The young man looked at her. His eyes were quick and black,

and inhuman. He saw, in the full evening light, the faint sub-smile of assurance on her rather large, calm, fresh-complexioned face; the weary, bluish lines under her large blue eyes; and in her eyes, as she looked down at him, a half-childish, half-arrogant confidence in her own female power. But in her eyes also, a curious look of trance.

"*Usted es Señora?* You are a lady?" the Indian asked her.

"Yes, I am a lady," she replied complacently.

"With a family?"

"With a husband and two children, boy and girl," she said.

The Indian turned to his companions and translated, in the low, gurgling speech, like hidden water running. They were evidently at a loss.

"Where is your husband?" asked the young man.

"Who knows?" she replied airily. "He has gone away on business for a week."

The black eyes watched her shrewdly. She, for all her weariness, smiled faintly in the pride of her own adventure and the assurance of her own womanhood, and the spell of the madness that was on her.

"And what do *you* want to do?" the Indian asked her.

"I want to visit the Chilchui Indians—to see their houses and to know their gods," she replied.

The young man turned and translated quickly, and there was a silence almost of consternation. The grave elder men were glancing at her sideways, with strange looks, from under their decorated hats. And they said something to the young man, in deep chest voices.

The latter still hesitated. Then he turned to the woman.

"Good!" he said. "Let us go. But we cannot arrive until tomorrow. We shall have to make a camp to-night."

"Good!" she said. "I can make a camp."

Without more ado, they set off at a good speed up the stony trail. The young Indian ran alongside her horse's head, the other two ran behind. One of them had taken a thick stick, and occasionally he struck her horse a resounding blow on the haunch, to urge him forward. This made the horse jump, and threw her back in the saddle, which, tired as she was, made her angry.

"Don't do that!" she cried, looking round angrily at the fellow. She met his black, large, bright eyes, and for the first time her spirit really quailed. The man's eyes were not human to her, and they did not see her as a beautiful white woman. He looked at her with a black, bright inhuman look, and saw no woman in her at all. As if she were some strange, unaccountable *thing,* incomprehensible to him, but inimical. She sat in her saddle in wonder, feeling once more as if she had died. And again he struck her horse, and jerked her badly in the saddle.

All the passionate anger of the spoilt white woman rose in her. She pulled her horse to a standstill, and turned with blazing eyes to the man at her bridle.

"Tell that fellow not to touch my horse again," she cried. She met the eyes of the young man, and in their bright black inscrutability she saw a fine spark, as in a snake's eye, of derision. He spoke to his companion in the rear, in the low tones of the Indian. The man with the stick listened without looking. Then, giving a strange low cry to the horse, he struck it again on the rear, so that it leaped forward spasmodically up the stony trail, scattering the stones, pitching the weary woman in her seat.

The anger flew like a madness into her eyes, she went white at the gills. Fiercely she reined in her horse. But before she could turn, the young Indian had caught the reins under the horse's throat, jerked them forward, and was trotting ahead rapidly, leading the horse.

The woman was powerless. And along with her supreme anger there came a slight thrill of exultation. She knew she was dead.

The sun was setting, a great yellow light flooded the last of the aspens, flared on the trunks of the pine-trees, the pine-needles bristled and stood out with dark lustre, the rocks glowed with unearthly glamour. And through this effulgence the Indian at her horse's head trotted unweariedly on, his dark blanket swinging, his bare legs glowing with a strange transfigured ruddiness in the powerful light, and his straw hat with its half-absurd decorations of flowers and feathers shining showily above his river of long black hair. At times he would utter a low call to the horse, and then the other Indian, behind, would fetch the beast a whack with the stick.

The wonder-light faded off the mountains, the world began to grow dark, a cold air breathed down. In the sky, half a moon was struggling against the glow in the west. Huge shadows came down from steep rocky slopes. Water was rushing. The woman was conscious only of her fatigue, her unspeakable fatigue, and the cold wind from the heights. She was not aware how moonlight replaced daylight. It happened while she travelled unconscious with weariness.

For some hours they travelled by moonlight. Then suddenly they came to a standstill. The men conversed in low tones for a moment.

"We camp here," said the young man.

She waited for him to help her down. He merely stood holding the horse's bridle. She almost fell from the saddle, so fatigued.

They had chosen a place at the foot of rocks that still gave off a little warmth of the sun. One man cut pine-boughs, another erected little screens of pine-boughs against the rock for shelter, and put boughs of balsam pine for beds. The third made a small fire, to heat *tortillas*. They worked in silence.

The woman drank water. She did not want to eat—only to lie down.

"Where do I sleep?" she asked.

The young man pointed to one of the shelters. She crept in and lay inert. She did not care what happened to her, she was so weary, and so beyond everything. Through the twigs of spruce she could see the three men squatting round the fire on their hams, chewing the *tortillas* they picked from the ashes with their dark fingers, and drinking water from a gourd. They talked in low, muttering tones, with long intervals of silence. Her saddle and saddle-bags lay not far from the fire, unopened, untouched. The men were not interested in her nor her belongings. There they squatted with their hats on their heads, eating, eating mechanically, like animals, the dark *sarape* with its fringe falling to the ground before and behind, the powerful dark legs naked and squatting like an animal's, showing the dirty white shirt and the sort of loin-cloth which was the only other garment, under-

217

neath. And they showed no more sign of interest in her than if she had been a piece of venison they were bringing home from the hunt, and had hung inside a shelter.

After a while they carefully extinguished the fire, and went inside their own shelter. Watching through the screen of boughs, she had a moment's thrill of fear and anxiety, seeing the dark forms cross and pass silently in the moonlight. Would they attack her now?

But no! They were as if oblivious of her. Her horse was hobbled; she could hear it hopping wearily. All was silent, mountain-silent, cold, deathly. She slept and woke and slept in a semi-conscious numbness of cold and fatigue. A long, long night, icy and eternal, and she aware that she had died.

2

Yet when there was a stirring, and a clink of flint and steel, and the form of a man crouching like a dog over a bone, at a red splutter of fire, and she knew it was morning coming, it seemed to her the night had passed too soon.

When the fire was going, she came out of her shelter with one real desire left: for coffee. The men were warming more *tortillas*.

"Can we make coffee?" she asked.

The young man looked at her, and she imagined the same faint spark of derision in his eyes. He shook his head.

"We don't take it," he said. "There is no time."

And the elder men, squatting on their haunches, looked up at her in the terrible paling dawn, and there was not even derision in their eyes. Only that intense, yet remote, inhuman glitter which was terrible to her. They were inaccessible. They could not see her as a woman at all. As if she *were* not a woman. As if, perhaps, her whiteness took away all her womanhood, and left her as some giant, female white ant. That was all they could see in her.

Before the sun was up, she was in the saddle again, and they were climbing steeply, in the icy air. The sun came, and soon she was very hot, exposed to the glare in the bare places. It seemed to her they were climbing to the roof of the world. Beyond against heaven were slashes of snow.

During the course of the morning, they came to a place where the horse could not go farther. They rested for a time with a great slant of living rock in front of them, like the glossy breast of some earth-beast. Across this rock, along a wavering crack, they had to go. It seemed to her that for hours she went in torment, on her hands and knees, from crack to crevice, along the slanting face of this pure rock-mountain. An Indian in front and an Indian behind walked slowly erect, shod with sandals of braided leather. But she in her riding-boots dared not stand erect.

Yet what she wondered, all the time, was why she persisted in clinging and crawling along these mile-long sheets of rock. Why she did not hurl herself down, and have done! The world was below her.

When they emerged at last on a stony slope, she looked back, and saw the third Indian coming carrying her saddle and saddle-bags on his back, the whole hung from a band across his forehead. And he had his hat in his hand, as he stepped slowly, with the slow, soft, heavy tread of the Indian, unwavering in the chinks of rock, as if along a scratch in the mountain's iron shield.

The stony slope led downwards. The Indians seemed to grow excited. One ran ahead at a slow trot, disappearing round the curve of stones. And the track curved round and down, till at last in the full blaze of the mid-morning sun, they could see a valley below them, between walls of rock, as in a great wide chasm let in the mountains. A green valley, with a river, and trees, and clusters of low flat sparkling houses. It was all tiny and perfect, three thousand feet below. Even the flat bridge over the stream, and the square with the houses around it, the bigger buildings piled up at opposite ends of the square, the tall cotton-wood trees, the pastures and stretches of yellow-sere maize, the patches of brown sheep or goats in the distance, on the slopes, the railed enclosures by the stream-side. There it was, all small and perfect, looking magical, as any place will look magical, seen from the mountains above. The unusual thing was that the low houses glittered white, whitewashed, looking like crystals of salt, or silver. This frightened her.

They began the long, winding descent at the head of the *barranca*, following the stream that rushed and fell. At first it was all rocks: then the pine-trees began, and soon, the silver-limbed aspens. The flowers of autumn, big pink daisy-like flowers, and white ones, and many yellow flowers, were in profusion. But she had to sit down and rest, she was so weary. And she saw the bright flowers shadowily, as pale shadows hovering, as one who is dead must see them.

At length came grass and pasture-slopes between mingled aspen and pine-trees. A shepherd, naked in the sun save for his hat and his cotton loin-cloth, was driving his brown sheep away. In a grove of trees they sat and waited, she and the young Indian. The one with the saddle had also gone forward.

They heard a sound of someone coming. It was three men, in fine *sarapes* of red and orange and yellow and black, and with brilliant feather headdresses. The oldest had his grey hair braided with fur, and his red and orange-yellow *sarape* was covered with curious black markings, like a leopard-skin. The other two were not grey-haired, but they were elders too. Their blankets were in stripes, and their headdresses not so elaborate.

The young Indian addressed the elders in a few quiet words. They listened without answering or looking at him or at the woman, keeping their faces averted and their eyes turned to the ground, only listening. And at length they turned and looked at the woman.

The old chief, or medicine-man, whatever he was, had a deeply wrinkled and lined face of dark bronze, with a few sparse grey hairs round the mouth. Two long braids of grey hair, braided with fur and coloured feathers, hung on his shoulders. And yet, it was only his eyes that mattered. They were black and of extraordinary piercing strength, without a qualm of misgiving in their demonish, dauntless power. He looked into the eyes of the white woman with a long, piercing look, seeking she knew not what. She summoned all her strength to meet his eyes and keep up her guard. But it was no good. He was not looking at her as one human being looks at another. He never even perceived her resistance or her challenge, but looked past them both, into she knew not what.

She could see it was hopeless to expect any human communication with this old being.

He turned and said a few words to the young Indian.

"He asks what do you seek here?" said the young man in Spanish.

"I? Nothing! I only came to see what it was like."

This was again translated, and the old man turned his eyes on her once more. Then he spoke again, in his low muttering tone, to the young Indian.

"He says, why does she leave her house with the white men? Does she want to bring the white man's God to the Chilchui?"

"No," she replied, foolhardy. "I came away from the white man's God myself. I came to look for the God of Chilchui."

Profound silence followed, when this was translated. Then the old man spoke again, in a small voice almost of weariness.

"Does the white woman seek the gods of the Chilchui because she is weary of her own God?" came the question.

"Yes, she does. She is tired of the white man's God," she replied, thinking that was what they wanted her to say. She would like to serve the gods of the Chilchui.

She was aware of an extraordinary thrill of triumph and exultance passing through the Indians, in the tense silence that followed when this was translated. Then they all looked at her with piercing black eyes, in which a steely covetous intent glittered incomprehensible. She was the more puzzled, as there was nothing sensual or sexual in the look. It had a terrible glittering purity that was beyond her. She was afraid, she would have been paralysed with fear, had not something died within her, leaving her with a cold, watchful wonder only.

The elders talked a little while, then the two went away, leaving her with the young man and the oldest chief. The old man now looked at her with a certain solicitude.

"He says are you tired?" asked the young man.

"Very tired," she said.

"The men will bring you a carriage," said the young Indian.

The carriage, when it came, proved to be a litter consisting of a sort of hammock of dark woollen frieze, slung on to a pole which was borne on the shoulders of two long-haired Indians. The woollen hammock was spread on the ground, she sat down on it, and the two men raised the pole to their shoulders. Swinging rather as if she were in a sack, she was carried out of the grove of trees, following the old chief, whose leopard-spotted blanket moved curiously in the sunlight.

They had emerged in the valley-head. Just in front were the maize fields, with ripe ears of maize. The corn was not very tall, in this high altitude. The well-worn path went between it, and all she could see was the erect form of the old chief, in the flame and black *sarape*, stepping soft and heavy and swift, his head forward, looking to neither to right nor left. Her bearers followed, stepping rhythmically, the long blue-black hair glistening like a river down the naked shoulders of the man in front.

They passed the maize, and came to a big wall or earthwork made of earth and adobe bricks. The wooden doors were open. Passing on, they were in a network of small gardens, full of flowers and herbs and fruit trees, each garden watered by a tiny ditch of running water. Among each cluster of trees and flowers was a small, glittering white house, windowless, and with closed door. The place was a network of little paths, small streams, and little bridges among square, flowering gardens.

Following the broadest path—a soft narrow track between leaves and grass, a path worn smooth by centuries of human feet, no hoof of horse nor any wheel to disfigure it—they came to the little river of swift bright water, and crossed on a log bridge. Everything was silent—there was no human being anywhere. The road went on under magnificent cotton-wood trees. It emerged suddenly outside the central plaza or square of the village.

This was a long oblong of low white houses with flat roofs, and two bigger buildings, having as it were little square huts piled on top of bigger long huts, stood at either end of the oblong, facing each other rather askew. Every little house was a

dazzling white, save for the great round beam-ends which pro-
jected under the flat eaves, and for the flat roofs. Round each of
the bigger buildings, on the outside of the square, was a stock-
yard fence, inside which was garden with trees and flowers, and
various small houses.

Not a soul was in sight. They passed silently between the
houses into the central square. This was quite bare and arid, the
earth trodden smooth by endless generations of passing feet,
passing across from door to door. All the doors of the windowless houses gave on to this blank square, but all the doors were
closed. The firewood lay near the threshold, a clay oven was still
smoking, but there was no sign of moving life.

The old man walked straight across the square to the big
house at the end, where the two upper storeys, as in a house of
toy bricks, stood each one smaller than the lower one. A stone
staircase, outside, led up to the roof of the first storey.

At the foot of this staircase the litter-bearers stood still, and
lowered the woman to the ground.

"You will come up," said the young Indian who spoke Spanish.

She mounted the stone stairs to the earthen roof of the first
house, which formed a platform round the wall of the second
storey. She followed around this platform to the back of the big
house. There they descended again, into the garden at the rear.

So far they had seen no one. But now two men appeared,
bare-headed, with long braided hair, and wearing a sort of white
shirt gathered into a loin-cloth. These went along with the three
newcomers, across the garden where red flowers and yellow
flowers were blooming, to a long, low white house. There they
entered without knocking.

It was dark inside. There was a low murmur of men's voices. Several men were present, their white shirts showing in the
gloom, their dark faces invisible. They were sitting on a great log
of smooth old wood, that lay along the far wall. And save for this
log, the room seemed empty. But no, in the dark at one end was a
couch, a sort of bed, and someone lying there, covered with furs.

The old Indian in the spotted *sarape*, who had accompanied
the woman, now took off his hat and his blanket and his sandals.

Laying them aside, he approached the couch, and spoke in a low voice. For some moments there was no answer. Then an old man with the snow-white hair hanging round his darkly-visible face, roused himself like a vision, and leaned on one elbow, looking vaguely at the company, in tense silence.

The grey-haired Indian spoke again, and then the young Indian, taking the woman's hand, led her forward. In her linen riding habit, and black boots and hat, and her pathetic bit of a red tie, she stood there beside the fur-covered bed of the old, old man, who sat reared up, leaning on one elbow, remote as a ghost, his white hair streaming in disorder, his face almost black, yet with a far-off intentness, not of this world, leaning forward to look at her.

His face was so old, it was like dark glass, and the few curling hairs that sprang white from his lips and chin were quite incredible. The long white locks fell unbraided and disorderly on either side of the glassy dark face. And under a faint powder of white eyebrows, the black eyes of the old chief looked at her as if from the far, far dead, seeing something that was never to be seen.

At last he spoke a few deep, hollow words, as if to the dark air.

"He says, do you bring your heart to the god of the Chilchui?" translated the young Indian.

"Tell him yes," she said, automatically.

There was a pause. The old Indian spoke again, as if to the air. One of the men present went out. There was a silence as if of eternity, in the dim room that was lighted only through the open door.

The woman looked round. Four old men with grey hair sat on the log by the wall facing the door. Two other men, powerful and impassive, stood near the door. They all had long hair, and wore white shirts gathered into a loin-cloth. Their powerful legs were naked and dark. There was a silence like eternity.

At length the man returned, with white and dark clothing on his arm. The young Indian took them, and holding them in front of the woman, said:

"You must take off your clothes, and put these on."

"If all you men will go out," she said.

"No one will hurt you," he said quietly.

"Not while you men are here," she said.

He looked at the two men by the door. They came quickly forward, and suddenly gripped her arms as she stood, without hurting her, but with great power. Then two of the old men came, and with curious skill slit her boots down with keen knives, and drew them off, and slit her clothing so that it came away from her. In a few moments she stood there white and uncovered. The old man on the bed spoke, and they turned her round for him to see. He spoke again, and the young Indian deftly took the pins and comb from her fair hair, so that it fell over her shoulders in a bunchy tangle.

Then the old man spoke again. The Indian led her to the bedside. The white-haired, glassy-dark old man moistened his finger-tips at his mouth, and most delicately touched her on the breasts and on the body, then on the back. And she winced strangely each time, as the fingertips drew along her skin, as if Death itself were touching her.

And she wondered, almost sadly, why she did not feel shamed in her nakedness. She only felt sad and lost. Because nobody felt ashamed. The elder men were all dark and tense with some other deep, gloomy, incomprehensible emotion, which suspended all her agitation, while the young Indian had a strange look of ecstasy on his face. And she, she was only utterly strange and beyond herself, as if her body were not her own.

They gave her the new clothing: a long white cotton shift, that came to her knees: then a tunic of thick blue woollen stuff, embroidered with scarlet and green flowers. It was fastened over one shoulder only, and belted with a braid sash of scarlet and black wool.

When she was thus dressed, they took her away, barefoot, to a little house in the stockaded garden. The young Indian told her she might have what she wanted. She asked for water to wash herself. He brought it in a jar, together with a long wooden bowl. Then he fastened the gate-door of her house, and left her a prisoner. She could see through the bars of the gate-door of her house, the red flowers of the garden, and a humming bird. Then from the roof of the big house she heard the long, heavy sound of a drum, unearthly to her in its summons, and an uplifted voice calling from the house-top in a strange language, with a far-away emotionless intonation, delivering some speech or message. And she listened as if from the dead.

But she was very tired. She lay down on a couch of skins, pulling over her the blanket of dark wool, and she slept, giving up everything.

When she woke it was late afternoon, and the young Indian was entering with a basket-tray containing food, *tortillas* and corn-mush with bits of meat, probably mutton, and a drink made of honey, and some fresh plums. He brought her also a long garland of red and yellow flowers with knots of blue buds at the end. He sprinkled the garland with water from a jar, then offered it to her, with a smile. He seemed very gentle and thoughtful, and on his face and in his dark eyes was a curious look of triumph and ecstasy, that frightened her a little. The glitter had gone from the black eyes, with their curving dark lashes, and he would look at her with this strange soft glow of ecstasy that was not quite human, and terribly impersonal, and which made her uneasy.

"Is there anything you want?" he said, in his low, slow, melodious voice, that always seemed withheld, as if he were speaking aside to somebody else, or as if he did not want to let the sound come out to her.

"Am I going to be kept a prisoner here?" she asked.

"No, you can walk in the garden to-morrow," he said softly. Always this curious solicitude.

"Do you like that drink?" he said, offering her a little earthenware cup. "It is very refreshing."

She sipped the liquor curiously. It was made with herbs and sweetened with honey, and had a strange, lingering flavour. The young man watched her with gratification.

"It has a peculiar taste," she said.

"It is very refreshing," he replied, his black eyes resting on her always with that look of gratified ecstasy. Then he went away.

And presently she began to be sick, and to vomit violently, as if she had no control over herself.

Afterwards she felt a great soothing languor steal over her, her limbs felt strong and loose and full of languor, and she lay on her couch listening to the sounds of the village, watching the yellowing sky, smelling the scent of burning cedar-wood, or pine-wood. So distinctly she heard the yapping of tiny dogs, the shuffle of far-off feet, the murmur of voices, so keenly she detected the smell of smoke, and flowers, and evening falling, so vividly she saw the one bright star infinitely remote, stirring above the sunset, that she felt as if all her senses were diffused on the air, that she could distinguish the sound of evening flowers unfolding, and the actual crystal sound of the heavens, as the vast belts of the world-atmosphere slid past one another, and as if the moisture ascending and the moisture descending in the air resounded like some harp in the cosmos.

She was a prisoner in her house and in the stockaded garden, but she scarcely minded. And it was days before she realised that she never saw another woman. Only the men, the elderly men of the big house, that she imagined must be some sort of temple, and the men priests of some sort. For they always had the same colours, red, orange, yellow, and black, and the same grave, abstracted demeanour.

Sometimes an old man would come and sit in her room with her, in absolute silence. None spoke any language but Indian, save the one younger man. The older men would smile at her, and sit with her for an hour at a time, sometimes smiling at her when she spoke in Spanish, but never answering save with this slow, benevolent-seeming smile. And they gave off a feeling of almost fatherly solicitude. Yet their dark eyes, brooding over her, had something away in their depths that was awesomely ferocious and relentless. They would cover it with a smile, at once, if they felt her looking. But she had seen it.

Always they treated her with this curious impersonal solicitude, this utterly impersonal gentleness, as an old man treats a child. But underneath it she felt there was something else, something terrible. When her old visitor had gone away, in his silent, insidious, fatherly fashion, a shock of fear would come over her; though of what she knew not.

The young Indian would sit and talk with her freely, as if with great candour. But with him, too, she felt that everything real was unsaid. Perhaps it was unspeakable. His big dark eyes would rest on her almost cherishingly, touched with ecstasy, and his beautiful, slow, languorous voice would trail out its simple, ungrammatical Spanish. He told her he was the grandson of the old, old man, son of the man in the spotted *sarape*: and they were caciques, kings from the old, old days, before even the Spaniards came. But he himself had been in Mexico City, and also in the United States. He had worked as a labourer, building the roads in Los Angeles. He had travelled as far as Chicago.

"Don't you speak English, then?" she asked.

His eyes rested on her with a curious look of duplicity and conflict, and he mutely shook his head.

"What did you do with your long hair, when you were in the United States?" she asked. "Did you cut it off?"

Again, with the look of torment in his eyes, he shook his head.

"No," he said, in a low, subdued voice, "I wore a hat, and a handkerchief tied round my head."

And he relapsed into silence, as if of tormented memories.

"Are you the only man of your people who has been to the United States?" she asked him.

"Yes. I am the only one who has been away from here for a long time. The others come back soon, in one week. They don't stay away. The old men don't let them."

"And why did you go?"

"The old men want me to go—because I shall be the Cacique—"

He talked always with the same naïveté, an almost childish candour. But she felt that this was perhaps just the effect of his Spanish. Or perhaps speech altogether was unreal to him. Anyhow, she felt that all the real things were kept back.

He came and sat with her a good deal—sometimes more than she wished—as if he wanted to be near her. She asked him if he was married. He said he was—with two children.

"I should like to see your children," she said.

But he answered only with that smile, a sweet, almost ecstatic smile above which the dark eyes hardly changed from their enigmatic abstraction.

It was curious, he would sit with her by the hour, without even making her self-conscious, or sex-conscious. He seemed to have no sex, as he sat there so still and gentle and apparently submissive, with his head bent a little forward, and the river of glistening black hair streaming maidenly over his shoulders.

Yet when she looked again, she saw his shoulders broad and powerful, his eyebrows black and level, the short, curved, obstinate black lashes over his lowered eyes, the small, fur-like line of moustache above his blackish, heavy lips, and the strong chin, and she knew that in some other mysterious way he was darkly and powerfully male. And he, feeling her watching him, would glance up at her swiftly with a dark, lurking look in his eyes, which immediately he veiled with that half-sad smile.

The days and the weeks went by, in a vague kind of contentment. She was uneasy sometimes, feeling she had lost the power over herself. She was not in her own power, she was under the spell of some other control. And at times she had moments of terror and horror. But then these Indians would come and sit with her, casting their insidious spell over her by their very silent presence, their silent, sexless, powerful physical presence. As they sat they seemed to take her will away, leaving her will-less and victim to her own indifference. And the young man would bring her sweetened drink, often the same emetic drink, but sometimes other kinds. And after drinking, the languor filled her heavy limbs, her senses seemed to float in the air, listening, hearing. They had brought her a little female dog, which she called Flora. And once, in the trance of her senses, she felt she *heard* the little dog conceive, in her tiny womb, and begin to be complex, with young. And another day she could hear the vast sound of the earth going round, like some immense arrow-string booming.

But as the days grew shorter and colder, when she was cold, she would get a sudden revival of her will, and a desire to go out, to go away. And she insisted to the young man, she wanted to go out.

So one day, they let her climb to the topmost roof of the big house where she was, and look down the square. It was the day of the big dance, but not everybody was dancing. Women with babies in their arms stood in their doorways, watching. Opposite, at the other end of the square, there was a throng before the other big house, and a small, brilliant group on the terrace-roof of the first storey, in front of wide open doors of the upper storey. Through these wide open doors she could see fire glinting in darkness and priests in headdresses of black and yellow and scarlet feathers, wearing robe-like blankets of black and red and yellow, with long green fringes, were moving about. A big drum was beating slowly and regularly, in the dense, Indian silence. The crowd below waited—

Then a drum started on a high beat, and there came the deep, powerful burst of men singing a heavy, savage music, like a wind roaring in some timeless forest, many mature men singing in one breath, like the wind; and long lines of dancers walked out from under the big house. Men with naked, golden-bronze bodies and streaming black hair, tufts of red and yellow feathers on their arms, and kilts of white frieze with a bar of heavy red and black and green embroidery round their waists, bending slightly forward and stamping the earth in their absorbed, monotonous stamp of the dance, a fox-fur, hung by the nose from their belt behind, swaying with the sumptuous swaying of a beautiful fox-fur, the tip of the tail writhing above the dancer's heels. And after each man, a woman with a strange elaborate headdress of feathers and seashells, and wearing a short black tunic, moving erect, holding up tufts of feathers in each hand, swaying her wrists rhythmically and subtly beating the earth with her bare feet.

So, the long line of the dance unfurling from the big house opposite. And from the big house beneath her, strange scent of incense, strange tense silence, then the answering burst of inhuman male singing, and the long line of the dance unfurling.

It went on all day, the insistence of the drum, the cavernous, roaring, storm-like sound of male singing, the incessant swinging of the fox-skins behind the powerful, gold-bronze, stamping legs of the men, the autumn sun from a perfect blue heaven pouring on the rivers of black hair, men's and women's, the valley all still, the walls of rock beyond, the awful huge bulking of the mountain against the pure sky, its snow seething with sheer whiteness.

For hours and hours she watched, spell-bound, and as if drugged. And in all the terrible persistence of the drumming and the primeval, rushing deep singing, and the endless stamping of the dance of fox-tailed men, the tread of heavy, bird-erect women in their black tunics, she seemed at last to feel her own death; her own obliteration. As if she were to be obliterated from the field of life again. In the strange towering symbols on the heads of the changeless, absorbed women she seemed to read once more the *Mene Mene Tekel Upharsin*. Her kind of womanhood, intensely personal and individual, was to be obliterated again, and the great primeval symbols were to tower once more over the fallen individual independence of woman. The sharpness and the quivering nervous consciousness of the highly-bred white woman was to be destroyed again, womanhood was to be cast once more into the great stream of impersonal sex and impersonal passion. Strangely, as if clairvoyant, she saw the immense sacrifice prepared. And she went back to her little house in a trance of agony.

After this, there was always a certain agony when she heard the drums at evening, and the strange uplifted savage sound of men singing round the drum, like wild creatures howling to the invisible gods of the moon and the vanished sun. Something of the chuckling, sobbing-cry of the coyote, something of the exultant bark of the fox, the far-off wild melancholy exultance of the howling wolf, the torment of the puma's scream, and the insistence of the ancient fierce human male, with his lapses of tenderness and his abiding ferocity.

Sometimes she would climb the high roof after nightfall, and listen to the dim cluster of young men round the drum on the bridge just beyond the square, singing by the hour. Sometimes there would be a fire, and in the fire-glow, men in their white shirts or naked save for a loin-cloth, would be dancing and stamping like spectres, hour after hour in the dark cold air, within the fire-glow, forever dancing and stamping like turkeys, or dropping squatting by the fire to rest, throwing their blankets round them.

"Why do you all have the same colours?" she asked the young Indian. "Why do you all have red and yellow and black, over your white shirts? And the women have black tunics?"

He looked into her eyes, curiously, and the faint, evasive smile came on to his face. Behind the smile lay a soft, strange malignancy.

"Because our men are the fire and the daytime, and our women are the spaces between the stars at night," he said.

"Aren't the women even stars?" she said.

"No. We say they are the spaces between the stars, that keep the stars apart."

He looked at her oddly, and again the touch of derision came into his eyes.

"White people," he said, "they know nothing. They are like children, always with toys. We know the sun, and we know the moon. And we say, when a white woman sacrifice herself to our gods, then our gods will begin to make the world again, and the white man's gods will fall to pieces."

"How sacrifice herself?" she asked quickly.

And he, as quickly covered, covered himself with a subtle smile.

"She sacrifice her own gods and come to our gods, I mean that," he said, soothingly.

But she was not reassured. An icy pang of fear and certainty was at her heart.

"The sun he is alive at one end of the sky," he continued, "and the moon lives at the other end. And the man all the time have to keep the sun happy in his side of the sky, and the woman have to keep the moon quiet at her side of the sky. All the time she have to work at this. And the sun can't ever go into the house of the moon, and the moon can't ever go into the house of the sun, in the sky. So the woman, she asks the moon to come into her cave, inside her. And the man, he draws the sun down till he has the power of the sun. All the time he do this. Then when the man gets a woman, the sun goes into the cave of the moon, and that is how everything in the world starts."

She listened, watching him closely, as one enemy watches another who is speaking with double meaning.

"Then," she said, "why aren't you Indians masters of the white men?"

"Because," he said, "the Indian got weak, and lost his power with the sun, so the white men stole the sun. But they can't keep him—they don't know how. They got him, but they don't know what to do with him, like a boy who catch a big grizzly bear, and can't kill him, and can't run away from him. The grizzly bear eats the boy that catch him, when he want to run away from him. White men don't know what they are doing with the sun, and white women don't know what they do with the moon. The moon she got angry with white women, like a puma when someone kills her little ones. The moon, she bites white women—here inside," and he pressed his side. "The moon, she is angry in a white woman's cave. The Indian, can see it—And soon," he added, "the Indian women get the moon back and keep her quiet in their house. And the Indian men get the sun, and the power over all the world. White men don't know what the sun is. They never know."

He subsided into a curious exultant silence.

"But," she faltered, "why do you hate us so? Why do you hate me?"

He looked up suddenly with a light on his face, and a startling flame of a smile.

"No, we don't hate," he said softly, looking with a curious glitter into her face.

"You do," she said, forlorn and hopeless.

And after a moment's silence, he rose and went away.

3

Winter had now come, in the high valley, with snow that melted in the day's sun, and nights that were bitter cold. She lived on, in a kind of daze, feeling her power ebbing more and more away from her, as if her will were leaving her. She felt always in the same relaxed, confused, victimised state, unless the sweetened herb drink would numb her mind altogether, and release her senses into a sort of heightened, mystic acuteness and a feeling as if she were diffusing out deliciously into the harmony of things. This at length became the only state of consciousness she really recognised: this exquisite sense of bleeding out into the higher beauty and harmony of things. Then she could actually hear the great stars in heaven, which she saw through her door, speaking from their motion and brightness, saying things perfectly to the cosmos, as they trod in perfect ripples, like bells on the floor of heaven, passing one another and grouping in the timeless dance, with the spaces of dark between. And she could hear the snow on a cold, cloudy day twittering and faintly whistling in the sky, like birds that flock and fly away in autumn, suddenly calling farewell to the invisible moon, and slipping out of the plains of the air, releasing peaceful warmth. She herself would call to the arrested snow to fall from the upper air. She would call to the unseen moon to cease to be angry, to make peace again with the unseen sun like a woman who ceases to be angry in her house. And she would smell the sweetness of the moon relaxing to the sun in the wintry heaven, when the snow fell in a faint, cold-perfumed relaxation, as the peace of the sun mingled again in a sort of unison with the peace of the moon.

She was aware too of the sort of shadow that was on the Indians of the valley, a deep, stoical disconsolation, almost religious in its depth.

"We have lost our power over the sun, and we are trying to get him back. But he is wild with us, and shy like a horse that has got away. We have to go through a lot." So the young Indian said to her, looking into her eyes with a strained meaning. And she, as if bewitched, replied:

"I hope you will get him back."

The smile of triumph flew over his face.

"Do you hope it?" he said.

"I do," she answered fatally.

"Then all right," he said. "We shall get him."

And he went away in exultance.

She felt she was drifting on some consummation, which she had no will to avoid, yet which seemed heavy and finally terrible to her.

It must have been almost December, for the days were short, when she was taken again before the aged man, and stripped of her clothing, and touched with the old finger-tips.

The aged cacique looked her in the eyes, with his eyes of lonely, far-off, black intentness, and murmured something to her.

"He wants you to make the sign of peace," the young man translated, showing her the gesture. "Peace and farewell to him."

She was fascinated by the black, glass-like, intent eyes of the old cacique, that watched her without blinking, like a basilisk's, overpowering her. In their depths also she saw a certain fatherly compassion, and pleading. She put her hand before her face, in the required manner, making the sign of peace and farewell. He made the sign of peace back again to her, then sank among his furs. She thought he was going to die, and that he knew it.

There followed a day of ceremonial, when she was brought out before all the people, in a blue blanket with white fringe, and holding blue feathers in her hands. Before an altar of one house, she was perfumed with incense and sprinkled with ash. Before the altar of the opposite house she was fumigated again with incense by the gorgeous, terrifying priests in yellow and scarlet and black, their faces painted with scarlet paint. And then they threw water on her. Meanwhile she was faintly aware of the fire on the altar, the heavy, heavy sound of a drum, the heavy sound of men beginning powerfully, deeply, savagely to sing, the swaying of the crowd of faces in the plaza below, and the formation for a sacred dance.

But at this time her commonplace consciousness was numb, she was aware of her immediate surroundings as shadows, almost immaterial. With refined and heightened senses she could hear the sound of the earth winging on its journey, like a shot arrow, the ripple-rustling of the air, and the boom of the great arrow-string. And it seemed to her there were two great influences in the upper air, one golden towards the sun, and one invisible silver; the first travelling like rain ascending to the gold presence sunwards, the second like rain silverily descending the ladders of space towards the hovering, lurking clouds over the snowy mountain-top. Then between them, another presence, waiting to shake himself free of moisture, of heavy white snow that had mysteriously collected about him. And in summer, like a scorched eagle, he would wait to shake himself clear of the weight of heavy sunbeams. And he was coloured like fire. And he was always shaking himself clear, of snow or of heavy heat, like an eagle rustling.

Then there was a still stranger presence, standing watching from the blue distance, always watching. Sometimes running in upon the wind, or shimmering in the heat-waves. The blue wind itself, rushing as it were out of the holes in the earth into the sky, rushing out of the sky down upon the earth. The blue wind, the go-between, the invisible ghost that belonged to two worlds, that played upon the ascending and the descending chords of the rains.

More and more her ordinary personal consciousness had left her, she had gone into that other state of passional cosmic consciousness, like one who is drugged. The Indians, with their heavily religious natures, had made her succumb to their vision.

Only one personal question she asked the young Indian:

"Why am I the only one that wears blue?"

"It is the colour of the wind. It is the colour of what goes away and is never coming back, but which is always here, waiting like death among us. It is the colour of the dead. And it is the colour that stands away off, looking at us from the distance, that cannot come near to us. When we go near, it goes farther. It can't be near. We are all brown and yellow and black hair, and white teeth and red blood. We are the ones that are here. You with blue eyes, you are the messengers from the far-away, you cannot stay, and now it is time for you to go back."

"Where to?" she asked.

"To the way-off things like the sun and the blue mother of rain, and tell them that we are the people on the world again, and we can bring the sun to the moon again, like a red horse to a blue mare; we are the people. The white women have driven back the moon in the sky, won't let her come to the sun. So the sun is angry. And the Indian must give the moon to the sun."

"How?" she said.

"The white woman got to die and go like a wind to the sun, tell him the Indians will open the gate to him. And the Indian women will open the gate to the moon. The white women don't let the moon come down out of the blue coral. The moon used to come down among the Indian women, like a white goat among the flowers. And the sun want to come down to the Indian men, like an eagle to the pine-trees. The sun, he is shut out behind the white man, and the moon she is shut out behind the white woman, and they can't get away. They are angry, everything in the world gets angrier. The Indian says, he will give the white woman to the sun, so the sun will leap over the white man and come to the Indian again. And the moon will be surprised, she will see the gate open, and she not know which way to go. But the Indian woman will call to the moon, *Come! Come! Come back into my grasslands. The wicked white woman can't harm you any more.* Then the sun will look over the heads of the white men, and see the moon in the pastures of our women, with the Red Men standing around like pine trees. Then he will leap over the heads of the white men, and come running past to the Indians through the spruce trees. And we, who are red and black and yellow, we who stay, we shall have the sun on our right hand and the moon on our left. So we can bring the rain down out of the blue meadows, and up out of the black; and we can call the wind that tells the corn to grow, when we ask him, and we shall make the clouds to break, and the sheep to have twin lambs. And we shall be full of power, like a spring day. But the white people will be a hard winter, without snow—"

"But," said the white woman, "I don't shut out the moon—how can I?"

"Yes," he said, "you shut the gate, and then laugh, think you have it all your own way."

She could never quite understand the way he looked at her. He was always so curiously gentle, and his smile was so soft. Yet there was such glitter in his eyes, and an unrelenting sort of hate came out of his words, a strange, profound, impersonal hate. Personally he liked her, she was sure. He was gentle with her, attracted by her in some strange, soft, passionless way. But impersonally he hated her with a mystic hatred. He would smile at her, winningly. Yet if, the next moment, she glanced round at him unawares, she would catch that gleam of pure after-hate in his eyes.

"Have I got to die and be given to the sun?" she asked.

"Sometime," he said, laughing evasively. "Sometime we all die."

They were gentle with her, and very considerate with her. Strange men, the old priests and the young cacique alike, they watched over her and cared for her like women. In their soft, insidious understanding, there was something womanly. Yet their eyes, with that strange glitter, and their dark, shut mouths that would open to the broad jaw, the small, strong, white teeth, had something very primitively male and cruel.

One wintry day, when snow was falling, they took her to a great dark chamber in the big house. The fire was burning in a corner on a high raised dais under a sort of hood or canopy of adobe-work. She saw in the fire-glow, the glowing bodies of the almost naked priests, and strange symbols on the roof and walls of the chamber. There was no door or window in the chamber, they had descended by a ladder from the roof. And the fire of pinewood danced continually, showing walls painted with strange devices, which she could not understand, and a ceiling of poles making a curious pattern of black and red and yellow, and alcoves or niches in which were curious objects she could not discern.

The older priests were going through some ceremony near the fire, in silence, intense Indian silence. She was seated on a low projection of the wall, opposite the fire, two men seated beside her. Presently they gave her a drink from a cup, which she took gladly, because of the semi-trance it would induce.

In the darkness and in the silence she was accurately aware of everything that happened to her: how they took off her clothes, and, standing her before a great, weird device on the wall, coloured blue and white and black, washed her all over with water and the amole infusion; washed even her hair, softly, carefully, and dried it on white cloths, till it was soft and glistening. Then they laid her on a couch under another great indecipherable image of red and black and yellow, and now rubbed all her body with sweet-scented oil, and massaged all her limbs, and her back, and her sides, with a long, strange, hypnotic massage. Their dark hands were incredibly powerful, yet soft with a watery softness she could not understand. And the dark faces, leaning near her white body, she saw were darkened with red pigment, with lines of yellow round the cheeks. And the dark eyes glittered absorbed, as the hands worked upon the soft white body of the woman.

They were so impersonal, absorbed in something that was beyond her. They never saw her as a personal woman: she could tell that. She was some mystic object to them, some vehicle of passions too remote for her to grasp. Herself in a state of trance, she watched their faces bending over her, dark, strangely glistening with the transparent red paint, and lined with bars of yellow. And in this weird, luminous-dark mask of living face, the eyes were fixed with an unchanging steadfast gleam, and the purplish-pigmented lips were closed in a full, sinister, sad grimness. The immense fundamental sadness, the grimness of ultimate decision, the fixity of revenge, and the nascent exultance of those that are going to triumph—these things she could read in their faces, as she lay and was rubbed into a misty glow, by their uncanny dark hands. Her limbs, her flesh, her very bones at last seemed to be diffusing into a roseate sort of mist, in which her consciousness hovered like some sun-gleam in a flushed cloud.

She knew the gleam would fade, the cloud would go grey. But at present she did not believe it. She knew she was a victim; that all this elaborate work upon her was the work of victimising her. But she did not mind. She wanted it.

Later, they put a short blue tunic on her and took her to the upper terrace, and presented her to the people. She saw the plaza below her full of dark faces and of glittering eyes. There was no pity: only the curious hard exultance. The people gave a subdued cry when they saw her, and she shuddered. But she hardly cared.

Next day was the last. She slept in a chamber of the big house. At dawn they put on her a big blue blanket with a fringe, and led her out into the plaza, among the throng of silent, dark-blanketed people. There was pure white snow on the ground, and the dark people in their dark-brown blankets looked like inhabitants of another world.

A large drum was slowly pounding, and an old priest was declaring from a housetop. But it was not till noon that a litter came forth, and the people gave that low, animal cry which was so moving. In the sack-like litter sat the old, old cacique, his white hair braided with black braid and large turquoise stones. His face was like a piece of obsidian. He lifted his hand in token, and the litter stopped in front of her. Fixing her with his old eyes, he spoke to her for a few moments, in his hollow voice. No one translated.

Another litter came, and she was placed in it. Four priests moved ahead, in their scarlet and yellow and black, with plumed headdresses. Then came the litter of the old cacique. Then the light drums began, and two groups of singers burst simultaneously into song, male and wild. And the golden-red, almost naked men, adorned with ceremonial feathers and kilts, the rivers of black hair down their backs, formed into two files and began to tread the dance. So they threaded out of the snowy plaza, in two long, sumptuous lines of dark red-gold and black and fur, swaying with a faint tinkle of bits of shell and flint, winding over the snow between the two bee-clusters of men who sang around the drum.

Slowly they moved out, and her litter, with its attendance of feathered, lurid, dancing priests, moved after. Everybody danced the tread of the dance-step, even, subtly, the litter-bearers. And out of the plaza they went, past smoking ovens, on the trail to the great cotton-wood trees, that stood like grey-silver lace against the blue sky, bare and exquisite above the snow. The river, diminished, rushed among fangs of ice. The chequer-squares of gardens within fences were all snowy, and the white houses now looked yellowish.

The whole valley glittered intolerably with pure snow, away to the walls of the standing rock. And across the flat cradle of snow-bed wound the long thread of the dance, shaking slow-ly and sumptuously in its orange and black motion. The high drums thudded quickly, and on the crystalline frozen air the swell and roar of the chant of savages was like an obsession.

She sat looking out of her litter with big, transfixed blue eyes, under which were the wan markings of her drugged weari-ness. She knew she was going to die, among the glisten of this snow, at the hands of this savage, sumptuous people. And as she stared at the blaze of blue sky above the slashed and ponderous mountain, she thought: "I am dead already. What difference does it make, the transition from the dead I am to the dead I shall be, very soon!" Yet her soul sickened and felt wan.

The strange procession trailed on, in perpetual dance, slowly across the plain of snow, and then entered the slopes between the pine-trees. She saw the copper-dark men dancing the dance-tread, onwards, between the copper-pale tree trunks. And at last she, too, in her swaying litter, entered the pine-trees.

They were travelling on and on, upwards, across the snow under the trees, past the superb shafts of pale, flaked copper, the rustle and shake and tread of the threading dance, penetrating into the forest, into the mountain. They were following a stream-bed: but the stream was dry, like summer, dried up by the fro-zenness of the head-waters. There were dark, red-bronze willow bushes with wattles like wild hair, and pallid aspen trees looking like cold flesh against the snow. Then jutting dark rocks.

At last she could tell that the dancers were moving forward no more. Nearer and nearer she came upon the drums, as to a lair of mysterious animals. Then through the bushes she emerged into a strange amphitheatre. Facing was a great wall of hollow rock, down the front of which hung a great, dripping, fang-like spoke of ice. The ice came pouring over the rock from the precipice above, and then stood arrested, dripping out of high heaven, al-most down to the hollow stones where the stream-pool should be below. But the pool was dry.

On either side the dry pool, the lines of dancers had formed, and the dance was continuing without intermission, against a background of bushes.

But what she felt was that fanged inverted pinnacle of ice, hanging from the lip of the dark precipice above. And behind the great rope of ice, she saw the leopard-like figures of priests climbing the hollow cliff face, to the cave that, like a dark socket, bored a cavity, an orifice, half way up the crag.

Before she could realise, her litter-bearers were staggering in the footholds, climbing the rock. She, too, was behind the ice. There it hung, like a curtain that is not spread, but hangs like a great fang. And near above her was the orifice of the cave sinking dark into the rock. She watched it as she swayed upwards.

On the platform of the cave stood the priests, waiting in all their gorgeousness of feathers and fringed robes, watching her ascent. Two of them stooped to help her litter-bearer. And at length she was on the platform of the cave, far in behind the shaft of ice, above the hollow amphitheatre among the bushes below, where men were dancing, and the whole populace of the village was clustered in silence.

The sun was sloping down the afternoon sky, on the left. She knew that this was the shortest day of the year, and the last day of her life. They stood her facing the iridescent column of ice, which fell down marvellously arrested, away in front of her.

Some signal was given, and the dance below stopped. There was now absolute silence. She was given a little to drink, then two priests took off her mantle and her tunic, and in her strange pallor she stood there, between the lurid robes of the priests, beyond the pillar of ice, beyond and above the dark-faced people. The throng below gave the low, wild cry. Then the priests turned her round, so she stood with her back to the open world, her long blond hair to the people below. And they cried again.

She was facing the cave, inwards. A fire was burning and flickering in the depths. Four priests had taken off their robes, and were almost as naked as she was. They were powerful men in the prime of life, and they kept their dark, painted faces lowered.

From the fire came the old, old priest, with an incense-pan. He was naked and in a state of barbaric ecstasy. He fumigated his victim, reciting at the same time in a hollow voice. Behind him came another robeless priest, with two flint knives.

When she was fumigated, they laid her on a large flat stone, the four powerful men holding her by the outstretched arms and legs. Behind stood the aged man, like a skeleton covered with dark glass, holding a knife and transfixedly watching the sun; and behind him again was another naked priest, with a knife.

She felt little sensation, though she knew all that was happening. Turning to the sky, she looked at the yellow sun. It was sinking. The shaft of ice was like a shadow between her and it. And she realised that the yellow rays were filling half the cave, though they had not reached the altar where the fire was, at the far end of the funnel-shaped cavity.

Yes, the rays were creeping round slowly. As they grew ruddier, they penetrated farther. When the red sun was about to sink, he would shine full through the shaft of ice deep into the hollow of the cave, to the innermost.

She understood now that this was what the men were waiting for. Even those that held her down were bent and twisted round, their black eyes watching the sun with a glittering eagerness, and awe, and craving. The black eyes of the aged cacique were fixed like black mirrors on the sun, as if sightless, yet containing some terrible answer to the reddening winter planet. And all the eyes of the priests were fixed and glittering on the sinking orb, in the reddening, icy silence of the winter afternoon.

They were anxious, terribly anxious, and fierce. Their ferocity wanted something, and they were waiting the moment. And their ferocity was ready to leap out into a mystic exultance, of triumph. But still they were anxious.

Only the eyes of that oldest man were not anxious. Black, and fixed, and as if sightless, they watched the sun, seeing beyond the sun. And in their black, empty concentration there was power, power intensely abstract and remote, but deep, deep to the heart of the earth, and the heart of the sun. In absolute motionlessness he watched till the red sun should send his ray through the column of ice. Then the old man would strike, and strike home, accomplish the sacrifice and achieve the power.

The mastery that man must hold, and that passes from race to race.

LEONAUR

ALSO FROM LEONAUR
AVAILABLE IN SOFTCOVER OR HARDCOVER WITH DUST JACKET

THE COLLECTED SCIENCE FICTION AND FANTASY OF STANLEY G. WEINBAUM 1—INTERPLANETARY ODYSSEYS *by Stanley G. Weinbaum*—Classic Tales of Interplanetary Adventure Including: A Martian Odyssey, its Sequel Valley of Dreams, the Complete 'Ham' Hammond Stories and Others.

THE COLLECTED SCIENCE FICTION AND FANTASY OF STANLEY G. WEINBAUM 2—OTHER EARTHS *by Stanley G. Weinbaum*—Classic Futuristic Tales Including: *Dawn of Flame* & its Sequel The Black Flame, plus The Revolution of 1960 & Others.

THE COLLECTED SCIENCE FICTION AND FANTASY OF STANLEY G. WEINBAUM 3—STRANGE GENIUS *by Stanley G. Weinbaum*—Classic Tales of the Human Mind at Work Including the Complete Novel The New Adam, the 'van Manderpootz' Stories and Others.

THE COLLECTED SCIENCE FICTION AND FANTASY OF STANLEY G. WEINBAUM 4—THE BLACK HEART *by Stanley G. Weinbaum*—Classic Strange Tales Including: the Complete Novel The Dark Other, Plus Proteus Island and Others.

THE COLLECTED SCIENCE FICTION & FANTASY OF JACK LONDON 1—BEFORE ADAM & OTHER STORIES *by Jack London*—included in this Volume Before Adam The Scarlet Plague A Relic of the Pliocene When the World Was Young The Red One Planchette A Thousand Deaths Goliah A Curious Fragment The Rejuvenation of Major Rathbone.

THE COLLECTED SCIENCE FICTION & FANTASY OF JACK LONDON 2—THE IRON HEEL & OTHER STORIES *by Jack London*—included in this Volume The Iron Heel The Enemy of All the World The Shadow and the Flash The Strength of the Strong The Unparalleled Invasion The Dream of Debs.

THE COLLECTED SCIENCE FICTION & FANTASY OF JACK LONDON 3—THE STAR ROVER & OTHER STORIES *by Jack London*—included in this Volume The Star Rover The Minions of Midas The Eternity of Forms The Man With the Gash.

THE CRETAN TEAT *by Brian Aldiss*—The Cretan Teat is a wry and comic novel that interweaves its own fiction with an inner fiction about the discovery of a Byzantine painting of the Mother of the Blessed Virgin Mary suckling the infant Jesus and a fake ikon that becomes an instrument of Nemesis.

LEONAUR

ALSO FROM LEONAUR
AVAILABLE IN SOFTCOVER OR HARDCOVER WITH DUST JACKET

THE FIRST BOOK OF AYESHA *by H. Rider Haggard*—Contains *She & Ayesha: the Return of She.*

THE SECOND BOOK OF AYESHA *by H. Rider Haggard*—Contains *She and Allan & Wisdom's Daughter.*

QUATERMAIN: THE COMPLETE ADVENTURES—1 *by H. Rider Haggard*—Contains *King Solomon's Mines & Allan Quatermain.*

QUATERMAIN: THE COMPLETE ADVENTURES—2 *by H. Rider Haggard*—Contains *Allan's Wife, Maiwa's Revenge & Marie.*

QUATERMAIN: THE COMPLETE ADVENTURES—3 *by H. Rider Haggard*—Contains *Child of Storm & Allan and the Holy Flower.*

QUATERMAIN: THE COMPLETE ADVENTURES—4 *by H. Rider Haggard*—Contains *Finished & The Ivory Child.*

QUATERMAIN: THE COMPLETE ADVENTURES—5 *by H. Rider Haggard*—Contains *The Ancient Allan & She and Allan.*

QUATERMAIN: THE COMPLETE ADVENTURES—6 *by H. Rider Haggard*—Contains *Heu-Heu or, the Monster & The Treasure of the Lake.*

QUATERMAIN: THE COMPLETE ADVENTURES—7 *by H. Rider Haggard*—Contains *Allan and the Ice Gods, Four Short Adventures & Nada the Lily.*

TROS OF SAMOTHRACE 1: WOLVES OF THE TIBER *by Talbot Mundy*—55 B.C.--an adventurer set during the Roman invasion of Britain.

TROS OF SAMOTHRACE 2: DRAGONS OF THE NORTH *by Talbot Mundy*—55 B.C. —Caesar plots, Britons war among themselves and the Vikings are coming.

TROS OF SAMOTHRACE 3: SERPENT OF THE WAVES *by Talbot Mundy*—55 B.C.--Caesar is poised to invade Britain—only a grand strategy can foil him!.

TROS OF SAMOTHRACE 4: CITY OF THE EAGLES *by Talbot Mundy*—54 B.C.—Rome—Tros treads in the streets of his sworn enemies!.

TROS OF SAMOTHRACE 5: CLEOPATRA *by Talbot Mundy*—Tros and the Roman Empire turn to the Egypt of the Pharaohs.

TROS OF SAMOTHRACE 6: THE PURPLE PIRATE *by Talbot Mundy*—The epic saga of the ancient world—Tros of Samothrace—draws to a conclusion in this sixth—and final—volume.

LEONAUR

ALSO FROM LEONAUR
AVAILABLE IN SOFTCOVER OR HARDCOVER WITH DUST JACKET

THE CIVIL WAR NOVELS: 1 *by Joseph A. Altsheler*—*The Guns of Bull Run &*
The Guns of Shiloh—the first and second novels of a series of eight adventures which
follow the momentous events, campaigns and battles of the great American Civil War
between the Northern and Southern states.

THE CIVIL WAR NOVELS: 2 *by Joseph A. Altsheler*—*The Scouts of Stonewall*
& The Sword of Antietam—the third and fourth novels of a series of nine adventures
which follow the momentous events, campaigns and battles of the great American
Civil War between the Northern and Southern states.

THE CIVIL WAR NOVELS: 3 *by Joseph A. Altsheler*—*The Star of Gettysburg*
& The Rock of Chickamauga—the fifth and sixth novels of a series of nine adventures
which follow the momentous events, campaigns and battles of the great American
Civil War between the Northern and Southern states.

THE CIVIL WAR NOVELS: 4 *by Joseph A. Altsheler*—*The Shades of the Wil-*
derness & The Tree of Appomattox—the seventh and eighth novels of a series of nine
adventures which follow the momentous events, campaigns and battles of the great
American Civil War between the Northern and Southern states.

THE CIVIL WAR NOVELS: 5 *by Joseph A. Altsheler*—*Before the Dawn: a Story*
of the Fall of Richmond—the last of a series of nine adventures which follow the momentous events, campaigns and battles of the great American Civil War between the
Northern and Southern states.

THE FRENCH & INDIAN WAR NOVELS: 1 *by Joseph A. Altsheler*—*The*
Hunters of the Hills & The Shadow of the North—In this three volume, six novel set the
story of the war, with many of its real life characters, is told through the adventures
of its principal characters, Robert Lennox, the hunter Willet and his Indian companion Tayoga.

THE FRENCH & INDIAN WAR NOVELS: 2 *by Joseph A. Altsheler*—*The*
Rulers of the Lakes & The Masters of the Peaks—In this three volume, six novel set the
story of the war, with many of its real life characters, is told through the adventures
of its principal characters, Robert Lennox, the hunter Willet and his Indian companion Tayoga.

THE FRENCH & INDIAN WAR NOVELS: 1 *by Joseph A. Altsheler*—*The Lords*
of the Wild & The Sun of Quebec—In this three volume, six novel set the story of the
war, with many of its real life characters, is told through the adventures of its principal
characters, Robert Lennox, the hunter Willet and his Indian companion Tayoga.

LEONAUR

ALSO FROM LEONAUR
AVAILABLE IN SOFTCOVER OR HARDCOVER WITH DUST JACKET

THE COMPLETE FOUR JUST MEN: VOLUME 2 *by Edgar Wallace—The Law of the Four Just Men & The Three Just Men*—disillusioned with a world where the wicked and the abusers of power perpetually go unpunished, the Just Men set about to rectify matters according to their own standards, and retribution is dispensed on swift and deadly wings.

THE COMPLETE RAFFLES: 1 *by E. W. Hornung—The Amateur Cracksman & The Black Mask*—By turns urbane gentleman about town and accomplished cricketer, life is just too ordinary for Raffles and that sets him on a series of adventures that have long been treasured as a real antidote to the 'white knights' who are the usual heroes of the crime fiction of this period.

THE COMPLETE RAFFLES: 2 *by E. W. Hornung—A Thief in the Night & Mr Justice Raffles*—By turns urbane gentleman about town and accomplished cricketer, life is just too ordinary for Raffles and that sets him on a series of adventures that have long been treasured as a real antidote to the 'white knights' who are the usual heroes of the crime fiction of this period.

THE COLLECTED SUPERNATURAL AND WEIRD FICTION OF WILKIE COLLINS: VOLUME 1 *by Wilkie Collins*—Contains one novel 'The Haunted Hotel', one novella 'Mad Monkton', three novelettes 'Mr Percy and the Prophet', 'The Biter Bit' and 'The Dead Alive' and eight short stories to chill the blood.

THE COLLECTED SUPERNATURAL AND WEIRD FICTION OF WILKIE COLLINS: VOLUME 2 *by Wilkie Collins*—Contains one novel 'The Two Destinies', three novellas 'The Frozen deep', 'Sister Rose' and 'The Yellow Mask' and two short stories to chill the blood.

THE COLLECTED SUPERNATURAL AND WEIRD FICTION OF WILKIE COLLINS: VOLUME 3 *by Wilkie Collins*—Contains one novel 'Dead Secret,' two novelettes 'Mrs Zant and the Ghost' and 'The Nun's Story of Gabriel's Marriage' and five short stories to chill the blood.

FUNNY BONES *selected by Dorothy Scarborough*—An Anthology of Humorous Ghost Stories.

MONTEZUMA'S CASTLE AND OTHER WEIRD TALES *by Charles B. Cory*—Cory has written a superb collection of eighteen ghostly and weird stories to chill and thrill the avid enthusiast of supernatural fiction.

SUPERNATURAL BUCHAN *by John Buchan*—Stories of Ancient Spirits, Uncanny Places & Strange Creatures.

AVAILABLE ONLINE AT **www.leonaur.com**
AND FROM ALL GOOD BOOK STORES

07/09

www.ingramcontent.com/pod-product-compliance
Lightning Source LLC
Chambersburg PA
CBHW031122030726
47496CB00002BA/642